OSWALD

THE

THIEF

A MEDIEVAL CAPER

NOVELS BY JERI WESTERSON

Paranormal

BOOKE OF THE HIDDEN SERIES

Booke of the Hidden

Deadly Rising

Shadows in the Mist

The Darkest Gateway

MOONRISER WEREWOLF MYSTERIES

Moonrisers

Baying for Blood

THE ENCHANTER CHRONICLES TRILOGY

The Daemon Device

Clockwork Gypsy

Library of the Damned

Medieval Mysteries

THE CRISPIN GUEST MEDIEVAL NOIR MYSTERIES

Veil of Lies / Serpent in the Thorns / The Demon's Parchment

Troubled Bones / Blood Lance / Shadow of the Alchemist

Cup of Blood (a prequel) / The Silence of Stones / A Maiden Weeping

Season of Blood / The Deepest Grave / Traitor's Codex

Sword of Shadows / Spiteful Bones / The Deadliest Sin

Historical Fiction

Though Heaven Fall

Roses in the Tempest

Native Spirit, writing as Anne Castell

Oswald the Thief

LGBTQ Mysteries

THE SKYLER FOXE MYSTERIES writing as Haley Walsh

Foxe Tail / Foxe Hunt / Out-Foxed

Foxe Den: A Holiday Collection (novella) / Foxefire / Desert Foxe

Foxe Den 2: Summer Vacation (novella)

Crazy Like A Foxe / Stone Cold Foxe/ A Very Merry Foxemas (novella)

Oswald the Thief

A Medieval Caper

JERI WESTERSON

Old London Press

Cover design by Mayhem Cover Creations

Book design by Jeri Westerson

Map: Charles Knight, London (Volume II), 1841, with alterations

ISBN: 978-1-7356160-4-9

Sign up for my newsletters at JeriWesterson.com

Old London Press
PO Box 799
Menifee, CA 92586

To Craig, who stole my heart all those ages ago.

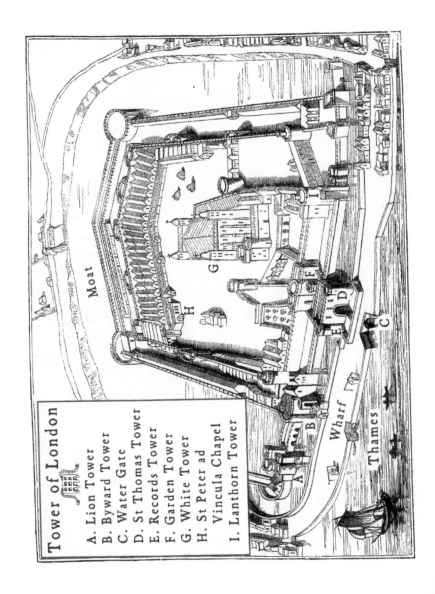

Tower of London

A. Lion Tower
B. Byward Tower
C. Water Gate
D. St Thomas Tower
E. Records Tower
F. Garden Tower
G. White Tower
H. St Peter ad
   Vincula Chapel
I. Lanthorn Tower

Moat

Wharf

Thames

ACKNOWLEDGEMENTS

Much thanks to my agent Joshua Bilmes from JABberwocky Literary Agency for trying hard to get this published. Alas.

Thanks always to my beloved husband who graces me with his support and encouragement and who reads it all first before it ever gets to you.

Thank you Mayhem Cover Creations for the awesome cover.

And finally, thanks to my readers for your continual encouragement.

Thanks to you all!

GLOSSARY

Ach-y-fi – Exclamation of frustration. Welsh.

Bouget – A yoke including water skins or buckets for carrying water.

Brewster – Female brewer.

Dagged – Decorative edges to garments sleeves or hem in various shapes like leaf patterns or crenellations.

Gadeling – "Kinsman" in Old English.

Greek Fire – An incendiary weapon used since the Byzantine empire circa 672 CE. Possibly made of naphtha and quicklime.

Saint Dafydd – Saint David, the patron saint of Wales, pronounced "DAYV-ith".

tegan – A toy. Welsh, pronounced "tee-GAHN".

twpsyn – A fool. Welsh, pronounced "TOOP-sin".

CHAPTER ONE

London, 1308

TWO THINGS I'M good at. One, is the Game. Second, are the women. Now, with a lad like me, young, one score and three, with golden hair curled like an angel's and eyes blue as woad, well. The women fall into my lap, so to speak.

But the Game. Sometimes my fair face is beguiling enough to work for the Game as well. My knife is sharp and good for snipping a purse. At times, deft fingers don't even need to cut it but can slip inside, touching gold. But that takes more skill, more time.

Then there's the other Games. Stealing into a man's house to take his goods. That's a tougher Game and dangerous but more generous.

And then there is the Shell. I like the Shell. It's simple, to the point, and does the job.

This is what I mean. You have three walnut shells and one pea. The *twpsyns* gather and you make a show of placing the one pea under one shell, shuffle them about, and the *twpsyn* guesses where the pea is. Simple.

You allow the *twpsyn* to follow your hands, which are clever and fast. He thinks he's cleverer because he's reckoned it out, thinks you aren't half as clever as him. Any sober man with the sense God gave 'em can reckon it out. He wins coin and walks away happy.

Except. You don't let him walk away. "Just once more, lad. Just once more," you tell him. And, quick as a wink, his coin is on the table. That's when the pea mysteriously disappears. And how does it do that?

Now, why would I tell you?

Any corner of London will do. I find myself a good spot almost every day and set up my little folding board.

Like the other day. My fingers were moving fast, switching shells madly, but I could tell the *twpsyn* had a good eye. So I coughed. He blinked. The pea was now gone. I lifted my hands and said for the hundredth time, "Where is it?"

He was proud of himself. Oh aye. He pointed to the shell it *should* have been under. But when I lifted it and there was nothing there, his mind stumbled. I could see it in his eyes. He scratched his head, then his stubbled jaw, and put his hand on the board. "Again," he said. They always do.

But by and by, it happens that the *twpsyn* sees just what I'm up to. In that instance, he tries to grab me and give chase.

I'm also good at running.

But tonight was different. Tonight there was no Shell. Instead, I stood in a man's house while all were asleep. That's the Greater Game. You see a lass I met in the marketplace two days ago tried to impress me with talk of her rich master, of his gold and plate and candlesticks and other rich ornaments. I had been intrigued at first by her generous bosom but talk of gold soon led my eyes upward to her face and I found m'self in her bed...that second thing I'm good at.

So here I was, in her master's house in the dead of night. She had finally fallen asleep. A talkative lass after a swive, more talk than a sleepy man usually desires. "Oswald, you have such beautiful golden hair!" and "Oswald, do you love me?" And all the time, me reassuring her with coos and kisses.

Well, a man's got to do his best to get by.

I crept out of her room and shut out the sounds of the wind outside and instead listened to all within. I stood in a passageway between the buttery and the hall. I wondered if a servant was sleeping in or near the buttery and I took a few cautious steps forward, peering around the corner. No servants. From my layman's description, I would have to make it across the hall to a tower stairway which would lead to the master's solar. There, she said, he seemed to keep his moveable riches.

I kept my eyes skinned for sleeping servants as I approached the hall but saw none. The hall's entrance ahead of me was a grand arch of carved wood. It opened into a spacious room of twenty feet wide and twice as long with a high open-beamed ceiling of dark, carved corbels and bosses. The tiled floor was a checkered courtyard, with benches pushed up against the walls, each with cushions of what looked like red velvet with gold thread. The rooms smelled of candle smoke, feasts, and spiced perfumes. All ghosts of gathering people and eating. The hearth in the center was cold and ash-free. A well-kept household was this...except for the thief in the midst of it.

Well, nothing but God is perfect.

And just so you don't think badly of me, I'm not a thief all the time. I'm proud of my trade as a tinker, too. Most of my fellow tinkers are travelers. Indeed, I learned my trade from one of them travelling sorts. He found his way to Harlech — that's in Wales — my little village at the foot of the castle. When my mother, God save her, passed from this world, I left for England, just like she told me. My sire... I never knew the man. My mother said he was an English bard, name of Oswald. Named me after him. He could sing a pretty tune right enough, I suppose. Left her with a babe to raise on her own. And I would have stayed the rest of my days in Harlech but my sainted mother told me to make something of m'self, and in order to do that I should take after my father and go to London. It was so far. I dreaded the thought.

But just as I wondered how the sarding hell I was to do that, a tinker, Master Edmund, came through town and was heading back to London. He took a fancy to me and my clever ways. Said he'd teach me his trade and I listened right well. Learned it good. Took us two years to get close to London what with all the places we got to in between. I learned quite a few tricks by then and he turned a blind eye when I showed up back to his fire with more coins than I left with. Never grizzled once, not with food in the pot.

When Master Edmund died, I sort of inherited his goods and tools. Finally got to London and set up shop on corners and alleys until I could rent my own shop. Aye. It's a good life. I work my trade, sell my pilgrim badges to the Hospital of St. Thomas of Acon, fix a pot or two, cuddle the occasional fair wench, and...well. Do a bit on the side. You see, I like to have a Plan. My mother always said, "Money is the key that opens all locks." And in truth, having it is better than not.

———◆———

THE CUSHIONS AND grand tapestries lining the walls interested me but only for a moment. These were not things I was equipped to carry away. My mind was instead on gold, and for that a man could bend his back. Softly, I made my way through the darkened room, lit only by clerestory windows of clear glass. Before me was the doorway which led to the tower stairs and I hastened across the floor to the safety of its shadows. I looked back, measuring the way I'd have to return and then made my way up the stairs. When I neared the top, I crouched low, lying down on the last few steps and raised as much of my head as I dared so to scan what was before me.

Another lonely passage with a lit oil lamp sitting in a wall niche.

I stood and slid against the wall, stepping carefully down the passage with several closed doors. My talkative laymen said that the solar was the second door past the stairwell, but she had neglected to tell me on which side of the passage.

Two doors ahead, both closed. One a bed chamber, the other a solar.

Saint Dafydd's bollocks, which was it?

I passed other rooms, doors slightly ajar. Bare floors, dark shapes that might be beds or sideboards. When I reached the two rooms I licked my lips, made a quick prayer, and chose the one of the left. Grasping the door handle, I slowly squeezed, hoping the latch would whisper instead of clank. My prayers were heard, for they opened softly and I pushed the door. Peering inside, my heart began to flutter. The shape of a curtained bed slowly formed in the darkness. Bare floors, tapestries, coffers. With a wince, I hastened to shut the door again.

I waited. No sound. Thank Christ for that!

The right door, then. I moved across the passage, grasped that door latch, and pushed the door open. Heavy tapestries, an ornate table covered with a decorative cloth, a rug with a boar hunt depicted on its surface with a dark wine stain in one of its corners, several chairs with embroidered cushions, a cold hearth, silver candlesticks perched on an ambry, and a tall arched window. No coffers, no boxes of any kind. Had I got the right room?

I carefully closed the door behind me and glanced about. No niches, no hiding places. Nothing but four walls. It was clearly a solar, it could be for nothing else. Had the wench lied to me? I almost chuckled. For I had lied to many a wench to get them into bed, but I was seldom the victim in such a deception. Could my charming face have been my undoing?

As my mother was fond of saying, "At the end of the song comes payment." If this was my due, well. There were silver candlesticks. At least I wouldn't leave empty-handed.

But something was not right. I could feel it in my bones. For if this *was* the place the man kept his riches, then something was amiss. There would at least be a coffer. And if there was not something as simple as that, then his treasure was hidden and hidden well. I moved about the room running my hands over the tapestries covering most of the walls. I lifted the edge of one and looked behind. I thought, perhaps, there might be a secret niche or a hidden door, but no such thing. I checked behind all the tapestries, but there was only blank wall. Disappointed, I paced the room. Something was not right in my mind but I could not rein it in. I kicked at the rug, feeling the time slip away. I could not tarry long. Should I simply take those candlesticks and be done?

Looking down, the boar hunt played out in a riot of colorful yarn on a black background. The rug. Neither the bedchamber nor the other rooms had rugs. Why this one?

I crouched and took up the corner, lifting. The floor had a seam. Folding the rug away, the floor had more than one seam. It had four and an inset iron ring.

I pulled the ring and lay the trap door back. Below was a dark passage and a stair. I was going to need a light. Quickly, I went back to the corridor and snatched the oil lamp from its niche and returned to the narrow square passage through the floor. Down I went, to Hell or Heaven, I knew not which.

Holding the little lamp aloft, its sparse light gave only a small halo of radiance. The staircase was well-dusted and worn and sported a few spilled wine stains. Much celebration had occurred because of this stash, I'd wager. I followed the stairs down and soon emerged into a vaulted room of stone and brick filled with many coffers, both small and large. That greedy old *gadeling*.

I descended the last steps into the room and approached the first coffer. Locked, of course, but I learned a trick or two from my companion Geoff and, using his instruments that I made for him m'self, I had it opened in no time. *Ach-y-fi!* What beauteous gold lay inside! Coins, plate, rings, bracelets. I untied the sack from my belt and began filling. Ach, what a pity I could not carry more. Foolish that I did not take Geoff or Walter with me. We could have gotten away with three times the amount. But a man must not be greedy.

See where it gets you? A room full of coffers and a man stealing from you.

I filled the bag with as much as I could safely carry and closed the coffer lid. It could be that I might return with Geoff and Walter in tow. That would suit. If we kept taking small amounts, it might be a long time till the master was the wiser.

Nicely burdened, I turned to the staircase and put my foot on the first riser. Something made a clicking noise, yet I took no heed of it until I was further up the stairs. But all of a sudden, the staircase jolted. I stopped, my heart pounding. What the devil—? And then the staircase swung free and began teetering.

I bent forward and grabbed the stairs with my free hand, trying to steady myself. What the hell was going on? I moved upward but the stairs before me suddenly tilted downward. I took a step back and the stairs above rose.

That devil! He'd made a sarding trap. The stairs were on a pivot of some kind and only he knew the secret to his devilish puzzle. And if I didn't reckon it right quick, I'd be caught come morning.

I moved upward, just to see. Aye. The steps lowered away from the trap door and freedom above. I dropped down to the last step, considered, and then stepped off onto the floor. The staircase began to rise and if I didn't get right back on, it would soon be beyond my reach. Sarding bastard! It's one thing locking a door to keep a thief away, but it's another to make a sly trap to ensnare him like he was a coney or a ferret. That was not to be borne!

I took a few steps up and sat. Very well, then. If I was not to be trapped all night and discovered I would have to get m'self out of it. Oh for some rope!

I glanced at my sack. I was not going to leave that behind. Not after all this! And so that could not be part of the scheme. Or could it?

I trotted down to the last step again, placed the heavy sack on it, and stepped off. Like a saint's own miracle, it kept the stairs in place. So now all I needed was a substitute.

I looked around. Ah! A small coffer just for the asking. I leaned over, grasped it from the sides…and nearly jerked out my entrails trying to pick it up. Something was amiss. It wasn't *that* heavy. I fiddled with the lock, opened it, and pushed its contents aside. There! Bolted to the floor. *Jesu*! Was there nothing this devil had not thought of?

I glanced back at my sack of treasure and scowled. I would best this rogue yet *and* get away with my plunder.

An idea. I pulled up my tunic and reached for the top of my stocking. Untying it from my braies, I slid it down my leg, scuffed off my boot, and slipped the stocking free of my foot. Stumping my naked foot back in my boot I began to fill the stocking with more coins — a whole leg of them!

I tied the opened end up tight when it had taken its fill. I worried about the seams and whether they would hold but it needn't be for too long. I laid it over the bottom step, lifted off my treasure sack, and watched. The stairs wobbled but they stayed upright. Now, the trick was to get it just right. I filled the stocking further and then laid it over the edge. Now or never.

I stole up the stairs with the sack of treasure over my shoulder, feeling the steps sway gently beneath me. The square of light above tantalized, teased. The stairs dipped slightly as I neared it and I held my breath. I took each step carefully, one at a time. Each step I took made the whole unsteady, for I weighed more than that leg of gold, especially with a sack over my shoulder filled with the same. So as I neared the trap door, I hoisted the sack up and over the rim of it and that gave the stairs the extra bit it needed to lift me to freedom.

I grabbed hold of the rim and hauled m'self up but I quickly turned about and lay on the floor, looking back down. The stairs seemed steady now but that was not good enough. I grasped them and shook, wiggling it this way and that. Inch by inch, the stocking of gold slipped further away from the stair until...plop! It fell off. With a satisfied snort, I let the stairs go and they fell away, pivoting on its axis, away from the gold and away from the trap door. Let the bastard sort *that* on the morrow!

I closed the trap door and replaced the rug just as I had found it. I hefted the bag again and smiled. Aye, it was a goodly haul. Though with his trap sprung, I knew I would not be returning. Pity.

It was a simple thing for me to steal down the passage, down the stairs, and into the hall again. Easy. The buttery and escape was beyond. And I was almost there until a voice came from behind. "Oi! Who are you?"

Slowly, I turned. A man-at-arms with surcote and mail stood before me.

He looked at me and I at him. And then he smiled and unsheathed his weapon.

Now I'm a peaceful man. I *am*! And I carry no blade except my eating knife, which is good for no kind of fighting. But as a tinker, I do carry my hammer, a hammer by the name of Saint Joseph of Arimathea, the patron saint of tinkers. More often than not, I've used old Saint Joseph as a weapon of discouragement, for I am no fighter.

But I measured the gleaming sword and thought of my little hammer sitting in its belt loop...and swung that heavy bag instead.

It caught the tip of his sword and yanked it from his grip. He made a cry as the sword clanged far too loudly across the floor. I turned to run, but he scrambled after the weapon and cried out good and loud.

Movement upstairs. Christ!

He came at me again, and again I swung the sack, but I could see that this kind of defense was too slow. I grabbed the sack instead and used it close like a shield. The blade sliced it open and all the plunder spilled out upon the floor.

We were both stunned by the splendor. Then we looked up at the same time. I dropped the empty bag and ran. But the way was blocked by a sleepy servant.

I thought about diving forward and chancing it, but he awakened fully upon noticing the man-at-arms and I ducked and ran the other way. The man-at-arms swung his blade, I dived beneath it, and the servant fell back with a cry.

I tore the other direction up the narrow stairs. The lord emerged from his bedchamber. I only caught a glimpse of his fearsome visage but that was enough. I pushed him out of the way, shoved him to the other side of the door, and slipped into his bedchamber, barring it. I'd have to get out from his window.

I spun and froze.

My lady clutched her sheets about her as she stood at the end of the bed, its curtains thrown wide.

She was a fair thing, too. Auburn hair spun in waves over her shoulder, and her face was round, eyes wide.

I jumped away from the pounding on the door and the lord's cries from without. I could hear more men rushing to help him.

But we were quite alone in the dim chamber.

"I will not harm you," I said to appease. "All I want is a window and my freedom."

Her eyes softened from their fearful tenor. Perhaps she believed me. I had no intension of molesting the lady. For one, it wasn't the best of circumstances with the husband and his guards pounding on the door to get in. And for another, well. Let's just say my *mind* was not on it.

I rushed to the window and threw open the shutter. I was some feet from the ground. Damn!

I looked back. She crept toward the door.

"No, no, my lady." I hastened back to her and took hold of her arms. She struggled.

Shouldn't she swoon? Why was there no swooning?

"My lady, please! I will not harm you but I cannot allow you to assist in my capture."

"Unhand me!"

"Stop struggling!"

"Help! Help!"

I clasped my hand over her mouth. The very last thing I needed was to be accused of rape. Thievery was one thing, but rape of a lord's wife? I'd be hanged thrice over.

"Be still!" I said. I stood uncertainly, my arms wrapped around a nearly naked woman, my hand over her mouth, the window and the door between us. I dragged her to the window.

"There is no use in your crying out," I hissed in her ear. "They know we are both in here and they will presently batter down the door. So you might as well help me escape."

Her brows rose.

"Well, you've nothing else to do," I told her. "I'm going to remove my hand. Are you going to be still?"

She shrugged, eyes narrowing. So it was that way, was it?

"Please?" I added.

Her eyes softened and I took that as a good sign. Slowly, I peeled my palm away from her lips. She pulled away from me and scowled. "You are in very great peril."

"Aye, I know that!"

A deep thud hit the door. They were using an ax.

I looked at her and then at the sheets. "I'll need a rope."

She clutched tighter at the sheets wound about her, hiding her modesty. Creamy shoulders distracted me. "I have no rope," she said.

"Aye, but...er...perhaps the sheets." The door creaked under the onslaught. "Not much time to debate, my lady. I...er...I need those sheets. Now you can either hand them over willingly or...or I shall have to take them."

Her hand covered her bosom, holding the sheets before them but framing their plump roundness so that my thoughts were other than pious.

I stepped closer. "Decide, my lady. I am" —I looked at the shivering door— "running out of time."

She heaved a deep breath. "Turn around."

"What?"

"Turn around!"

God knows why I did it. She could have coshed me right good and *then* where would I be?

But I am a fool for women and I did as she bid and heard the rustle of fabric and then the sheets pooled at my feet. I desperately wanted to turn and as I leaned down to take the sheets, I did peek.

She had wrapped herself in the bed curtains, but a long pale strip of her leg showed beyond it. Christ Almighty.

My voice was rough when I nodded and said, "Thank you." I tore it into strips and set to tying them together. When I made it as long as I could, I tied one end to the bed post and threw the other out the window, praying mightily.

I climbed over the sill when she stopped me.

"Wait! You truly are just going to escape?"

"Aye, my lady." I tried not to look at her and over the mounds and strips of flesh glowing creamy pale in the firelight.

"Oh." She stared at the floor, her hair cascading over her eyes before she hastily brushed it back. "Did...did you get what you came for?"

"Alas, my lady. My burglary was unsuccessful. I leave with nothing but my life—"

The door crashed again, rattling the doorposts.

"—if I am lucky," I added.

"Then—"

Saint Dafydd's bollocks. What ailed the woman? I was halfway out the window.

"You took nothing and you were honorable to me. I offer you…a kiss…as recompense."

"*Eh?*" If I had till Doomsday, I will never understand the female mind.

"A kiss, Master Thief. For your trouble."

"My lady? I was in the process of burgling your husband and it was only my poor luck that I didn't get away with naught. Should that be rewarded?"

"You have treated me honorably and kept your word." She licked her lips, a little too anxiously, I thought. "And so I feel certain that I should bestow some token."

Not coin? Not jewelry? For I could see a fine gold ring on her smallest finger, sporting a beauteous crimson stone. Ah well. I'd take what I can get.

I spared an eye for the door and climbed back out of the window. She was, after all, a comely lass. And so that the night wasn't a complete waste of time…

I leaned down and pressed my lips chastely to hers…until she dug her fingers into my hair and forced my lips open with her own.

Soft lips and a quick tongue. She tasted me good and long, and I'd be a liar if I said I didn't enjoy it. Perhaps too much.

I pulled away with a gasp, though her fingers were still threaded through my locks. "Er…my lady," I murmured against her lips. I confess, she was good at this art. "I still have an escape to make."

Reluctantly, it seemed, she let me go. Her mouth was wet and it lifted into a secret smile. "Farewell, Master Thief. My lord is a vengeful man. I would not come here again."

"Aye, my lady." I took a breath to get my land legs back. "I think that most wise advice." I didn't look back as I slipped over the sill, clutching tight to the sheets, and climbed down into a back garden.

Where I promptly stumbled over a body.

CHAPTER TWO

I NEARLY SCREAMED but slammed a hand over my mouth. Blessed *Jesu*! What was here? A house of carnage! I swallowed my scream and merely stared.

He lay all a-crumbled as if he had fallen from a great height. I looked up the wall to the master's bedchamber window and the lady had hauled in the sheets and closed the shutter. *Just how many men had been in that chamber this night?*

But had he truly come from there? There was another window beside the bedchamber.

Why the hell was I debating it? But I couldn't tear my eyes away. He was young and handsome and his face was forever locked in a great grimace, blue eyes looking skyward.

The shutters above were cast open and someone lowered a lantern. A shout. I looked up and men had crowded in the open window, pointing down.

Toward me.

And a dead man.

Over the wall I went into the night, and didn't stop running till I reached my shop on Cornhill Street.

I didn't go in to my own shop directly. I feared it too much. Feared the closed space, feared I'd see the dead man's eyes in the hearth fire. So I wandered the dark and deserted streets of London, never too far from my shop, but not going in it.

My leg was cold, the one without a stocking, but if I kept moving, I felt a bit warmer.

Finally, the sun rose and the market bells rang, signaling the start of the days' transactions. Tense, I wove in and out of the shoppers and sellers, never meeting anyone's eyes. To take the edge off, I snipped a purse from a fat merchant who was beating a sorrowful-faced apprentice. When the boy was allowed to wash the tears from his face at a nearby bucket, I left a coin from the purse beside it. I winked at him and he gave me a small, grateful smile.

When I finally arrived home, Geoff was peering around the doorframe worriedly. I felt a weight of guilt on my chest, for I knew my absence had put that look on his face. I tried on a less mournful expression and called out to him. "Oi! Geoff! Looking for me?"

He came running and closed me in a crushing hug. For a mite of a dab, he had a good grip.

"Geoff, I can't breathe. Give us some air, eh?" He released me and looked up with his sorrowful brown eyes and hedgehog hair. There were tracks of tears on his dirty cheeks.

"Oz! I was so worried! You always tell me when you're to be out all night. I thought something happened to you and I didn't know what to do—"

"Now, lad, dry your tears and come inside. I'm perfectly all right."

Ah Geoff. There is no more honest, God-fearing man than is my Geoff. But he's so dim he don't know he's scratching his own bum if you don't tell him.

He dragged me inside. A poor little shop, little more than a stall, but a place I called home. All my tools were there and my small forge. Geoff never could master tinkering.

I know what you're asking. Who was Geoff to me? Well, the Gospels tell us that we are our brother's keeper, and I guess I keep Geoff right enough, even though he isn't my brother. He's just a man from London town with a head full of wool and a hand that was born to pick locks.

He and me shared this shop for nigh on five years. Truth to tell, I never knew exactly where he came from and neither did he. But I didn't have the heart to send him away. We didn't have much, but between us at least we weren't lonely. I suppose he was the brother I never had…were my mother to ever have a lackwit for a son. He and I each had a pallet bed beside the hearth with a table and two chairs, one of which was occupied with the bum of my landlord, Walter Pomfret, and I could see with a grunt of displeasure that he was consuming the last of my ale.

He lowered the jug from his lips and looked at me with them lackluster eyes of his. I know you've seen people with black clouds over their heads. You know my meaning. Folk who can't do nothing right no matter what saint they pray to. Well, that was Walter, right enough. Here he was, a man of learning, a wool merchant, mind you, but who never seemed to have two coins to rub together. Oh, his clothes were fine enough. He was wearing a bright green houppelande with long dagged sleeves and shoes with long pointed toes. Perhaps his garb was a little shabby, but they'll do. He had a habit of talking in a long drawl, too, each word pronounced as if they were to be his last.

My usual grin was in place. "Greetings, Wat!"

He wiped his lips of *my* ale and frowned. "Oswald, I have asked you innumerable times never to address me in that manner. If my sire had desired to call me 'Wat'" —and here he said the word like spittle—" he would have named me so. It is *WALTER*. By rights it is '*Master* Walter' to you."

There was never a man who could draw out a sentence like Master Pomfret. It was a thing to behold.

I bowed low to him and his pompous palace accent. "My dear Master Walter," I clarified. "I beg your mercy."

"Didn't get caught, I see," he said.

Panic burned my chest. "Caught at what?" Did he know about the dead man? Was it all over London already? No, no he couldn't have. And besides, it wasn't my fault.

Geoff snatched the purse from my hand, the one I was still absently holding. "Bless me, Oz! You got a *fat* purse."

Relief cooled my veins. Oh, *that* was his meaning. I slung my arm around that wiry frame of Geoff's. The lad smiled a bright grin that crinkled his eyes.

"I did!"

Walter held his hand out. "And that's thruppence for the rent. Which is late."

No, all was well. No one knew. No one *would* know. As long as I kept my own counsel.

"Right you are, Master Walter. Give it to him, Geoff." In a moment or two, I knew I'd win it back in a game of dice.

Geoff's animated face fell a bit as he reached into the pouch but he pulled out three silver coins and slowly placed them into Walter's open palm. The fingers closed over them like Doomsday and they slipped one, two, three into his pouch. And do you think that made him happy? Not old sour Walter. He leaned back and scowled. "Well that's one more quarter."

I took the seat beside him and gave him the elbow. "Don't nothing make you happy, Walter? Look here." I showed him the blue sky without and waved my arm to encompass the small shop. It made me happier to think about it. "All this, Walter. A lovely London day, a fine little shop where I am in the most holy occupation of making pilgrim badges–" He snorted. "Making pilgrim badges," I went on, "and fixing pots and such. And if I weren't, where would you be spending your days, eh? Some ale house? A stew? Naw, you got me and Geoff for company."

"And you have to ask why I'm not happy?" he said sullenly.

"Aw Walter. You do make me laugh."

"Oz." Geoff looked at me oddly. "What happened to your stocking?"

I thrust out my naked leg and forced a chuckle. "Er...lost it. Last night."

Walter snorted into his ale. Most likely he thought I left it in some lass's bedchamber and more often than not he'd be right. I let him think what he would. I went to my coffer and took out another patched stocking, kicked off my shoe, and slipped it on.

I sat again and we remained silent for a bit whilst Geoff fidgeted with my tin snips. I wish he wouldn't play with those. He hurts himself so easily.

"So Walter," I said after a long pause. "How about a game of dice?"

————◆————

IT'S LIKE THIS. A man has got to know his limitations. And Walter didn't know his. It's the Game, is what it is. He can't pass it up. And on no account should he ever gamble with me. He knows this. But he can't help himself. It's like the fools picking the shell and the pea just one more time. They never learn.

So after a few moments, I pocketed the three coins and then some. Not that I play a crooked game of dice. Well, it's a might bent. But he truly should know better.

Walter isn't married so he is his own man. But that has its pitfalls. For me, that is. The man wouldn't go home. It got later and later. He sent Geoff next door to his own lodgings to get more ale. I'm not one to turn away a beaker of spirits and in truth, I learn a lot listening to Walter's slow amble over the language. He's a learned man. Reads and writes. Has ideas. It's just none of them work out to gold.

"Oswald," he said, a slur just at the edge of his speech. He sloshed his ale on his lap, turning the fabric's bright green darker.

"You're a wily fellow. Why is it you are not wealthy by now? You certainly know how to make a coin or two."

I sighed and drank a fat dose of Walter's good ale. I wiped my mouth with the back of my sleeve then cast a glance at Geoff, but his face had disappeared behind his bowl accompanied by slurping sounds.

I picked up my *tegan*—it's what I call my pieces of little gears and pulleys I like to make and trifle with—and filed one of the splines down to a smooth rod. It helped me think, and in truth, I could not get thoughts of last night out of my head, of that sack of hard-won gold and how it spilled all over the floor like the entrails of a slaughtered animal. I shivered a bit, also thinking of that stiff dead man at my feet. An accident, surely. Folk are always falling out of windows in London. It's a dangerous place.

"Well, Walter, I'll tell you. I believe the right opportunity just hasn't yet come along. I'm waiting for it to walk through my door."

The hard *knock, knock* made us all jump. We looked at one another, then at the door.

"Oi, Oz," said Geoff, a sloppy smile on his face. "It's at the door now."

Was that the tingle of someone walking on my grave? I shook it off and set down my *tegan*. With a spike of trepidation, I approached the door. Whether responsible for it or not, the thought of the dead man—whoever he was—kept my thoughts dark and jittery.

When I opened the door, there stood a man, a lord, all dressed in a long, velvet cote-hardie riotously embroidered with vines and leaves. I marked right away the thick gold chain about his neck, the bejeweled dagger at his belt, and bulging money pouch.

All this took less than a heartbeat. But he looked at me, right enough. A long, slow look he gave me, too. He had dark beetle eyes and a trimmed brown beard. A tall man and handsome. He wore his power like a cloak.

And it was only then I recognized him. Christ Almighty! The lord whose house I burgled!

CHAPTER THREE

"ARE YOU OSWALD the Welshman?"

I bowed shakily. I had tried hard when I was with Master Edward the Tinker to lose that Welsh accent, and it had left me, more or less. But sometimes I still sounded a bit foreign to the average Londoner's ear.

"Aye, my lord. In the flesh," I answered. Surely he didn't recognize me. Surely not! Else the sheriff would be in tow. Yet, still, this was terrible. Terrible! I kept my face low, trying to find shadows where there were none

He peered over my shoulder and noticed Walter and Geoff. "I would speak with you alone."

Christ. I turned reluctantly to my companions and jerked me head. Walter took the hint but Geoff stood like a toadstool. Walter grabbed his sleeve and tugged him along. They skirted past the lord and bowed before they made haste next door to Walter's lodgings.

I motioned for the man to enter and he hesitated before he moved forward, pulling his cloak taut about him as if he were unwilling to soil it with my lodgings.

I offered him a chair but he would not take it. "This is no social call. It is business. I will speak plainly. You are a thief and a murderer."

My palms sweated and a trickle beaded its way down my back. I could feel the manacles slide over my wrists. Shuffling, I looked down at m'feet. "Good my lord, I am but a humble tinker, sir. I earn my wage—"

"I know well what you are. I remember you well…thief."

What had his wife told him? Did she tell him about the kiss? That mattered so little now. I was caught stealing from him though I had no gold for my trouble. I *had* stolen a kiss from his wife and I had been eye to eye with a dead man. I was done for. My knees felt weak.

I grasped at straws. "I…I think you are mistaken, my lord."

He suddenly grabbed my tunic and shoved me hard against the wall. My eyes watered.

"You are a lying dog, Welshman. I know all about you. Oh yes. Apparently, you are well known in London. Your little gambling games and your thievery. Some seem to think your life is charmed in some way. Always getting out of trouble, always avoiding the law. But now there is murder on your list of accomplishments."

"No, my lord! I never murdered nobody!"

"Murder." He seemed to like the sound of it and his lips cracked open over his teeth.

I kept silent. Especially when he drew his dagger.

He held it to my neck. "Give me a good reason why I should not slit your good-for-nothing throat right now. I could rid London of one more miscreant, one more foul knave."

"I…I…" The blade made a mute of me. I stared at it cross-eyed. Holy Mother!

"No?" But he sheathed it again and pushed me back, letting go of my shirt. "I own you, Welshman. Know that. I own your miserable hide and I can do with it what I will. I can as easily put you in Newgate or the grave. It matters little to me. That is, unless you would be of some use. Then I might find my way into letting you live rather than drop you into a dank cell awaiting the hangman." His feral eyes held me tight until they changed, a subtle glint now deep inside them.

His smile was slow and dangerous. "But perhaps you don't fear the hangman as you should. You can easily slip out of that noose, can you not? You've done it before. Yes, I asked about you and you are notorious in certain circles. They knew you were a tinker, for instance, and they knew where you lived and that you shared this disreputable place—" His eyes darted to the other cot, rumpled and untidy from Geoff's tossing and turning, "with the dim-witted one."

All hope fled and with it my breath.

"Yes," he said, getting right up to my face again. "That knave. What is his name?"

"Geoff," I choked out involuntarily.

"Geoff. Indeed. Yes, they say he is slow-witted. More like a pet than a man." He looked at his nails as if his words meant little. "Verily, they say he is little more than your lap dog. But they also say he is a thief as well. Surely your accomplice in these foul deeds, in murder. They'd hang him certainly."

"No! Please. Not Geoff!"

He was satisfied and stepped back from me, appraising his handiwork. He was the Devil's own apprentice, right enough, knowing all the proper words and gestures. I trembled as I recognized each of them. "Then perhaps," he went on, "you might be willing to listen to a little proposition I have for you." He pulled absently on the cuff of his sleeve. "For a bit of remuneration."

Remuner-*what?*

He sighed and rolled his eyes. "You do something for me, and I won't surrender you, or that half-wit, to the authorities."

Oh. *Oh!*

My fear eased, but only a little. There was still a dead man. What was to be done about that? "Er...good my lord, what is it you would have me do?" If he wanted me to kill someone I would have to refuse. While it was true I was many things—and a thief among them, aye, I confess it—I was *not* a murderer. My heart wasn't in it. Blessed Saint Dafydd knew that well.

If a snake could smile, I rather think it would have looked like his grin. I was beginning to think that maybe the hangman was a better choice.

"I am gratified to hear you agree with me," he said. "I have been a firsthand witness to your various…accomplishments. I am certain you can accomplish this particular task."

"I did not kill that man, my lord. You must believe me! I…I never saw him before. I just climbed out the window and there he was."

"Climbed out of my *bedchamber* window."

"I…erm…didn't steal nothing, my lord."

"Not for lack of trying."

"*Trying* is true, my lord, but not *accomplishing* has got to be good for something!"

"*Intention*, Welshman, is the sin."

"Well…I didn't *intend* to kill nobody…and I *didn't*!"

"That is a matter for the sheriffs. At the moment, I don't intend to help them find the murderer. But if I do not get the help I desire…"

"I hear you well, my lord," I said softly.

"Very well. I am Percy de Mandeville, the Keeper of the Wardrobe for the King…at the Tower of London."

Saint Dafydd's bollocks. I was in deep, *deep* trouble. I harkened well to him.

"I'm a man with great responsibilities. But I am ill compensated for them. Indeed, I am treated no better than a lackey. His grace the king has no appreciation for the sacrifices I have made, the indignities I have endured. Years and years of it. And then, he committed an injustice against me and my family. Well. The less said of that the better. His nobles are thieves and so I have no compunction about joining their ranks." He was breathing heavily. I think he forgot for a moment that I was even there. But when he remembered, his eyes slid over me again. He stepped closer and said in a quiet voice, "I have thought long and hard about his grace's jewels that are kept there. Yes, long and hard." Despite his earlier misgivings, he sat himself on my chair with his back to the fire. He stared dreamily into the distance.

Oh Christ. Here was a man in love with a single idea. There was greed written on his face to be sure.

But…did he not just mention the *crown jewels*? Surely he didn't mean…I mean, he didn't mean to say…

"The crown jewels," he said quietly. "Welshman, I mean to take them."

I becrossed m'self. "Ah now. That…that…is a…a… Good Christ!" I sat, in spite of him being a lord and him not giving me leave. My legs just wouldn't hold me up no more. I shook my head. "Lord Keeper, I am good at what I do, but not *that* good."

"Oh I think you are. If you do not wish for your friend to be turned over to the king's sheriff, I think you shall *make* yourself that good."

"But my lord! I never done anything like that! Shell games and…and the occasional foray into a manor house." I said the last sheepishly. "But *this*! This is big! How am I to get into the Tower? And get to the jewels? I don't know nothing about how — "

"You are forgetting that I know where they are and how they are guarded. This is my expertise. Yours is in taking them." He leaned back and stroked the smooth fabric over his wide chest. "But I am a generous man. I will not take all the profits from this venture. I realize the danger involved. I will offer you and your friend your freedom as well as one percent of the booty."

My ears were ringing like a Sunday. Did he just say one percent of the crown sarding *jewels*?

"Er…well, my lord. That is a feat worthy of the saints. Not that the saints would be, well…" I lowered my voice. "Robbing the king. Isn't that treason? I'm no traitor."

He puffed up like a mallard facing a gander. "Of course not! And may I remind you that you have no choice in the matter. It is this or you and your friend in the noose."

I sobered. He *did* own me.

He toyed with his dagger. "I need not tell you that this must be kept in the strictest confidence," he went on.

"I can't do it alone, my lord. I need help from my trusted friends."

He considered. "Then beware that they are under the same onus. And that is one percent in total, not for each of your accomplices."

I chewed on it. Well, Saint Margaret's dugs, that was still a tidy sum. But, the organization of the thing was a hellish nightmare.

"How will I—?"

He rose and pushed me aside. "I will send you a message when I will speak to you again. I shall not return here. We must not be seen together."

"Aye, I can see that." I bowed awkwardly. "Thank you, my lord. You are mercy itself, my lord. They'll be no need to speak of this to Geoff, now is there, my lord?"

"You do your part and you and your little friend keep your freedom." He swept away like it was nothing at all planning to steal the king's crown and jewels right out from under his royal nose.

I was cooked. What was I to do? There was no one in all of London town who seemed to care for Geoff but me. My hammer hung heavy at my side. I slipped it out of its loop of leather and looked at it. A tinker was a traveling sort. But traveling is tiring and dangerous. And if I left London, they'd never let me back in. I was no citizen, after all. Yet it was my home just as sure as Harlech gave me my birth. *Ach-y-fi!* What was a man to do?

"Oz?"

I jumped three feet in the air and whirled about, Saint Joseph in hand, ready to crown him good, and I doused Geoff instead with all the curses and oaths I knew. But it wasn't his fault. My mind had been miles away on a fair road far away from London.

"Geoff." I shook my head and sank back to my chair, slipping Saint Joseph back in his loop.

Geoff shuffled in. I looked at his kind face. Some might call it handsome in a boyish way. He wore a bright smile most times, though now his face was drooped in worry. His short, spiked hair reminded me of a hedgehog and usually caused me to smile. But not today.

He dropped down on his stool. That was Geoff's place more often than not, for Walter usually occupied the second chair. "What did that lord want?"

Out of the edge of my eye I saw movement at the doorway. "You might as well come in, Walter," I said. "No sense in eavesdropping."

"I was *not* eavesdropping," he said, the curl of his nostril signifying his resentment. He took his place in his chair. "I was merely curious."

Geoff gazed up at me with his innocent eyes. No, I was never going to tell him what danger he was in. What we were *both* in. That wouldn't do.

I placed my hands square on the table. "That was Percy de Mandeville, the Keeper of the Wardrobe for the King. And he...er...caught me. Last night. Robbing him."

Geoff gasped and threw his hand over his mouth. I could see tears welling in his eyes. I rushed to him and patted his head. "No, Geoff. Don't be afraid. He did threaten to call in the sheriff but instead he'd rather I did a job for him."

Walter immediately straightened. He was a quick fellow and he knew the lay of the land.

"He wants me to—"

"Don't say it!" Walter was on his feet and heading toward the door with his hands over his ears. "I know that whatever it is, it is highly illegal and possibly treasonous."

"Now how did you know *that*, Walter?"

He stared at me. I swear by Saint Michael, that the whites nearly filled his eyes. "Treason?" he squeaked.

"Well, I don't rightly know. Is stealing the crown jewels treason, after all?"

"No, no, NO!" He rushed about closing shutters and barring the door. "I was not party to it before you said it! Damn you, Oswald. I don't want to be involved."

"I can't do it alone, Walter. Geoff is as good as it gets, but I still need help. It's a big job."

"You are utterly mad! You cannot contemplate stealing the crown jewels!" He seemed to realize how loud he was and dropped down to a harsh whisper. "And I will not help you!"

"I've got to, Walter. They'll hang me sure. I know there is a good chance I deserve it."

"Ha!"

I stared at my feet. Aye, I could be man enough to admit it. It was God's truth. I was a thief and a rogue. But I never hurt no one and I never robbed no one that couldn't spare it. "It's Geoff I'm worried about," I said soft so that Geoff couldn't hear. "What would happen to him?"

I'd never seen Walter hysterical. Angry, aye. Drunk, more than I can count. But never as red and flustered as he was now. "What are you talking about? He's a thief same as you!"

I stood toe to toe with him. "No, he isn't. Geoff is a good lad. He does what I tell him 'cause he don't know no better. If he steals, it's because I tell him to and he's got a rare talent for it. But he's a God-fearing man just as he should be. And I'll cry it from the highest bell tower that Geoff is no thief."

Walter's bugged eyes stared at me in disbelief. I saw them shift toward Geoff cowering by the fire, back to me, back to Geoff, until finally he threw his hands up. "Very well. Geoff is not the thief. You are."

"That's so. I wish it weren't but there you are. And I have no choice. I must do as this lord says. I must try." But then the weight of the thing fell to my shoulders. I thought I could just look at it as a problem, a new Plan. If I saw it that way I could do it, I knew I could. But Walter was right. I'm just a thief.

I stumbled back, looking for the chair and nearly missed it till Geoff reached out and helped me to the seat. "And...there's another thing."

"God help us," muttered Walter.

But I caught sight of Geoff and knew he couldn't know about it. I sent him on an errand instead, to get more fuel. I knew that would take him a good while and I could have a hard talk with Walter. Geoff shambled outside, looking back over his shoulder at us. There was a kernel of a thought behind his eyes, but like a good lad, he did as told.

Once the door closed, I canted toward Walter. "Last night, there was...a dead man. Stiff as wood. I don't know if it was an accident or if someone killed him, but that lord is blaming me for it and it's that he's holding over my head."

"Oswald," he gasped. "You didn't—"

"No!" I cried. "Of course not. Me? Kill a man? I'm not one for the sight of blood, Walter, and that's God's truth. I found him there."

Walter looked at the door that Geoff had closed after him. "Maybe you'd best tell me everything, Oswald."

I toyed with my *tegan*, fingers finding comfort in the familiar slide over wood and steel. "Well, I've been bedding that sweet lass for the last few nights, you know the one—" and I gestured with hands cupped large over my chest. "Well, she works as a servant in my lord's manor house. She relayed to me the times that the lord takes to his bed and all manner of details of his schedule and I thought 'why not?' So I laid my plans, so to speak, and last night I snuck out of her bed when she fell asleep and made my way into the main house. I found his treasure, just like she said I would, bagged it, and was making my way out when one of the house guards caught me. We fought, and I ran up the stairs and nearly tumbled over Lord de Mandeville. I slipped past him and locked m'self in his bedchamber."

Hmm. Tell him about m'lady? No need to complicate matters.

"I tore the bedsheets and climbed down out the window while all Hell was breaking loose in the house. And when I got safe to the ground, I almost tripped over the body. He could have fallen out that bedchamber or out of another. He just looked like he took a right good tumble."

"Could the fall have killed him?"

I nodded. "It was a good way down. And stony. But I'm not familiar with corpses so…"

"Are you certain he was dead?"

"Good Christ, Walter!" I shot to my feet and paced. "His eyes were staring up at nothing. Maybe at God, but he wasn't moving no more. Trust me. He was dead."

Walter sat in thoughtful silence for a while.

"You should leave London, Oswald," he said softly. I looked up at his earnest face, that long nose, those sunken cheeks. He nodded. "You should leave London," he said again.

He lied a lot, did Walter. He was always saying how I vexed him and how I should leave him be, but in his eyes, I could tell he loved me well. I offered a weak smile. "Aw, Walter. I can't. They wouldn't let me back. A Welshman isn't exactly the sort they want living in their fair city. And it's my home. Where would I go?"

And Geoff, of course. Couldn't leave him. The girls always called Geoff fair-looking and sweet, giving him the eye right enough, but he was too much of a lackwit to do anything about their trifling. I reckoned he was my age, and that would make him three and twenty...going on ten years. I couldn't leave Geoff behind to fend for himself. He was a right mess when I first met him. And he couldn't take to the road anyway. He gets too confused in new places. And then there was the noose awaiting him...

Walter shook his head. "Oswald."

"What am I to do, Walter? I can't become an outlaw. I did enough traveling just to get here safe. So I have to stay and try to do this thing. Is it even possible?"

I went to the window, opened the shutter a crack, and stared out onto the street. The mud made it a hard trudge for those on foot. Horses drawing carts had a better time of it but not by much. The mud was churned up after all the traffic, and new storm clouds were looming. I could just make them out between the tall buildings shadowing the lane. Smoke curled down from chimneys and pranced along the tiled rooftops.

I inhaled a good whiff of mud and sweat and smoke and loved it. How could I be defeated by the likes of this? I was a clever lad, no boasting. I could think my way out of it.

But the Tower. A mighty keep in the heart of London. Surrounded by high walls all around it as well as a moat. Guards, flaming cressets at night to light its walls, gates and portcullis with its sharp teeth. Impossible! Impenetrable! Insane!

But like a bolt of lightning, I felt all tingly with the thought. For no one but the Keeper of the Wardrobe wished to entertain the idea that I might just be able to do it. Me. Oswald of Harlech. Steal the biggest cache of gold and gems in the realm. And why not? It was only five years ago a man with less sense than me managed to steal the old king's treasure right out of the bowels of Westminster Abbey. True, it was now stored in the Tower. A bit harder, but still.

Aye, I remember the crime well. It was all over London. But he was a fool and deserved to hang and hang he did. The difference between a fool and a clever man was a Plan.

And I always had a Plan.

I felt the warmth of pride stirring my chest. But just as quickly, it snuffed out like a candle flame. No. A master thief I might be, but it would all be for naught if I was ever thought of as a murderer. Before anything was accomplished, I had to find out about that dead man and who killed him.

CHAPTER FOUR

I LEFT THE safety of Cornhill Street and headed toward Newgate at the west end of town. I shook my head, thinking that it was madness itself going *toward* the sheriffs. Usually, I was headed in the other direction. But it had to be so. I had to know who the man was, for surely the hue and cry had been made and the sheriffs had been alerted last night.

Grimly, I headed up Newgate Market and stared up at the great arch of Newgate prison. "I must be mad," I muttered to m'self, and walked up to the guard.

He glanced at me, glanced away, and then looked again. "Oswald? What the hell are you doing here?"

"Greetings, Robert. Fine day, isn't it?"

He stared. His eyes were large through the nose plate of his helm.

I coughed. "Well. I'm here to see the sheriffs."

"On your own?"

"Aye. It's just a friendly chat."

"You're jesting."

"No. Wish I were. But…no."

He scratched his whiskered chin, gave me a look once more, and pivoted. "Oi, Falkes!"

A smart page, a lad of ten, poked his head out the dark entrance. He grinned when he saw me. "Oz! God keep you."

"He does, lad. He does."

"For the love of Christ," said Robert. "Oswald wishes to see the sheriffs."

Falkes snapped back. "He *does*?"

I rolled my eyes. "Just take me up, Falkes."

The lad shrugged and rambled up the stone stairwell, me at his heels.

Mind you, I had taken these same stairs many a time. Sometimes I was dragged up by Robert on one side and one of the sheriffs' heftier minions on the other. Mostly I made the journey with heavy iron manacles around my wrists with chains dragging after me.

But never on my own two feet and willingly.

Falkes approached the landing and spun about. "You know the way," he said over his shoulder and descended.

What was today's youth coming to when they couldn't bother to make the simple journey up a flight of stairs?

I stood before that all too familiar oak door and felt the hammering of my heart. "Saint Dafydd," I prayed aloud. "Watch over your poor Welsh son."

I knocked. The clerk, William de Wengrave, a short man with knobby knees, opened it quickly. I heard agitated voices behind him. The sheriffs were preoccupied, apparently.

William wore the same surprised expression as everyone else I encountered. "Oswald? What do *you* want?"

"I came to see the sheriffs. But it sounds as if they are busy."

"*You* came to see them?"

"Aye. For the love of Heaven." I was starting to get annoyed.

"Well." He looked back over his shoulder past the arched portico at the figures in the room. "You'd best come in and wait."

He opened the door wider to allow me in and ushered me quickly and quietly into a corner of the portico, beside a small brazier glowing red with coals. I was well familiar with this particular portico, for I had kept company with William many a time before the sheriffs could see me. Each year, a new pair of sheriffs would make my acquaintance. This year it was a mild-mannered vintner Nicholas Pigot and a squat-faced draper Nigellus Drury.

The voices were raised and the other man facing them, seemed furious and near to tears.

"What's all that?" I asked quietly.

William peered at them from the shadows. "That's Master Hamo Aubery. His son died last night under suspicious circumstances."

I perked up. "His s-son?"

"Yes. Master Aubery is the steward for Lord Percy de Mandeville. I don't suppose you'd know who that is."

Wouldn't I? But silence is sometimes the wisest course. "Even a fool is counted wise when he holds his peace," my mother used to say.

"The boy, Hugh Aubery, died falling out a *locked* window."

"Did he now? That's...suspicious."

"Indeed! He's getting no satisfaction from his master, Lord de Mandeville. That's why he's here. The poor man. Struck with grief. He only had the one son."

I gnawed on my fingernail without even realizing it. "So...so...they didn't arrest anyone yet, then?"

"I shouldn't be telling you this—" but I knew he would. William de Wengrave was a terrible gossip, thank Christ. "But the sheriffs aren't so certain it *wasn't* an accident. Could have fallen out the window, and then a servant could have closed it after him without even knowing, you see. No one would have found him till morning if there hadn't been a burglary at the manor house. The thief got away. So it's either a coincidence or it's the thief that did it. Or perhaps not. It's a puzzle."

"A...a burglary."

William suddenly gave me the eye. "*You* wouldn't happen to know anything about that, would you, Oswald?"

"Who? Me?" I blustered for a moment or two, truly looking like the offended party. "It's a sin, is what it is, you thinking that about me, Master William. Here I came of my own free will to talk to them sheriffs."

"Yes, about that. Just what did you come here to talk to them about?"

I pulled at my soiled tunic to straighten it. "You know, I have a mind not to tell you. In fact, I am so offended, I shall depart this moment."

I turned on my heel, and with a stunned William in my wake, I opened the door and marched out of it.

After all, I got what I came for.

Hugh Aubrey. God rest his soul. Why did you have to be killed the moment I was robbing that household? You have complicated my life, rest you. But something was amiss about it. Fell out a window only to have a servant close the shutter after you? I suppose it could happen. Odder things have happened. But it didn't feel right. Not at all.

I walked through the shadows of the arch once more, with the serjeant Robert looking after me. I hit a puddle hard and it splashed, speckling my stockings with dark mud, but I paid it no heed, so deep in thought was I.

I hated the very idea that he had died right when I was there, doing my utmost to steal fine gold. It galled. It took away my enjoyment of the thing, even though I didn't get no gold that night. I should at least get a good feeling from it. But that was robbed of me.

And I realized something else, some other feeling as well. I felt guilty. Aye. As if I were somehow culpable and *that* wouldn't do at all! For I was not. I just happened to be there at the same time of these dreadful events.

Or was I? For when I had tried to rouse him, he felt a bit stiff to me. I'm not one to know about corpses but I do know that a body gets stiff only when it's been dead long enough. I'm not so much of a fool not to know that!

So it couldn't have happened when I was there, but much earlier. *Much* earlier.

Walking up the Shambles, I sidled past a man pushing a cart full of stinking offal. I glanced at it and my belly turned, thinking of corpses. I couldn't take a fresh breath on the butcher's street so I hurried along, hoping my stomach would stay calm enough for me to reach Cornmarket.

I grabbed a fence and leaned over, inhaling the stink of pigs, but it was better than the metallic smell of blood in my nose.

"Here!" cried a man from the house. "If you're going to be sick, do it in the gutter, not my pigsty."

I waved him off—I must have looked a sight, probably pale as bone—and turned toward the street. My belly calmed itself and I had a chance to think. I leaned against his fence, feeling the sharp wattled twigs poke into my back. If Hugh Aubery died much earlier, why was he not found? A man falling out a window in the daytime would have been discovered, would he not? Or was that household so careless that anything could happen?

I was troubled enough by every thought imaginable. And I still had a burglary to plan! I took my vexed self back to Cornhill as fast as the mud allowed me. I needed an alehouse and right quick!

CHAPTER FIVE

I COLLECTED GEOFF and Walter. Walter wanted nothing to do with it until I offered to pay for the ale. There was still the problem of planning to steal the crown jewels. Walter still insisted he was not part of that plan but I knew better. I might need a man who could read and write. And he'd do it, too. After all, Walter was always in need of coin. We headed for our favorite ale house, but when we turned the corner, we all stopped dead.

Smoke billowed out the doors and we could see flames rising. Men with buckets ran back and forth until the black smoke turned white. We scurried to help. Shoulder to shoulder, we passed buckets and ran back and forth, pulling benches and stools out the door, but it was all for nothing. Our favorite alehouse. Gutted.

An hour later we stood around with other men from the lane, now sooty and tired. The tavern keeper was consoled by his friends and though we were frequent clients, we were not close. Instead, one by one, we stepped forward to the weeping man and offered our condolences. I felt badly but we needed a place to plan...and to drink. I called Geoff over from where he was chatting close with another young lad. "Gentlemen, I regret to say that we have no alternative but to find another alehouse."

The look Walter gave me, you'd think I suggested an outrage with the Holy Virgin. "But this is our tavern," he said, gesturing toward the blackened maw of the broken building. "It's always been our tavern."

"It don't look like much now," said Geoff. A big daub of soot smeared his cheek.

"I need a drink," I said again and marched down the lane. I know, I know. A man is a creature of habit and a man's tavern is as sacred as his parish church, though he frequents his tavern more than he ever sees the rood. Still, a usual chair, a usual chipped beaker, a usual smiling wench. These things can be homey to men like me and Geoff and Walter who haven't got the soft sameness of wife and hearth.

There were many on the lane, some who had just come from helping put out the fire. I recognized their faces and singed clothing. Others were merchants and still others those buying from them. I watched a proud boy walking up the street with a prize pair of dead coneys tied at the feet slung over each shoulder, their long ears bobbing with every stride. And as I watched him walk by me, I caught a glimpse of two men, well-dressed in long fur-trimmed gowns, swords at their hips, standing in the shadows. I wouldn't have taken any heed of them except that they appeared to be watching me. I faced the road ahead of me again but I couldn't help but look behind one more time for another nervous glance at those gentlemen.

But of a sudden, they weren't there.

"I'm seeing things," I muttered, but I was quickly drawn from my mood by Geoff pulling on my hand. He trotted ahead like some anxious pup and kept looking back at me with a wide grin.

We turned down Birchin Lane though I was not wholly familiar with the shops. There! Almost at the end of the street was an ale stake projecting over the avenue and a painted sign with two animals, a cockerel and a bullock. That was the place for us. I motioned them to follow and I stepped proudly up to the front entrance. Inside was warm and raucous, smelling of spilled ale, smoke, and savory meats. A man slid a bow across a rebec lying on his lap, making a merry tune, and some drunkards were dancing to it. Others were talking in earnest taut voices, their arms curved protectively around their beakers and bowls.

We found a spot on a long table. A small oil lamp gave us a pool of light and we settled on the stools. Geoff craned his neck, looking all about with wide eyes, already forgetting his troubles. Ah me. What I wouldn't give to be as addle-pated as Geoff sometimes.

"Masters, what may I bring you?"

I was looking about, too, and paid little attention to the woman who asked our pleasure. But when I turned, I beheld a sight that sent a jolt of yearning through me.

She was beautiful. Though a wimple framed her sweet face, I could see dark, lustrous hair peeking through the edges. And her skin was pale and smooth. Color blushed her cheeks, and her lips were rosy though a bit chapped. She fixed her brown eyes on me and waited.

Christ, could she hear what I was thinking? It *had* been a while since I had some quim. A whole day, in fact.

"Are you deaf?" She waved her hands in front of my face.

Walter glared at me and told her to bring three cups and a jug of ale. She left, but glanced over her shoulder, frowning.

"Who is that?" I asked, but of course Walter did not know.

"She's a wench, is all."

"Oh no! No, Walter. She is no wench. She's an angel. A wood nymph. She's something from a minstrel's song. That is no wench."

His mouth made a sour expression and he rolled his eyes. What was the matter with the man? Did he not see what I saw?

Walter did not wish to speak until the girl returned with the drink and we were finally left alone, and I did not wish to speak in anticipation of her arrival. And there! Parting the curtain to the buttery, she strode forth, three bowls and a jug on a tray. Her gown was yellow like a buttercup but her stockings, which I could see when her mannish stride kicked up the skirt, were sky blue. "Fair maiden," I said as she placed the bowls before us. There's nothing like a fair lass to make a man forget his troubles. "Pray, tell me your name so that I may sing its praises to the angels."

She sneered. My heart broke a little.

"And why would you possibly need to know that?"

A sour one, she was, if not on the outside, then on the inside. I smiled at her. It never failed to win a lass' heart, or so they tell me.

She poured the ale roughly and some of it sloshed upon the table. I scooted back so that I wouldn't get soaked. "I'm Alison." She held up a hand stopping me from replying. "And I don't care who you are. Mark me, I'm the brewster here. This is my place and I'll serve who I like…or toss out who I like, make no mistake."

She flounced away, her long plait swishing from under her kerchief. She was a fair sight retreating as well. A nice round-arsed lass.

Alison. And a widow. So no men to get in my way. I stood.

Walter grabbed my tunic and yanked me back down to my seat and I thumped down, blinking from the smarting in my bum. "What—?"

"Oswald!" he hissed. "Keep your mind off of quim and on your current situation! You are in trouble."

Oh, aye. Almost forgot! I grabbed my bowl and drank the whole thing. Good ale, this. Cockerel and Bullock was the name of the alehouse. I tasted tansy and gillyflower and a bit of sweetness. I liked the flavor of their ale. And the flavor of their maker, Alison. But there was much to do before I could attempt to partake of that.

Looking around I saw we were quite alone. I leaned in close and the others followed. Walter looked paler than usual and Geoff still had the tinge of fear in his eyes. This was a solemn thing, to be sure, and it was childish of me to be putting my thoughts elsewhere. "Right then," I said, my voice low. "The crown jewels."

"What makes you think you are any cleverer than Richard of Pudlicott?"

"Richard who?"

"Pudlicott! *Pudlicott!* The one who planned the burglary of the crown jewels five years ago."

"I know the gist but what exactly happened, Walter?"

Walter straightened. His palace accent got thicker and his words came out slower the drunker he got. "This was when the jewels were kept in the chapter house of Westminster Abbey. He was a poor wool merchant, in debt more often than not and got himself thrown into a Flemish gaol. Blamed the king for not getting him out. He fell in with a raucous crowd and discovered about where the crown jewels were kept and how the monks guarding them became slovenly and corrupt. He conspired with them to steal the treasure and succeeded…until they were all caught."

"And just how was that again?" I asked though I was fairly certain of his answer.

"The thieves were careless and exchanged the treasure through the goldsmiths and silversmiths of London. The thieves had even been so careless as to drop some of their booty into the Thames, and fishermen pulled objects up in their nets. They stashed them behind headstones in the church of St. Margaret's graveyard. These loyal citizens of London recognized what was in their possession, naturally, and alerted the authorities. When he was caught, Pudlicott declared that he had acted alone."

"An honorable man, then."

"I doubt it was for honor. More likely he would avoid anyone testifying against him if other conspirators were found. The man was a onetime clerk and pleaded benefit of clergy."

"Right smart that."

"Did him no good. He was hanged two years later."

Unconsciously, I rubbed my neck. "Well, rest assured I would plead that I did it alone because it is the honorable thing, not to save my own neck which wouldn't have a hope in Hell of being saved. It's that I don't want you nor Geoff getting into any trouble."

Walter saluted with his cup. "I admire your fortitude. But I'll believe that when I see it."

Christ, Walter. I hoped to God you never did see it! But that was Walter.

"He made his mistakes," I declared. "But we will not fall into that same trap. He relied on drunken monks and foul gentlemen. The

Tower is an entirely different affair, is it not? What of the Tower, then, Walter? In your memory, have you ever heard of anyone breaking into the Tower and stealing anything?"

Walter shook his head. "No. Oswald, it's a castle. No one man can break into a castle if the castle keepers do not wish it."

"Aye. You have a point. But, when you hear the tales, some army or other is besieging a castle, eh? That's many men. I think it is more difficult with many men. But I think that one man stands a better chance."

"Why?" Walter drank his ale thirstily and poured more. Walter was thirstiest on another man's coin. "What could possibly make you think that?"

"Well…a castle…is just a very large manor house, isn't it? I've been in many a manor house. A manor house has a gatehouse and guards, too."

"They usually don't have a moat," he growled.

"Harken, Walter. It's fortified, is my meaning. A gathering of men-at-arms clattering up to the gate and making a general ruckus calls attention to them."

"Your point?"

"I'm getting there. The point is, all them men focused on one point can be a distraction. A distraction for the man alone to creep round the other side and sneak in through a crack in the wall. Where they are least expected."

Walter opened his mouth but nothing came out. He frowned, swallowed a dose of ale, and frowned again. "Go on," he said, slowly.

I looked at Geoff. He was staring at me with them excited eyes.

"So I was thinking, that a man alone going in by extraordinary means has got a better chance than storming the gates."

Walter stared at me with lowered lids. "I'm listening. What is your plan?"

I drank a deep one and set the bowl down. "I'm working on it."

———— ◆ ————

WE WERE AT it, plotting and arguing and drinking for the better part of the evening. Walter would offer an idea and I'd point out the flaws and then I'd make a suggestion and Walter would beat it down. It was late when Alison came round again. She held a fire iron. "Good masters, it is time I close my doors."

"Mistress Alison," I said and bowed. Perhaps my speech slurred just a wee bit. "We are pleased to make your acquaintance and we shall return to enjoy your fine mead and ale."

She raised the poker to her hip. "I can hardly wait."

"Aw now, sweeting!"

She shied back and stuck the poker into my chest. "Don't call me 'sweeting.' I've given you no leave."

I leaned away and rubbed the soreness off my chest. "You've given me nothing at all but sourness. I'm a fine lad. Truly."

The poker was still aimed at my heart. "I'm certain you are. But I have no time for your mummery. Out with you."

Geoff tugged on my arm and we stumbled out the door. I looked back and there she stood, with the firelight blazing behind her. Truly, a woman of rare beauty. Beautiful enough to be a Welshwoman.

Walter was in his cups and poor Geoff did his best to herd the two of us back where we belonged. I slept like the dead. At least I think I must have done. But I awoke the next day with a head pounding like a hammer on an anvil. Geoff was as cheerful as always. He was a-chatting with some lad in the doorway, his arm around his shoulders, and they were laughing when he noticed me awaken. Geoff waved his farewell and nearly pounced upon me.

"Come on, Oz! Time to get up!" He pushed a bowl of porridge into my hand but I couldn't look at it. I pushed it back.

"Ach, Geoff." I held my aching head. "You've got a bell on every tooth! Hush, now."

"You've got to finish them badges for St. Thomas today, Oz. The priest has already been by. I put him off but if he comes again, I won't know what to tell him."

It was Geoff that got me the pilgrim badge commission. Geoff is a religious soul. God took away all his wits but He gave him the skill to break through a lock and for that, I thank Him. So it was the least I could do and make them badges for all His pilgrims…at a good price.

It was good to have the work. Coin was satisfying to earn the honest way, and working with my hands always gave me time to think, and I needed that time to do my planning.

I settled in at my bench with my trusty Saint Joseph and a large kettle with a crack. I'd have to make a patch to fit over the crack and hammer it smooth, so the kettle lay sitting and heating in my little brazier. I watched the coals turn to orange and I gave the bellows a few squeezes to make them glow.

"Oz?" Geoff did his best to mend my cloak or toil at keeping the coals stoked or any little task I set him to. But it was dreamy work for him, too. At the moment, he was polishing a serving spoon I had repaired and it was ready to return to its owner.

"Aye, Geoff."

"Oz. I was thinking about the Tower. It's a big place, isn't it?"

"Aye, Geoff. That it is. A powerful big place."

"I was thinking. What if we got lost inside looking for them jewels? How would we find them?"

"When *you* get lost in London, how do you find your way back?"

"Well…" He looked up at the timber and beams above. A dove had found her way in and flapped about on a beam, sending down a shower of feathers and dried bird shite. "I look for things that look familiar. Just like you told me, Oz. But sometimes, I still get lost."

"What of that map I gave you?"

"Oh!" He pulled at his pouch and took out the scrap of cloth I drew a map on with a bit of charcoal. "I forgot, Oz. It's a fine thing you done. And I've used it plenty."

"And forget about it just as many times," I chuckled.

Geoff laughed, a light sound. "Aye. I forget it, right enough. Say, Oz. We could use a map of the Tower to get about, can't we?"

I scrubbed my eyes and stared at him. Aye, it was still Geoff, only he'd gotten an idea. "Blind me, Geoff! That's a right smart notion you got there!"

"It is?" He scratched his head, making his bird's nest of hair that much wilder. "Bless me. I don't get them very often, do I?"

"No, but son, when you do, they are as bright as the sky! We'll make a map. And that sarding Lord de Mandeville had best get it detailed or we are all in the gutter."

"Say, Oz." Geoff grinned. When Geoff smiled, his whole face was as cheerful as a cake drizzled with honey. "Maybe we should see the Tower. I mean, Lord de Mandeville should take us there."

"He don't want to be seen with us, so he says."

"Oh. But he could still let us in and allow us to look about. Won't it be easier that way, so's we know where we're going? The map is only good to me 'cause I remember where I'm heading."

I couldn't stop staring at the lad. Whatever he'd eaten this morning, I wanted him to get extra doses of it. "Geoff, that's another good idea you've got!" I leaned over and rubbed his head like he likes it. "You done good, Geoff, right good!"

He beamed and set to polishing the serving spoon in his lap with a vigorous stroke.

Aye, it was coming together. Between my ideas and Geoff's, I had hope yet.

———•———

I KNOW I was supposed to wait for Lord de Mandeville to send me a message but I was chomping at the bit to get started. Geoff and I set out along Cornhill Street toward the Tower to see what we could discover on our own.

But when we turned the corner, I ran smack into someone and nearly knocked her off her feet. I grabbed hold of her arms and found m'self looking into the eyes of the lass with whom I shared a bed the night of the burglary.

"Oswald!" Her lovely face crumpled and she began to weep.

There is nothing more uncomfortable for a man than to have a woman weeping all over him. I patted her back awkwardly. "Now, now, lass." What the devil was her name? "I would have come to call again. There's no need for this." It was a small lie. Honey may be sweet, but no-one licks it off a briar.

"Oh Oswald." She lifted her face from the damp spot on my tunic. "A terrible thing has happened in my master's house."

A chill went through me. I gently pushed her back.

"There was a thief and he killed our steward's son. Oh, and such a fair lad was he. I tried to catch his eye many a time, but he kept his nose in his master's business and would not look my way. Such a pity."

"Y-you think this thief killed this lad?"

"What thief, Oz?"

I snapped my head toward Geoff. I'd forgotten about him. He might say something he shouldn't. "Geoff, go on ahead and wait for me by the Tower. There's a good lad."

"Go on without you?"

"I'll be there anon. You wait there for me, Geoff, you ken?"

He nodded reluctantly and walked away, glancing back with a troubled look on his face.

The girl pushed a ginger lock of hair back under her kerchief. "The master was ranting about a thief, is all I know. Poor, poor lad. And the steward is so distraught."

"Did you see the boy?"

"Aye. They got him in the chapel." She sidled up to me and slipped her arm in mine. She was almost cheek to cheek with me, and her breath was hot on my ear. "Come tonight, Oswald. I'm frightened to be alone."

"Oh…well…you see, lass…I don't think I can just yet. I mean…"

She drew back sharply and frowned. "You've run cold of a sudden. You think I don't know who you are. You're Oswald the Welshman. They say *you* are a thief. Coincidence, that. You being in my bed the same night the master was burgled. When I awoke from all the noise, you were nowhere to be found."

I clambered back from her. "That don't mean nothing. And you can't prove it."

A sneer pulled up her lip. "Go on, then! Back to your thief's lair. I'm done with your like."

She turned so sharply that a mud clod shot upward, splattering my stockings. That was that, I supposed. I certainly didn't want to return to Lord de Mandeville's manor. Except. The thought kept provoking me. As long as all were made to think that a thief was responsible, I'd never have a peaceful moment again. Of course, to prove I didn't do it was to also prove I was robbing the house. Was it possible to be free of both accusations?

I looked the one way up the street that would take me to the Tower where Geoff awaited. The other direction lay the manor.

Dammit!

With a silent apology to Geoff, I swept down the lane in the opposite direction and headed through the crowds to the manor house.

CHAPTER SIX

I KNEW THAT de Mandeville was probably at the Tower and not at his manor—at least I hoped he was—and no one else would recognize me at his house.

I had just hopped over the manor's wall and landed softly, when I came face to face with that man-at-arms I had encountered the night before.

He stared at me as if he couldn't believe it. *Oh, believe it,* I thought. *What half-wit would willingly return to the scene of the crime?* He had that smile again and then he drew his weapon.

I didn't wait. I bounded through the garden, tripping over stakes and fences in my hurry to flee. Why had I done it? Why? I was going to get caught and that would be the end of me!

I dived through a hedge and tumbled out the other side, rolling arse over ear until I came to a stop right side up. I shook off my dizziness and took off running. I skirted shrubs trimmed like dandelion clocks and skidded along the gravel path, knocking over a bird bath. If I could make it to the chapel, they'd never think to look for me there.

I ran and spotted a shutter wide open on a ground floor window and slid to a stop below it. I raised my head just enough over the sill to peer in. Finally! A bit of luck! I climbed in as quick as I could and slid to the floor, hiding in the shadows.

All was quiet. Hazy light filtered in from tall, arched windows of reticulated glass. A single candle flickered, standing in a sconce beside a bier. I becrossed m'self. I had stumbled upon Hugh Aubery.

As reverent as I could, I walked forth, head bowed. I stood at the head of him for a long time, not truly knowing what to say or think. Why had I come? What was I to gain from it except get m'self caught or killed? I know I didn't have anything to do with the lad, but I somehow felt responsible.

I pinched the gauzy cloth between my fingers and slowly peeled it away from his face. He looked a little bloated, more so than he had the day before, but I owed that to his being dead and all. "Master Hugh," I said softly. "I'm sorry this happened to you. I wish you could tell them I didn't have naught to do with it. But your master Lord de Mandeville is certain it was me and I have no choice but to do his bidding because of it." I sighed, for the lad, eyes now closed, thank Christ, could say nothing at all on the matter. He was beyond cares, was Master Hugh.

But as I looked at his quiet face, I noticed something at his neck. I slid the shroud down further and looked close in the dim candlelight. Bruises on his neck. You couldn't get those from a fall. Not out a window. "This boy was throttled," I whispered, for there they were, plain as day: fingermarks. I glanced around for any witnesses before leaning closer. I scoured his face and features, and moved to the other side and saw another deeper bruise on the other side at his temple and, God help me, a *dent*. "He was struck. He bled!"

"He will not answer you."

I jerked back and dropped the shroud over his face again. Stunned in place, I was unable to make my feet run.

But the man—the priest—dismissed my fear with a wave of his hand. He was older than me, perhaps in his thirties, fair-haired and broad-shouldered. He had the kind of face and bearing I should not be surprised to see in armor on the lists. A noble face. Of course, many a man from a noble family found himself in wont of an inheritance, especially if he was the youngest son. Some turned to the priesthood to find their way in life. I imagined he was such a man. He was not yet wizened by time and bent from reading close by a candle. "Calm yourself, young man," he said. "He may not be able to answer, but his soul lingers, at least for a month's time, so they say, so he can hear you and forgive you. For whatever sin you wish to confess to him."

"You...you didn't hear what I—?"

"No, no. Never fear. I did not hear you. Were you close to young Hugh?"

"No, my lord. We were not truly acquainted."

"Oh? Well, I suppose his father knew everyone on the estate."

I kept silent. The less lying I did to a priest the better.

"Poor Master Aubery. A good son, he had. Perhaps a bit too inquisitive but he made up for it in hard work. Strong. Honest. That is a commodity here sorely lacking."

I perked up but said nothing. What did this priest know of this household that I did not? Maybe he knew well the character of Lord de Mandeville, a man who was not afraid to steal from the king, the very goods that were in his keeping. That was a grave dishonesty indeed. Did he know? Did he know that his master was a bigger thief than I?

"Was he killed, my lord, or was it an accident? What are they saying?"

"Well, some say an accident and some say foul play. Some even say he jumped. But I don't see how that could be. A good soul, was Hugh. Alas. It is difficult to say, yet who would kill so innocent a lad?"

Who indeed?

It was dark, true enough, but I don't recall seeing no blood. Not on him and not on the ground. Nor on me, for I had tripped right over him. That means he did not die on the ground below the window. He was killed elsewhere and put out in the garden there to make it seem he fell from a window. He was already stiffening, as I recall.

But where? And by who?

"The mistress was most distressed. She doted on the boy, so they say, but a lad in his position should know better than to look beyond his status. Perhaps he was distraught over his love of her."

I blinked. "Of who?"

"My lady," he said quietly. "There was a rumor…dear me. I should say no more. If he took his own life, he cannot have Christian burial. That is very…troubling."

"Aye." But if it was murder instead… "That is a foul thing, my lord. I hope it is not true. Not that murder is better."

"Not at all." The priest patted my shoulder. "It is indeed very troubling. You must get back to your duties, as should I."

"Aye, my lord." I bowed to him but he had already turned away.

I pulled the sheet back over his face. I wanted to reassure him that he would find justice, but I didn't know if I could. "Master Hugh," I whispered close to his ear. "If I can, I will find you justice…and save m'self, too, in the bargain." Crossing myself, I left him.

But I wasn't done. A wild notion had taken hold of me. I thought about everything I'd seen the night before and I threw my hood up over my face and crept across the hall again, but this time I headed for the stairs to the upper floor. I passed a maid carrying linens but she did not look twice at me. I wondered if that guard was still on my trail. Though surely they thought I would have left over the wall by now.

I avoided the master's chamber and headed toward the solar. The door was ajar and I could tell that no one was within. I slipped through and quietly closed the door.

In the light of day all was easier to see. There was the rug on the floor before a table and cold hearth. I got down on my hands and knees on the rug and looked carefully. A wriggle in my belly like a live fish made all of me squirm. For what I had taken for a wine stain upon the rug the night before was surely blood. Blood, that looked to be hastily cleaned. With what?

I went to the hearth and grabbed the iron, rooting around in the gray ashes. My iron uncovered a half-burnt rag. I lifted it and could just make out a rusty stain. I swallowed. Had this cleaned the rug? Or the murder weapon?

I dropped it back in and set the iron aside. I scoured the room but didn't have far to look. A silver candlestick sat with its twin on the sideboard. But the one on the right was dented on one side and even listed a bit. I rushed over to examine it. Hastily cleaned but I sucked in a breath with a whispered prayer. There, inside the carvings, blood and…hair?

I felt sick. I breathed, trying to calm my belly.

Was it also wiped hastily with the burned rag? Someone throttled him but not happy with that they silenced him but good with the candlestick. And then…

"Good Christ!" I looked at the rug beneath my feet. The trap door was hidden beneath it and he must have thought to hide the body there till all was quiet. There were wine stains on the stairs as well, but now I knew they were not made by wine.

When the house was still, he had taken him to the room beside his chamber and chucked him out the window. Hugh would have looked like he took a bad tumble, maybe hit his head on a rock.

And the knave of a lord did it all himself and had the gall to blame me for it.

For I had the heavy feeling that Lord de Mandeville, who knew his house well, and was jealous of his pretty wife, did the deed and was now extorting *me* for the crime.

CHAPTER SEVEN

MY HEART WAS heavy as I climbed out the solar window. It led out to another garden and I easily scaled the wall and was free. I took my time down London's streets. I had committed many a sin. Fornication, stealing, adultery...but thou shalt not kill, and I never done.

Could he have killed him out of jealousy? The wife certainly had a roving eye. It roved toward me, after all. Might de Mandeville have killed Hugh for her?

It made me angrier the more I thought on it. How dare he kill someone and try to hang *me* for it!

Alas. He threatened but he also dangled the carrot, used my own pride and greed to hook me with the prospect of the crown jewels. Aye, he got me good and tied up.

I couldn't keep Geoff waiting any longer. I trudged down lane after lane. The houses trailed off to a wide field and a sloping hill reaching north to plains and copses beyond London town. To my left was Tower Hill where the gibbet stood, ready to take any poor soul to Heaven. I could see it gleaming in the sunshine, a body hanging from its open arm. Ravens were circling it, landing on the unfortunate's head, pecking at him.

I rubbed my neck in sympathy. Poor bastard.

I started looking for Geoff but got caught up in the magnificence of the Tower itself. I was raised in the shadow of Harlech Castle, saw it grow day by day and stone by stone. But this! This was different.

If you've never beheld the Tower, then you are the poorer for it. Such a proud structure. Oh, I suppose your cathedrals might be taller or more ornate, but this is the king's own palace, his castle in the heart of his proud city. And like London itself, the Tower is not fancy or decorous. It sports no gargoyles at its corners nor is it faced with beautiful stone. But it is an edifice of frightening strength. Tawny in the sunshine, its walls rose straight up overlooking a moat surrounding it. And then there are inner walls with round turrets and battlements. I could see chimneys, and timber and daub walls with peaked, tiled roofs. Must be where the household lived, for truly it is surely a hive within those intimidating walls.

I had to think about that. It wasn't as if the place was vacant but for a few crowns, a scepter, and some jewels. No. A whole household and a household within a household lived there, for there were lords like de Mandeville who spent his days there and they had servants, didn't they? And there were cooks and maids and blacksmiths and a constable and knights and horses and host of others who lived there day and night.

All food for thought.

But that was not the end to the structures within structures. It was like a puzzle box, with more nesting within. For I could see, if I stood on my toes, that within those inner walls, was the Keep itself, the White Tower. They say that William the Conqueror laid the cornerstones down for it himself but that later kings added their own walls and structures. The Keep was a square building with three square turrets and one rounded turret, each reaching up to a spire, pointing toward God Almighty. Pennons flew from those topmost spires, whipping in the wind. I could hear them even from where I stood as if they were singing the praises of the Tower's own strength. These were the king's apartments, with those ancient stone walls protecting him. But he needed no protection from me, for I would not hurt the king for anything, Welshman though I am, for I am no fool.

It was only last year that England mourned the passing of his father, King Edward Longshanks. There's no denying that King Edward I was a fine warrior, taking my people's homeland for his own. The Welsh don't think kindly of the English for that, but there was no stopping the king of England and his army. My mother suffered in our village, for she had loved an Englishman and bore his bastard, who was half and half but didn't belong with either. But I've managed.

And in truth, I sometimes find my heart filled with hate for these cursed English bastards who would take the fair land from peaceful folk with an ancient history, a history more ancient than theirs. But what are a people to do? Like a stalk in the wind, we must needs bend or we will surely break. As my mother said, "Adversity brings knowledge and with knowledge, wisdom." I tried to make m'self wise, mostly by living in the enemy's camp, but also by keeping my ears open and my eyes skinned.

Well, London is my home now. Nigh on ten years. Soon I'll have lived in London town longer than in my village. What is the stronger? The old dead days or the new days ahead?

Edward of Caernarfon, Edward II, was king now and...well. Even though he was not the man his father was, his father was still the man who invaded Wales. I didn't mind too much the thought of stealing from this family.

Standing at the edge of the moat was Geoff. He was laughing with another young man, sharing a jest, standing close and guarded. Geoff was a friendly sort, no mistaking. Many a patient young lad found him pleasing. But when Geoff spotted me, he ushered his companion away with a shy smile.

He loped forth, finding his place beside me and shook his head, gesturing toward the mighty Tower. "Oz, it's so big!"

"Aye," I whispered. "Might be as big as Heaven. I forgot how big. I'll never be able to make my plans work."

He turned that smile on me, the one like a torch in the wilderness. "'Course you will, Oz. You'll have your map! That was my idea."

The map. Maybe he was right. It felt a bit smaller with the idea of a map. Would Percy de Mandeville cooperate and provide one? The knave had better if he wanted me to get his jewels for him.

"How much gold do you suppose is in there, Oz?"

I shook my head. "I haven't rightly thought about it. Would have to be a lot to keep the king in furs and velvets, eh? Pay all them people living inside it."

"And at Westminster. Don't forget, Oz, the king has two houses."

"And more, Geoff. He's got them all over England, France, Scotland, and Wales. How much money does a man like that have to have?"

"He's not just a man, Oz. He's the king."

"I haven't forgotten that."

We drew closer and at my urging, he followed me around the outer walls. We were both studying them like a raven picking the best eggs out of a dove's nest.

The one entrance from land was the Lion Tower. And indeed, it was said that the king kept lions and all manner of animals as one might see in Noah's ark in that very tower. A big-bellied tower it was with a drawbridge running north and south connecting the city to it. There was our first hurdle directly before us. With this drawbridge up and shut tight at night—and surely nighttime was the best time to do our deed—then we'd have to cross to it on a boat or some such. But we couldn't lower that bridge in the middle of the night without giving warning. I'd have to return tonight and look it over, see if there were any chinks in it for a body to slip through.

Since the gate was open now, I could look my fill. Peering through that great mouth of a gate, I saw a road that curved and opened to a grand courtyard but it continued on and curved right into another tower which might also have a drawbridge. God blind me! Two drawbridges in a row. During the day the drawbridges lay down like tired dogs, but at night they'd be upright and shut tight. Perhaps daytime was the best time? Saint Dafydd's bollocks but this was a puzzle.

I turned to say so to Geoff but he wasn't there. Now where the hell—? I raised my chin to scout out for him and caught the tail of his cloak bouncing ahead. Oh Holy Virgin! Geoff had jumped onto a cart laden with straw, creaking over the first drawbridge and he was waving to me. Christ!

I gave chase. I pumped my arms in a dead run up the mound to the drawbridge but I was stopped at the point of a spear by a guard in mail and surcote.

"Back, knave!" he said and I felt the point jut into my chest. I backed away just glimpsing Geoff disappear past the great arch.

"But...but...." I pointed, but he wasn't having it.

"I said *back!*" The spear point—more like an ax with a long, sharpened spine—convinced me.

Geoff! You sarding fool! What are you doing? There was nothing for me to do but wait. I began to pace, wearing down the bit of road beneath my boots. The guard never stopped glaring at me, and then I reckoned that I had best not be someone worth remembering or recognizing. Scuffing my boots in the dirt and putting up my hood, I wandered away down the mound and along the road. Oh what was that dim-pated lad doing? He'd get himself killed and then what would I do? I took good care of him, I did. He ate, didn't he? Had a place to sleep. Had a trade of sorts. I didn't want nothing to happen to him. But the only help I could think of was Walter, so I hurried my steps and in no time found m'self back on Cornhill Street.

I pounded on Walter's door and his maidservant, Sibbe, answered it. "Oswald, I'd take a rod to you if you held still long enough," she groused. She was a wizened old thing with wild white hair barely contained under a kerchief. I used to jest that she must have been Walter's wetnurse, but he never laughed at that, which leaves me to conclude I might be right. She never liked me and there was nothing I could ever seem to do to change her mind.

"Sibbe, please, fetch Master Walter."

"What kind of trouble? Coin or gaol…or both?"

"Neither. Just get your master before I take a rod to *you*!"

"As if you could." She shook a little white fist at me, skin pale and pulled taut over her boney knuckle. "Master WAL-ter!" she cried. "That knave Oswald is at the door. Shall I toss him out?" There was too hopeful a tone in her voice.

But soon a grumbling Walter shuffled to the door. "What is it this time?"

I grabbed his arm and tugged him over his threshold. "Geoff's gone and done it. Christ have mercy but he's truly done it this time."

"What has that churl done now? And stop yanking me!" He wrested his arm back and glared at me down his large nose.

Suddenly I couldn't breathe. I leaned over and pressed my hands to my thighs, gasping. I felt Walter's tentative hand patting my shoulder.

"There, there. Sibbe, fetch the lad some water. Make haste!"

I shook my head. I could feel the curls slapping my temples. "No. I'm well. I am." I rose up. Sibbe, of course, had not moved a lazy muscle. "We were inspecting the Tower. Geoff and me. And suddenly he disappears. And the next thing I see, he's hopped on a cart heading inside."

Walter pulled me into the foyer and led me to a bench, pushing me on it. "Heading inside where?"

"The sarding Tower! Geoff's inside!"

"What? Why didn't you go after him?"

"I tried, didn't I? But I was turned away by the guard." I clutched at my head and started rocking. "What will become of him? They'll torture him. And it's all my fault!"

"You should have thought of that before you agreed to this idiocy. Now look what's happened. Geoff inside, surely to be incarcerated and you — Oh God! And *me*! God's teeth, Oswald! The guards will be baring down on us now! And all because of your stupid schemes. I never should have befriended you, never should listen to you." His usual woeful expression was filled with even more woe and he sank to a chair. "This is my punishment for befriending a thief."

That awakened me. "Walter! Thinking of yourself at a time like this when God knows what is happening to our Geoff! For shame!"

"He's not *my* Geoff."

I jumped to my feet. "He is, too! You've been his friend as long as I have."

He moaned. "Be still, for God's sake! Yes, very well. I *am* his friend."

"Then we should go down there — "

"And do what? They wouldn't let you in."

"But maybe they'd let *you* in. You've got fine clothes and a palace accent."

"No, they wouldn't let me in either. I've no business there."

"Then we must think of some!"

"Oswald, be reasonable. We'll just…wait. Surely they will let him go. Once they see he's a half-wit they'll send him on his way."

"Truly?"

"It's possible." That was Walter's way of saying he didn't know. But he was right. There was nothing we could do but wait. Such a terrible thing, is waiting. Waiting for good tidings or bad, it was all the same.

I decided to go home and Walter joined me. He had Sibbe bring us cold meats and fish dumplings. She brought it grudgingly but I couldn't touch it. I gnawed on a finger instead, staring out the window.

Hours passed. The shadows moved across the square and buyers and sellers waxed and waned. I was all worry now, my body thrumming with it. And then a figure—sopping wet by the look of him—stumbled down the lane. I knew that head of hedgehog hair anywhere! I tore out the door and ran, and at the end of the lane I grabbed him by both shoulders and hugged him tight. "Geoff! Geoff! Are you well, lad? Did they hurt you?" But I had only to push him at arm's length to see the damage. His face was bruised and there was dried blood at his nose and he was soaking and stinking of a sewer. "Aw Geoff!"

I expected him to be crying, but he wasn't. He had a stiff look about his face but he wasn't weeping and when Walter met him in my doorway, he gave Walter a nod and sat on his stool. I covered him with a blanket and brought a basin of water and a rag and began bathing his face. He let me.

"Welcome back, Geoff," said Walter, voice rough. He stood over him like a guardian angel.

"What happened, Geoff? What did you see?"

"Well," he said, pushing my hands away from his face. "I got a fair piece inside, Oz. You should see it, Walter. It's big. Bigger than any place I've ever been before. That map is what's needed, Oz, and no mistaking." He licked his lips. "You wouldn't have a spot of ale, would you, Oz?"

I looked to Walter who rolled his eyes and reluctantly ambled next door to call for Sibbe.

"It was big, Oz. I never seen anything as big."

"Aye, Geoff. I believe you. But tell me what you saw."

"Remember how you was pointing out the gates and the drawbridge, and remember how we could see the second tower inside? Well guess what, Oz? There's *three* drawbridges, one after the other."

I groaned. Impossible! This was becoming more and more impossible.

"There's a great gatehouse once past the moat to the inner ward. I could see guard rooms past the doors and great fireplaces. There were a lot of men, Oz."

Walter trotted back with a jug in hand. He gave it to Geoff who tipped it to his lips and drank and drank. I pulled it away impatiently and squatted before him. "Geoff! Go on!"

He smacked his lips again and wiped his chin with his wet sleeve. "The cart went past the bell tower and came to another gatehouse. We passed under the portcullis—no drawbridge this time—and into the inner ward. I saw it, Oz. I saw the White Tower. Up close! There were knights and guards with horses in the courtyard and one of them spotted me in the back of the cart. They dragged me out and beat me. But I wouldn't say nothing."

I patted his head. "My brave Geoff."

"Aye. They tossed me in the moat."

"No!"

"Oh, that was all right. I wanted them to."

"Geoff you dunder-pated *twpsyn*! Why did you want them to do that?"

"So I could swim around it and look for places to get in."

I sat back on my heels. God blind me! Either I was getting stupider or Geoff was getting smarter.

"So I swam and swam. There were eels, though. You know how I don't like eels. But I kept thinking of you, Oz, and I kept going. I was tired, though. And I couldn't make it around the whole thing, but I climbed out and came here."

"Well, Geoff." I was proud of him, and no mistaking. "You done right well. The best ever!"

"I did? Aye, I saw a lot."

"Aye, you did, but not quite enough. We can't wait for Lord de Mandeville to get off his arse and contact us. We got to send him a missive and make him take me into the Tower. I've *got* to see it for m'self!"

CHAPTER EIGHT

I STOOD OVER Walter as he penned the words. His quill scratched slowly, each loop and flourish like vines and flowers. He finished at last and carefully folded the parchment and sealed it with dripping wax.

He held it aloft. "How shall we deliver this?"

I hadn't thought of that. I couldn't very well take it m'self and I wasn't going to send Geoff into the lion's den. Sibbe wouldn't do it even if told.

Exasperated, Walter stomped to the door. "I'll get the boy next door to do it."

He sent him off with a coin and the missive and we set to waiting once more.

After a thoughtful silence, Walter cleared his throat. "Oswald, have you honestly thought this through? While it is true you are the cleverest man I ever met, you are also prone to missteps and disaster. What makes you think you can trust this man? I tell you. I think the best course is to run."

"And I already told *you*, Walter, I cannot do that." My eyes darted toward Geoff wrapped in a blanket and testing his steaming clothes drying before the hearth.

"And there is the little matter of a murder," I said.

"He may not have been murdered. You said so yourself. He could have fallen —"

"I went back to the manor."

His face changed in a heartbeat to fury. "You *what*? You *idiot*!"

"Shush!" But Geoff was already looking our way.

"Geoff, why don't you throw one of my tunics on and go get us some meat pies before the shops close."

"Very well, Oz." He grabbed my patched work tunic from a coffer and slipped it on. He had an unhappy look on him but he went anyway.

When the door closed, I rounded on Walter. "Don't you go telling him things. I don't want him to worry."

"I'm not the one who tumbled over a body, now am I?"

"That's why I went back." I sat, running my hand through my hair. It felt dry and crackly, like old leaves. I shivered. "I had to know. I...saw him in the chapel. His name was Hugh Aubrey. He was the son of the steward. He was younger than me, Walter. And I believe it was no accident. I saw the gash on his head and the bruises around his neck. He was murdered. And I also know where. In the very solar that the lord's treasure is hidden. I saw the blood stain for m'self on the rug...and down below in the treasure room, where that murdering knave stashed the body. He was killed right enough, Walter. And then tossed out the window like the contents of a chamber pot. And I think it was Percy de Mandeville what done it."

Walter's large hand covered his mouth. The horror in his eyes must have reflected my own.

"But if Lord de Mandeville did it, Oswald, then what can *you* do?"

"I don't know. All I know is, he's going to hold this over my head to make me steal the jewels."

"What makes you think he will be done with you once you've accomplished that?"

"I was thinking the same thing. He said he owned me. And he does. Until I can prove it was him, I've got to continue with this scheme. To save Geoff *and* my own neck."

We said very little after that. I poked at the fire and Walter sipped at my ale. We had a lot to think about, him and me. A scheme such as this was hard enough, but with a murder to prove, it was ten times harder.

———— • ————

WHEN GEOFF RETURNED, we ate, we drank. To pass the time, I thought of doing a bit of the Shell down the lane but I don't like to do it so close to home. So I got a dice game going instead. It was much harder for the fools to catch me out at cheating. It's the nimble fingers and weighted dice, you see. Three sets.

I wandered back with coins in my pouch. By this time Geoff's clothes were dry and he shrugged into his own tunic and tied his gaiters to his calves.

It was at Vespers when the messenger finally arrived. We huddled around Walter as he opened the letter with quivering fingers.

Walter read silently, his frown growing deeper and deeper still. "He says he is angry that we did not wait for his message but he says to meet him at the gate on Tower Street by Prime tomorrow. He says to come alone. I don't like it, Oswald."

"Oi!" said Geoff. "You're not taking me?"

"The man said for me to come alone and that's as I would have it. But while I'm gone, Walter, see what you can discover about this man, Percy de Mandeville. Does he have any enemies? What are his weaknesses? Does he owe anyone a debt?" De Mandeville wanted leverage, eh? I'd show him leverage.

Walter gave a quick jerk of the head. Walter wasn't good for much, but he could read and get folk to talk to him. That was a powerful skill, I say.

We parted company and, later, when I'd settled in my bed, I could find no sleep.

I guess Geoff couldn't either.

"Oz!" he hissed in the dark.

"Aye, Geoff?"

"What's troubling you? It's more than the Tower, isn't it?"

"Don't worry, Geoff. All will be well."

The straw under him rustled as he sat up. His silhouette was a dark shape against the coals casting their glow against the wall. "I may be a half-wit, but I still know when you're keeping something from me."

Taking a deep breath, I smelled the night heavy around us. The damp just outside the door, the musty smell of the straw in my own mattress, the smoke from the coals. Usually, these were comforting smells. But now, they only served to close the walls in on me. I did not know what I should tell him and what I should keep to m'self. Though maybe I was underestimating the lad. His voice was clear and far from the unsure man he had been five years ago. Maybe he learned, just slower than the rest of us.

I turned to look at him, though he was still only a dark shape. "That Lord de Mandeville," I said. "I don't trust him. I don't think he'll be done with me once this job is over. I think he will use me and use me until I'm all used up."

There was a thoughtful silence, until, "That's not good, Oz."

"No, it isn't. And I must find a way to rid us of him once we're through with this scheme."

"We could leave London, like Walter said." His voice was unsteady and small. God bless him for his liberality.

"Aw Geoff. You weren't supposed to hear that. I will not leave London except into the arms of God's angels. London is my home now, and yours, too."

"But if it isn't safe..."

"It's never safe. Don't worry, Geoff. I'll reason it out somehow. Go to sleep."

"God rest you, Oz."

"And you, Geoff."

He settled in the straw and left me wondering. If a man was capable of murder, to what lengths would he go to keep it secret?

———•———

THE TOWER WASN'T all that far from Cornhill. Just down the lane, south on Bridge Street, then over to Thames Street and cut up to Tower Street. As the sun rose, I left our shop. The church bells had not yet rung for Prime. I planned on going down to the wharves and listen and talk to some lads about boats that might come and go to the Tower. There was a lot to think about. But I couldn't wait to get m'self inside them walls.

Just as long as I was allowed *out* the gate as well.

I walked down Bridge Street and took a left at Thames. There were plenty of buildings along Thames, fine cookshops that filled the air with the savory aroma of meat and sage. I sniffed the sharp smell of lard in the baked pastie crusts just come from the ovens. My belly growled with the thought. I often came this way to buy a meal on the hoof. Skewered larks are one of my favorites. But the turrets of the Tower called to me, rising as they did above the shops and stalls, blazing gold with the dawn, until I finally cleared the vestiges of the city and beheld the Tower again. The wharves bustled in the mornings. I like to watch the wherrymen and fishermen at their barges and nets. Another man's job is always more interesting than one's own.

I spied a fisherman I knew, Tim, and he was busy passing a shuttle through his net, repairing it, I supposed. I watched him from a distance for a bit before I approached.

"'Day to you, Oz," he said. And then I saw him reach for his money pouch and slip it around to his back.

I let it go. The man had every right to worry. "God's blessings, Tim. Are you a fisher of men today or of fish?"

"I'm a fisher of nothing because of this damned net. Tore it again. The fishing's stinking today anyway." He squinted up at me. "Isn't it a bit early to be at whatever illegal thing you are about, Oz?"

I spread out my empty hands. Maybe a little dirty, but they were clean of misdeeds this hour. "Tim, I'm merely enjoying watching the boats."

He glanced toward the Thames. The grey churning waters sparkled like a mermaid's tail in the sunshine. If I took a deep breath I could catch a whiff of the sea, briny and heavy in the distance. But mostly I smelled fish, both fresh and rotting.

"The boats. They are pretty things, aren't they?" Talk to a man about his business and he'll be all jaw.

"Aye, they are. How far do you go up and down the Thames, Tim?"

His eyes narrowed. "Why do you want to know?"

"Can't a man talk to another without accusations?"

"No. Not you, at least. You want something, so you might as well come out with it."

I pretended to be affronted for another moment or two and then I dropped all pretense. It wasn't worth the trouble. "I was just wondering, Tim. Do you ever have occasion to make deliveries to the Tower?"

His gaze stretched along the bank until it reached the edifice. "The Tower...of *London*?"

"Aye."

"What business have you got there?"

"Harken, Tim, I am innocent of whatever it is you are thinking. There is just a wench who works as a laundress there and I wondered —"

He laughed. "Oh it's that, is it? Coins and quim, that's all you think about."

Aye, the man knew me well, there's no mistaking.

Tim resumed his net repair. "There's only one way in from the water, and that's at St. Thomas' tower at Water Gate."

"There's no other gates?"

"Naw."

"I see. Thank you, Tim. You're saving me trouble."

He laughed again. "There's no saving you, Oz. Christ's blessings on you. God knows you'll need it."

With a nod I moved on, gazing upon St. Thomas' Tower in the distance, the Thames lapping against its stony walls.

The rising sun and the sound of the bells of Prime told me I should hurry to the Lion Tower entrance. I didn't want Lord de Mandeville angrier than he already was. I trotted around the moat to the road and turned the corner sharply. I spied him immediately and made haste, bowing to him when I neared. "My lord."

He quickly looked around and motioned for me to follow him into the shadows. "You have incommoded me, Welshman. I gave you strict instructions—"

"And I beg your pardon heartily, my lord, but it has to be done. There is so much to plan that there is no time to waste."

"Well, your eagerness does compel me." He looked around again. "What is it you want of me?"

"I need to get into the Tower grounds, my lord. I have to see what I must conquer to do the deed. And I shall need a map of the environs both inside and outside."

He fit his thumbs into his bejeweled belt. I eyed them jewels long and hard. What was one percent of a fortune? With the profits, could I buy that selfsame belt twofold over? Threefold? I haven't a head for them kind of numbers. Walter could help with that.

"I could take you now, but we wouldn't have very long."

"It would help, my lord. It truly would." I felt bees buzzing in my innards. I was that edgy.

"Very well. Put your hood up and come with me."

I pulled my chaperon hood up over my hair, yanking it low over my brow. I had a time keeping my head down but my eyes up, scouring my surroundings, for I did not know what might be helpful for our scheme.

We approached the Lion's Gate and with a mere wave of his hand, the guards ignored us as we passed through. I looked up at the portcullis, the chains arcing upward, and once we passed through, I looked back but I realized the mechanism was high up in the tower, invisible from our vantage. I would have liked to have seen that but I didn't think we'd have the time. I'm a fair hand with delicate work, my *tegans*. I've done my share of carving gears and levers. And I did not yet know what I would need to conquer this edifice.

But it was not to be. We moved forth along a road to a wide courtyard, a good place to get trapped if I was an army. The battlements above could be crowded with archers and an army — or even a man alone — would have no chance at all.

I fell behind de Mandeville's steady gait and hastened to catch up to where he was already walking beneath the arch of that middle tower. Over another drawbridge we went where a host of guards were milling about, some with their halberds leaning lazily in the crooks of their arms, others with beakers of ale in their hands. They bowed to him but didn't pay me any heed.

This second road was a bridge taking us right over the moat to a third drawbridge. I gazed out to the muddy waters thinking of poor Geoff and them eels swimming and squirming about him. Can't say that I liked the thought of them much either. We passed through yet another tower. De Mandeville muttered that this was called Byward Tower.

It was difficult, what with the round bellies of the towers, but I paced off from where I thought the outside of the wall began to where it seemed to become the inside of the wall. Twelve feet thick, by my reckoning. Twelve sarding feet. It would take from now till the Second Coming to mine through that!

Once we passed through the arch, I looked up and spied the bell tower Geoff spoke of. A square tower atop a round turret. We were in the outer ward and there were high walls — forty feet high — all around. Saint Dafydd! I felt my knees getting weak. I glanced at de Mandeville's face. His expression was stern and he looked neither up nor down but straight ahead, never bothering to look at me while I kept a few steps behind him or to the many who bowed as he passed. I tried hard to keep my hate for him inside me. Any man who threatens an innocent like Geoff was fair game, to my way of thinking. And now him being a cold-blooded murderer...But thoughts of revenge were useless. He was a mighty lord and I was a tinker. The odds were against me.

'Course, that never stopped me before.

Ahead of us rose a large square-faced tower with a portcullis nestled beside the large round record tower, and we passed on through it a long way. A big structure was this square tower with rooms and stairs going in all directions. Blind me! Like a rabbit warren.

We emerged into the sunshine and to a long wide gravel avenue. There was a long dividing wall to the left with a garden — trees and hedges — and a taller embattled dividing wall to the right with some houses of timber and daub against it on the other side. After walking a way down the avenue, we turned right and passed through yet another arch and out to a greensward where a cluster of short towers and stone buildings hugged the knees of the White Tower itself. Gleaming in the sunshine, it stood tall and proud, each of its lead-covered turrets waving pennons. The windows were dark like staring eyes. I had stopped in my tracks and just now noticed de Mandeville looking back at me with a deep scowl. "Come!" he hissed with a jerk of his hand.

I girded my courage and trotted after him. We were to go inside the White Tower and as I looked across the expanse of greensward, more walls, and more buildings, and back the way we had come under arches and through walls, I wondered how I was to get through at all.

And knights. Aye, we encountered knights and guards and dogs and horses and men of all stripe all the way through. Holy Virgin! The deeper we stalked into the Tower grounds the more impossible it seemed.

I looked up at the south wall of the White Tower. It was called thus because the whole was whitewashed in lime and shined bright like a heavenly thing.

Just as we approached the stairs a page came running up to Lord de Mandeville and whispered something to him. He huffed and shook his head. He pointed to the spot I stood and said, "Stay there!" like he would to a dog before he hurried off, following the page.

I was no dog. And truly, I needed to see what I was up against. So I took a long, slow amble of the Keep's south side. It was the size of a large manor house with three levels of windows. They were all arched in the Norman fashion and got smaller as they marched up the walls with double windows on the left side.

I walked on and turned the corner, keeping my hood low over my face and nodding to a guard with a mail coif clutched around his chin, who kept giving me the eye. I had to pass through an arch in another dividing wall and when I emerged, I looked up the bright wall of the Keep. This side was different. The wide turret swelled outward and there were fewer windows, but the ground floor windows were just as tall and narrow as on the other side.

I turned the corner again and the north side was even plainer with both square turrets and five windows marching across the face going three high.

Finally, I rounded the other side and saw much the same, with three levels of windows. Each turret in each corner sported windows but not the same number or at the same height as the other windows, which must have meant that these were for a different use. Most likely they were stairwells, but of that, I couldn't be certain until I saw them for m'self.

I turned to go back and stopped short. In the distance stood two men in long gowns with swords at their hips. I could not see their faces for the shadows but they seemed to be studying me. I ducked my head, hiding my face under my hood, and made my way back to the south side of the fortress.

Were those the same two knaves staring at me back on Cornmarket?

A fist closed on my collar and yanked me to my toes. I twisted round, expecting the worst, but it was Lord de Mandeville, his eyes ablaze and his red mouth warped by ire. "I thought I told you to stay over there!"

I shook myself loose from him and straightened my tunic. "Now my lord, I have to see the outside as well as the inside. I have to know my course."

He leaned into me and jabbed a finger in my face. "I own you, Welshman. Never forget that. Never forget that I hold your companion's life in my hands."

I shrank a little. Couldn't have him taking it out on Geoff. "I beg your mercy, my lord." I bowed, wincing up at him through my hood.

He grunted his approval and without any signal to me, marched ahead. I followed like the good lackey I was and we headed for the foot of the stairs. It was certainly a building of impressive proportion but I can't say that the Conqueror had an eye for design. Maybe things were done different in those long-ago days.

Up the steps we came to a great hall. Pillars marched away from us like soldiers while servants flitted about. The floor was painted wood and it was a long rectangular space, some eighty feet long. De Mandeville leaned down to whisper to me and it so startled me that I jumped back. His patience was thinning, so I girded m'self and harkened to him. "I *said*, the walls here are seven feet thick, impossible to cut through."

I felt smaller and smaller. "My lord, I beg you to reconsider. Perhaps there is some other thing I can do for you. I do not think that this is possible."

His whisper was harsh. "You will find a way or I will hand your lap dog over to the authorities. Is that clear?"

I crumpled the hem of my tunic in my hands. "Aye, my lord. It's clear. But it isn't clear how I'm to do this thing. Walls many feet thick and forty feet high. Gateways with portcullises. It will take a miracle."

"You complain a great deal for a man who is supposed to be clever," he went on. "Have I been mistaken in that?" He withdrew his dagger and brandished it. I stumbled back, fear closing my throat. "You must die — here, now — or do as bid. Make your choice."

I gulped and ran a hand over my slender neck. "It isn't fair you blaming me for killing that lad. It wasn't me that strangled him or coshed him good. I swear, my lord."

His eyes bulged as he glared at me. "Who said anything of that?"

"It's true, my lord. He didn't just fall out that window. He was strangled and hit on the head. And I didn't do it."

He took a deep breath and straightened. "So! You are fiendish indeed. Tossing the poor lad from the window wasn't enough for you, eh? So you strangled him, did you? Smote him, too, in your passion? Such vile secrets. Which did which, hmm? Did your half-wit strangle him while you struck him down with a candlestick or did *he* do it? Perhaps it best I rid the streets of London of you and your foul companion. Perhaps I waste my time on this."

"M-my Lord —"

The dagger was in my face again and I cringed. "You've told me secrets only the killer would know. I have no wish to be party to your sins. But if you wish for me to keep them secret, too, then I suggest you be silent and do as I bid without argument."

"N-now my lord! There is no need. I will do as bid. I swear by Saint Michael. But I must think on it. I must have time."

"Very little time." He thrust his dagger back in its sheath and I breathed a relieved sigh. "It must be done before a fortnight, for the king shall return by then."

A fortnight! How can all be planned and implemented in the span of a fortnight?

I closed my lips and followed him as he led me near a guard hovering beside a spiral staircase. I lowered my head further as de Mandeville distracted the guard with small talk and shooed me down ahead of him behind his back down into the vaults below the keep.

Down the stairs I went and looked around. This space was divided into a maze of corridors. The only windows, if a body could call them that, were several arrow slits interspersed across the walls. They gave narrow bands of pale light. Cressets burned at intervals, leaving pools of flickering light upon the stone floor and weaving demon shadows beyond it on the walls. I did not like this place that seemed more tomb than palace. Made me think too much of my own grave. Strangely, it made me think of my mother as well and I prayed to her then. *Please, don't let this be my last act on this earth! Mother dearest, watch out for your poor son from Heaven.* But suddenly I could hear the words she would have said to me. *Oh Oswald, my love. How do you get yourself into such things?* A mystery, to be sure.

I was ready to follow this man into Hell, it seemed, however unwillingly, and I almost did just that when I made to step forward, but suddenly, he was there beside me and thrust an arm across my chest, stopping my progress just in time. I looked down. A dark maw opened before me, sinking into the earth God knows how far.

A pit? An infinite pit right in the floor before here and there? What sort of place was this?

"There are traps," said de Mandeville unnecessarily because I could see that well with my own eyes. "Many traps." I stared up at him. His face was hard to see in the dimness but his eyes shown with preternatural light. Oh, this man knew of traps, right enough. "This is the dangerous part," he said.

This is the dangerous part? Maybe he wasn't thinking of the forty-foot walls and the guards with their sharp weapons, but I was. What's a pit to all that?

"No one knows how far down this pit goes...or what is at the bottom." He shivered. Blind me! "First, you must cross this pit and once on the other side, there is one more trap before you get to the doors."

"What is that trap?"

"I don't know."

"You don't know? But you are the Keeper of the Wardrobe. How is it you do not know?"

"I leave it to my guards. They know. And if something is needed, I send them ahead."

"So, there is a pit here first and then another trap and then what?"

"Two sets of locked doors. Each has several locks that must be opened simultaneously."

"Saint Dafydd's bollocks," I muttered. "It takes an army just to get through."

"As it should. It was far too easy to steal the king's jewels when they were supposed to be safe at Westminster Abbey. The king has learned the lessons of his father."

"Aye, he has." I squinted into the darkness, trying to see whatever trap lay beyond the pit. "I suppose them guards use a ladder to get across."

"Something like that."

"But that next trap…"

"I understand it is something equally deadly."

"Of course it would be. And then two doors with multiple locks. Can you get me the keys?"

"No. The keys are on my person at all times and must never leave me, even to make a copy. These things are checked periodically and I would be immediately suspect if they were to turn up missing, even for an hour."

"Naught of that, then." But the thought finally occurred to me. "But sir, why is it if you have the keys and the means, that you do not do the job yourself?"

"Are you mad? That's the first place they would look? All suspicion must be removed from me if I am to accomplish it."

Of course. The sly devil.

I could just make out the door in the distant gloom. Tall, arched, with bands of iron and rivets pocking its surface. Two lock plates, one in the usual location and one directly above it. The doors were only thirty feet away but it might as well be a thousand.

I looked up to the rafters. "And what is above?"

"The chapel of St. John the Evangelist. A very plain chapel that rises to the top story. But each floor is heavy with mortar and stone, impossible to breach."

A chapel. But there were windows in the chapel, while here there were none.

I could feel him looking at me expectantly. I licked my lips, thumbing toward the locked doors. "How much is in there exactly?"

His eyes, the only bright spots I could see on his face, seemed to light up. "There are crowns and coronets, scepters, bejeweled swords, gold plates, candlesticks, gold florins and silver coins in bags, gold ingots, loose gems and jewelry. It will take many bags. Over one hundred thousand pounds worth."

My mouth went dry. It was the greed, I knew that. I had never heard of so much wealth before. But I could hear my mother's voice again, this time shaking a finger at me: "Too much pudding will choke a dog."

There was nothing for it. It had to be done. I could feel the cold steel of his dagger at my neck. But God help me, I couldn't wait to see that treasure for m'self, even as frightened as I was.

"There are two things I need, my lord."

"And what is that?" he asked, eyes narrowing.

"I will need a careful map of the environs and of the Keep, as detailed as you can give me. And I will need that guard above at the stair to be absent the night we are to accomplish it."

He nodded. "That is easily done. For you see, there are few guards needed here when there is an entire castle to breach."

And well I *did* see it. Saint Dafydd, but a solid Plan at last was forming!

I bowed to de Mandeville. "I think I have seen enough, my lord."

CHAPTER NINE

"I DON'T KNOW," Geoff was saying after I told him all I had seen and some of my ideas. "It seems dangerous."

"Of course it's dangerous, you dunder-pate! If it weren't, anyone could do it!"

"I'm scared, Oz. Scared for you."

"Don't be. I tell you, I've got a Plan!"

"Heaven preserve us," muttered Walter. He was drinking all my ale again and offering nothing but moanings and wailings. I tell you, sometimes the man was as useless as Geoff.

"Aye, a Plan. But we need to burgle something first."

Walter blanched. "What? Isn't one outlandish burglary enough for you?"

"We are going to need Greek Fire. Unless you know how to make some, we'd best steal it."

"Greek Fire?" Walter's eyes pinged back and forth in his head. "Why on earth would you need that?"

"It's a distraction. It's important. But we must get it quickly. I was thinking tonight."

"Tonight? From where?"

"An alchemist, of course."

Walter shook his head and paced a trough in the floor. "And do you even know what you are looking for?"

"Well, that's where you come in. I'll need you along, Walter."

"You are mad. I am not going with you."

"But Walter, you must. If the thing is labeled, I'll need a man who can read."

He threw up his hands and leaned heavily against the wall, his head hanging low. "Holy Saint Margaret. An alchemist. Who?"

"I know of a man, Benet Chigwell, who has served the king's army with Greek Fire before. He's down St. Martin's Lane. And I happen to know that he is out of town."

"Oswald...."

"We need it, Walter. So how about it? Shall we go?"

"What? Now?"

"Aye. Geoff, come hither and I'll show you both the Plan."

———◆———

I WAS NO fool. I had been to the place before. In disguise. It was a year ago, but no doubt all was the same. I sketched out the layout of the place on the table with a bit of charcoal. Master Chigwell had high walls around his house. It would need ropes and I had them. I explained to them the complicated stairwells, for Chigwell had many of them like a puzzle for he was a clever man and liked to keep his doings secret. We'd have to leave ourselves a trail so that we would not lose our way. I had the yarn ready on a spool just for that purpose.

The more I spoke on it the more tense Walter got. Well by the saints, if Walter could not help with this simple robbery, how was he to help with the Tower?

After an hour of explaining, Walter grudgingly agreed to go.

Geoff just grinned at me. Good old trusting Geoff.

We waited till nightfall. While others dreaded the night, looked on it with fear in their hearts, jumping at each little scraping of rat or howling of dog, I looked on it as the time for Opportunity. Night time was the time of my business, so to speak. Shadows were my friend and kept me safe from the Watch or danger from a nosy spy. I knew London by night and I led an excited Geoff and a tentative

Walter through those familiar lanes. Each had a coil of rope over their shoulders and as we got closer to the shop, I slowed them, gesturing for them to crouch a bit in the darkness while I looked about.

The alchemist lived in a tower-like structure. For all the world, it appeared to be akin to a windmill without the sails. A tower surrounded by a wall. Sound familiar? It was a good test for our future endeavors.

I'd been experimenting with my *tegans*, fashioning larger pieces with movable action. Tonight would be a good test of the equipment that might prove useful at the Tower. It was a four-pronged hook, but not truly a hook until the hook sprang free once it was launched. Light in weight, too. I was right proud of it and gave it a good look over in the moonlight. With its arms folded down it appeared to be more like a short javelin. I motioned for the others.

"Give me the rope," I said to Walter and he handed it over gratefully. I tied one end of the rope to my *tegan*/hook, making certain the knot was tight, before I swung it back and forth in my hand. I scanned the wall for the best place, gave the rope a good overhead whirl, and heaved it. The hook arced into the darkness. It stopped with a click as it opened and a soft satisfying clang. I pulled it and offered a smile to Geoff. "It works."

With one hand wrapped around the rope and one foot against the wall, I said over my shoulder, "Now, lads, up we go."

"Wait." Walter looked vexed. "We're to climb vertically up a wall?"

"Aye, Walter. What did you think I meant when I said we were going to 'climb the wall'?"

"Well, I..." He craned his neck looking upward. "I didn't think we would actually...I mean it didn't seem that we... God's teeth, Oswald! That's a wall!"

I lowered m'self. Sometimes Walter needed the coddling of a small child. I slid my arm over his shoulder and he stiffened at the contact, knowing as he did that I was about to do my best to talk him into something he didn't want to do. How long had the man known me?

"Walter. We're here to steal this man's goods. His goods are behind this wall. What other means would you suggest? Knocking on his door?"

He raised his chin with a huff. "I'm not a simpleton. You need not address me so."

"Then try not to act so." We could argue or we could get caught, but there was only the third choice as far as I was concerned. "Walter, we must go up the wall. Now you can help or go home, I care not which." I grabbed the rope again, set my foot upon the stone wall and pulled m'self up, walking up the wall. Out of the corner of my eye, I saw Geoff looking at the rope and then at Walter, wondering what to do. If I knew Geoff — and I did — he'd side with me. He always did. And sure enough, he grabbed the rope, but Walter pushed him aside. "Very well," he grumbled. "You'd best be there behind to catch me," he said to Geoff, who looked doubtful now about the whole thing.

The rope strained in my hands, getting stiff and taut and I reached the crest of the wall just as Walter scrambled with both feet against the stone, looking for purchase. "How is it done, Oswald?" he huffed. "You must be part fly."

If I had as easy a life as Walter with the rich food he always ate I'd not be able to lift m'self from a chair let alone up a wall.

I lowered my hand to him. "Not far now, Walter. Give us your hand."

With me clutching his hand and Geoff shoving him with his shoulder from behind, Walter managed to lay himself over the wall. His face was sweaty and he glared at me. He lay like a pelt, the top of him on one side and the back end of him on the other. "Now what?"

"Now...we jump."

"Down there?"

"Aye, Walter. Like this." And I pushed him over. He had the good sense not to holler when he landed. But he did jab two fingers in the air at me. I smiled. Geoff reached the summit and we both leaped down together. The rope was in my hand, and I yanked, sending the hook down. I stashed it amid the bushes. Walter, no worse for wear but fuming, waited for me in the shadows. "And now," I said in a whisper. "To the house."

I am partial to windows for entry. No soul is likely nigh, and one might have a bit of time to do the deed if you find the right one. I circled the house looking for just such a window and found it. A high corner window, its shutter closed tight. It was a good solid stone tower with plenty of handholds, and like a spider, I made my way up. Walter sputtered and gasped below me. Now what?

I grabbed the sill and looked down. Walter gestured upward. "How am I to scale that?"

I looked at my feet, secure on an inch of stone, and on my hands gripping the carved sill and didn't see the difficulty. I shrugged.

"Here, Walter," said Geoff, lifting Walter's foot and placing it on a foothold before the man snatched it back. "There," Geoff pointed, undeterred.

Walter bristled a bit and then lightly touched the wall as if it might burn him. He grabbed more firmly when he'd found a handhold and placed his foot back where Geoff had showed him. With a grunt he pulled himself up and lay with his cheek against the wall. I couldn't help but roll my eyes.

I let Walter be, listening with only half an ear to his grunts and groans as he slipped and climbed after me. My task was to get the shutters open. I pulled but naturally they were locked. I took out my eating knife, raised it high, and slid it into the gap between the shutters and ran it upward before I encountered the latch. I slid it up slowly until I could feel the latch swing back, and just like that the shutters opened for me.

I pulled them open enough to slip through and I landed softly on the floor, looking around. No one there. Good. I knew the alchemist had but one servant and he was an old, deaf man. We would get in easily.

I leaned over the sill and saw Walter's red face as he climbed and there I was again, reaching down and pulling the man up the rest of the way and yanking him bodily into the room where he landed in a heap. Geoff popped his head over the sill like he was a cat and looked this way and that. "Is Walter all right?"

Walter glared daggers. He rubbed his backside. "How did I let you talk me into this?"

"Because you're a good friend, Walter." I helped him to his feet and brushed him down. He slapped my hands away.

"Let us get this over with."

"Right." We had arrived on a landing and I led the way to the top of the stairs. With my back against the wall, I peered carefully down the darkened stairwell. It was black as pitch below and I dared not strike flint to steel to light a candle. Instead, I crept slowly down with two sets of footfalls behind me.

By the time I reached the bottom my eyes had adjusted and my gaze rose. The tower was an open structure with a web work of staircases spiraling upward. But here was the odd part. Only one led to the place we needed to go; the alchemist's parlor. The rest were set there as a trap for the unwary. A sly man, was Master Chigwell. But I had mastered this a year ago. I pointed to a staircase on the right, stepped forth, and they followed.

I took out my spool of yarn and began to unreel it. If we weren't to spend a sennight here getting out, we could follow the thread back the way we had come.

We climbed the spindly wooden structure. It swayed, for it hung from the rafters with cables that I hoped were strong. We reached the top and encountered a problem. It ended, rather abruptly. I bent forward and looked down into the chasm.

Well hell.

"Now what?" came Walter's caustic voice in my ear.

I scratched my chin. The first nubs of beard were peppering my jaw. Breathing deep I looked upward, then downward, then to the side. "Er...we took the wrong stairs."

"I can see that for myself! But what are we to do now?"

"Why, take another, Walter." I turned on my heel and led the way down, winding up the yarn again, and hopped onto another nearby staircase, allowing the thread to unwind behind me once more. If this went on too much longer, I'd run out of thread.

The staircase rocked back and forth with a low groan in the rafters. Geoff followed suit, giggling at the movement. He was fearless, that lad. But Walter stared sorrowfully at us as he stood on the stair Geoff and me had just left.

"I'll stay here, if it's all the same."

"It isn't, Walter. That one was a false stair. And I can't speak for its integrity. It might be designed to fall soon after a thief made his way on it."

If I blinked, I would have missed Walter's clumsy scrambling over to where we were. "I'm never listening to you again," he grumbled. "Are you certain this is the one?"

Now that he mentioned it... "Well, I thought that other was the right one. That crafty alchemist might have moved them about. It was a year since I been here last. And if that is the case then I don't know which is the right one."

My eyes, now fully adjusted to the dark, scanned the many staircases and the maze of light and dark they made. It was all lines and angles here in the dark and it was difficult to guess which went all the way and which terminated. I noticed something else, too. There wasn't much of a way down from where we stood either. It was go up or go nowhere.

I didn't tell Walter that.

Geoff's eyes shown with excitement. "Which way, Oz?"

"Er…" I didn't think the stair we were on was the right one either, but my eyes followed the lines of another, higher up and the only way to get to it was to climb the one we were on. "That way!" We climbed. I'd run out of thread suddenly and I just let it fall. It was no good to me now anyway, but I didn't tell Walter that either. I was beginning to worry, for the higher we climbed the more unstable the hanging staircase became. Rich men and their sarding trap staircases!

Walter must have been thinking the same thing. "Why does this alchemist make it so difficult to see him?"

"We're not exactly meeting him, are we? This is to keep thieves out."

"And does it?"

"Witness with your eyes, Walter."

"Oz, look!"

Geoff pointed upward. A stair crossed over our heads, and we clambered up that one, leaving the last stair to groan and lurch on its bolts and plates fastened to the beam above us.

Yet the new stair we were on proved fruitless, too. I had thought for certain that it was the right one. "Holy Mother, Geoff. Can you see which one it is?"

He squinted into the distance and shrugged. "That one, I think."

"Don't just *think*," said Walter. "Be *sure*." His fingers whitened over the cable and his head was shifting from side to side trying to see a way down. But now we were many feet above the floor.

"It's that one, Oz. I'm sure of it."

The one Geoff was sure of was a good fifteen feet away with a gap like the pits of Hell. We could never jump it. Then I got an idea.

"Very well, lads. Let us make this stair work for us. Lean this way." I pulled on the cable and swung the thing.

Walter held on with an arm slung around the cable. "What are you doing? You're swinging the stair!"

"I know, Walter. I plan to swing it into *that* stair, the one we want."

Geoff got it right quick and pulled the cable into rhythm. With us working together, the stair was soon swinging wide.

Above I heard a groan of metal against beam. We had best accomplish it in haste or this stair wouldn't last long either.

Walter had a death grip on the railing now, but he was beginning to help, bending his legs to sway his body along with me and Geoff.

I leaned out as far as I could with my outstretched arm. I was so close to reaching it. "More, Geoff. Put your back into it."

It lurched. We didn't have much time. If the cable snapped, we'd be dashed to the floor. "Walter, move in rhythm with Geoff."

"I'm trying!"

Now was not the time to discover he had no touch of rhythm!

A little more…a little more…got it! I grabbed the railing tight with fingers curled around it, and that stair swayed to meet us. "Make haste, you two. Get across."

Geoff was first, having no fear. He scrambled over the side and made the leap. He turned and held his hands out to Walter. "Come on, Walter. I'll help you."

Not to be outdone by a halfwit, Walter girded himself and sloppily jumped, catching his foot on the rail and nearly going over the other side. But Geoff was a man of his word and grabbed his coat and pulled him back before he became a blot on the floor below.

Geoff made certain Walter was secure before he reached over and grabbed the railing on my side. "You're turn, Oz."

I had one leg over the rail when, with a mighty shriek, the cable gave way, whipping about like a great serpent. I ducked, feeling the whoosh of air as it streamed by my hair nearly beheading me. The cable shot its way toward the floor and the staircase fell away with it.

I lunged for Geoff…and missed!

And yet, the angels must have borne me up for I did not fall into the pit of darkness as befitted a thief like me. When I got my wind back I opened my eyes and looked up.

Walter's fist was buried deep in my tunic, cloth wrapped tight around his hand and even with a trembling arm he would not let me go. He and Geoff hauled me in and we all sprawled like fish from a net onto the stair.

"Much thanks, Walter," I gasped. "And Geoff."

"That's nothing, Oz," said Geoff, smiling. "Look there."

I did, and saw the door at the top of the stair. God be praised!

Up we went and reached the door at last. There wasn't even a lock. There was no latch, come to think of it. I pushed on it, expecting it to open, but alas.

"And if you say 'Now what?', Walter, I'll skin you alive."

In silence—except for the ominous creaking of the hanging stairs—we contemplated the door that had not lock, latch, or way in. Tight as a castle.

Castle. Gate. Portcullis!

"Ah!" I bent and pushed my fingers under the door. "Lift!" I shouted to them, unmindful of that old servant that might still be about. If he was here, even deaf he couldn't have avoided *feeling* the stairs crash.

It moved. An inch. But now that there was more room, my companions slipped their own hands beneath. With grunts, we pulled and slowly, slowly it rose. But we were having a hard time of it, for no matter how we pulled, got under it and pushed, prayed and swore oaths, it would move no quicker. Finally, it lifted enough to slip under and I did, rolling. Geoff followed and Walter followed him, whimpering the whole way, and like some giant hedgehog, we rolled all together in a heap and stopped. The door slammed down again and I hoped by all the saints we could get it opened once more to leave.

When I gained my feet, I found myself staring into the sharp point of a crossbow quarrel aimed straight at my heart.

CHAPTER TEN

WE WERE NOT alone as I had supposed.

"Thief!" cried Benet Chigwell. His crossbow was cocked and ready to fire and I was the one who might soon be wearing an arrow-sized hole.

I raised my hands pleadingly. "Now Master Chigwell. Please." He was supposed to be out of town!

"Though I must admit," he said, a smile turning up his lips. He had a day-old beard of white stubble on a lean, lined face that had the look of boiled leather. "I have to admire you for your fortitude. Coming this far." He wore a dark cap over his long white hair whose tendrils reached to shoulders covered with a black wool gown rolling in folds down to his ankles.

"And we will leave more peacefully, sir," I said.

"Oh no. Not you, Master Thief. We must call in the sheriffs to dispatch you."

"There's no need for that, Master. We will leave quietly, with no harm done."

"No harm done?" He looked over my shoulder to Walter. "No harm, he says. This is quite out of the question. You have destroyed my stairwells."

"Master Chigwell," said Walter, in his best noble bearing. "I do not see why we cannot come to a comfortable agreement. It so happens that this lad was trying to get me in to see you and we came across your…interesting staircases. Surely a few silver coins might go far in assisting in their repair."

"Oh ho! And you have the coins? I see you are a gentleman. Why not just knock at the front door?" Geoff and me looked at one another sheepishly. Walter was smart enough to stand his ground. "What might you be doing in this thief's company?"

"As I said. He was merely assisting me in coming to you to buy a most precious commodity."

Slowly, the crossbow lowered and I breathed a sigh. "Precious commodity?" he said, eyes narrowing. "And what might that be?"

Walter was now in his element. He was a man who enjoyed negotiation though little he profited from it. Walter straightened and lifted his chin. "Sir, it is an unusual request. And it might even raise questions. But I hope that our silver will assuage that."

"Go on, go on," urged the alchemist.

"We seek…Greek Fire."

The alchemist blinked. Then he burst into laughter. I wanted to elbow Walter. Buy? We weren't here to *buy*. Though, come to think of it, I suppose we could have. I felt a bit of a fool.

Master Chigwell recovered and stumbled to a chair which he sat upon. He cast his crossbow on a table without care and looked at all of us. "Greek Fire? I'm to sell it to you, am I? And what makes you think I shall?"

Walter lurched forward to protest but the alchemist raised his hand. "It is dangerous," he said, sobering. "Extremely so. You must tell me to what purpose you intend to put it."

"No. That is out of the question."

"Well then. We are at an impasse. I must know its purpose else I cannot in good conscience sell it to you."

I saw my chance. I grabbed for the crossbow and held it up, aiming at the man with trembling arms. "Th-then you must surrender it to us without payment, good sir."

He looked at me and at the arrow pointed at him…and laughed again. What bedeviled the man? Did he not see that I — oh hell. By all the saints. I dropped my arm and looked at the sarding thing. This was no working crossbow. The quarrel was nailed to the stock and there wasn't even a trigger.

The man laughed again and snatched it out of my hand. "Foolish things, weapons. Someone could get hurt." He tossed it to the table again, and now I understood why he had done it so carelessly before. "So, thieves you are. Go ahead. Steal it. If you can find it."

He sat again with a self-satisfied smirk on his face and crossed his arms over his chest.

I looked at Walter. Another trick? "Look, old man," I said. "We are in dire need of your Greek Fire. A life depends upon it and we *will* have it. With your help or without it."

"A life, you say?" He didn't appear convinced. "As you say. Search for it. Very much without my help."

I fisted my hands. Sorcerer, that's what he was. "Come, Walter." I pulled him along and he seemed to wilt, losing his bravado.

"Shouldn't we have disguised ourselves?" he said quietly once we were at the other side of the room. "Now he can point a finger at us. Accuse us."

"He won't do any such thing," I assured, though I wasn't too certain of that. "He's mad. Search the room. Here, Geoff. Look about and search for anything like a jar or vessel with writing on it."

The room was vast. Noises like fluttering wings disappeared into the inky dark rafters and I knew there must be birds…or bats. I chilled at the thought. Shelves lined one wall, so high there was a ladder leaning against it. They were filled with jars and more jars, baskets, wooden coffers and the like. There were skulls, too, and stuffed ferrets and birds. What manner of place was this?

None of the jars or coffers seemed to have the labels I held such store in. How were we to tell what was what without the sarding man's help?

I glanced down at him. Aye, he knew the problem. His smirk turned into a full-blown grin. I stuck my foot into the first rung of the ladder. "You'll never find it," he cackled. "You think I would let simple thieves like you find such dangerous compounds?"

I continued to climb and push jars out of the way. One teetered on the edge and his shrill laughter turned to a gasp. "Be careful, you fool! Those are valuable."

Ah. I got me an idea.

I shoved a vessel to the edge of the shelf…and pushed it over. As it tumbled down, the lid flew off and a black powder dispersed like a fine mist before the jar shattered against the floor below. I looked down at the aghast alchemist. "Oops," I said.

"Young man. Stop that."

Another jar slid to the edge and plummeted over the side. A gray goo leaked from its shattered remains.

Chigwell was on his feet. "I said stop that! That took me weeks to formulate."

"Dear me, Master Chigwell. I am unable to find the substance I need. And I am afraid I am clumsy in my search." Another jar met the fate of the other two.

"That's enough!" He grabbed the ladder and shook. I nearly teetered over, but I grabbed on and glared.

"Give me what I want!"

"Why? Why do you need it?"

"I told you. To save a life. Or two."

He closed one eye and homed in on me with the other. "What is your name?"

"I'm Oswald of Harlech. What's that got to do—"

"Oswald the Welshman? The thief?"

No time to puff up my pride at being known. "So you know me."

"*Of* you, certainly. And you wish to use my Greek Fire for some nefarious purpose? To commit a burglary?"

I bit my lip. "Well, as I said, a life was at stake, Master Chigwell. Er…" I looked at Walter. Should we include him in this? Split that one percent yet more? But by Christ we needed that potion!

Walter could see in my eyes what I was up to and vigorously shook his head. *But Walter*, I pleaded silently. *Be reasonable.*

No, you idiot, he seemed to be saying back at me with his wide desperate eyes.

We could surely beat the information out of the man, but I was not a violent man and if he knew anything about me at all, he knew that, too. He would not sell it and we could not steal it so we had no choice but to gather him into our confidence and our scheme.

"Good Master Chigwell—may I call you Benet?" I climbed down the ladder and stood beside him. With an arm slipped around his shoulders I smiled. "Ben, I see that it is time to open my soul to you. There is in fact a burglary. Indeed, quite a burglary—"

"Oswald!"

"Calm yourself, Walter. I think we need to include Ben, here"

Ben chuckled. He slipped from my loose embrace and sat down again, threading his fingers over his belly. "I should like to hear this."

"Oh of *course* you would!" said Walter. "Perhaps you can oblige the sheriffs by looping the noose around our necks. No, Oswald. Geoff, you may stay with this lunatic but I, for one intend to leave."

He spun on his heel and approached the door but it was shut up tight again. The wheel was beside it and I could see the mechanism now. A clever man, was Ben.

Geoff wrung his hands and looked from Walter to me.

"We need to trust you, Ben," I said, "and that is no lie. 'Tis a very dangerous burglary. It might even be treason."

Ben's laughter subsided and he looked at me with concentrated interest. "Indeed. Treason, you say. I have certainly heard of you, Master Oswald. You are not a man to waste his time on foolishness. This must be an important venture. Profitable?"

"Most profitable, sir. More profitable than your wildest dreams."

"I have some fairly wild dreams, young man. Surprise me."

I licked my lips. "We're going to rob the Tower of London."

Silence. His lips quirked but when I didn't appear to have been jesting, he quickly frowned. "Hmm," he said. "And you need the Greek Fire because...?"

"Because I need it for a distraction. No one is meant to be hurt by it."

"I see." He rose. "Well, I must say, young man, you succeeded in surprising me."

I glanced at Walter, but he had dropped his face into his hands and was shaking it back and forth.

I have been told that I was sometimes too trusting a man. And it was true. I had the belief that most mean had pure hearts and that he would overcome his sinful ways if dealt with honestly. This was not always the case and I could certainly tell you stories where I had failed to judge a man with proper care.

The moment I saw Chigwell pace across his floor, silent except for a grunt or two and worrying his lip with his teeth, I thought that I might have mistaken the man. Was he about to call for the sheriffs after all? I hastily plotted how to get Walter and Geoff out of there. And just as I moved to grab Walter's arm, Ben spoke.

"There's audacity in you, to be sure. How the burglary of the Tower will save a life isn't exactly clear to me —"

"I ask you to trust me on that, Master Chigwell. Ben."

Those old, gray eyes glistened and covered me from head to foot. "A trustworthy thief. What is this world coming to?" His gaze swept Walter. "And you? Surely you are no thief."

Walter adjusted his gown. "Indeed not! However, I have seen it necessary...only from time to time, mind you...to assist Oswald in his endeavors."

"Your trade, sir?"

"Wool merchant." He bowed. I was in the presence of a strange transaction.

"Interesting. You vouchsafe for this man?"

Walter's lips twisted. "Oswald is..." He gestured vaguely. "He is...enthusiastic. But more times than not, thriving."

Ah, sweet words, Walter. Were they sweet enough, was the question?

The alchemist steadily approached Geoff and said not a word. His widespread fingers suddenly grabbed Geoff's scalp, turned his head this way and that in a jerking motion. All the while, Geoff's eyes were bulging like to pop out of his head. Chigwell still said nothing when he released him a moment later. A shiver ran up my spine, for it seemed as if he could see inside of Geoff, past the skin and bone, muscle and sinew. He could tell that Geoff was a halfwit just by looking at him and I should have been affronted and I was ready to say something to defend old Geoff when the alchemist tossed his head as if the notion of Geoff's inadequacies did not trouble him.

He stepped back and faced me again.

"Very well, Oswald. I shall join your company. But I will not participate in your burglary in a physical sense. I am an old man and have no desire to traipse all about in the middle of the night over mossy walls. I will make your Greek Fire for you and I shall take my cut of the plunder."

I grinned and took his hand, shaking it. "That is very fine, Ben, very fine indeed."

"Yes, well." He wiped his hands on his gown. "I take it you need this in a hurry."

"We do. That is, it must be done soon. Very soon."

"I do not wish to know details. The less involvement the better. I'd advise the same to you," he said to Walter but waved his hand in the air. "But that is as you will. Come back in a day or two and I will have it for you. I will teach you the proper way to use it. And I expect a goodly sum for my efforts."

"We were promised a percentage of the hoard, Ben, but I will do my best. You have my word."

"Your word, eh? Bless me. I'm an old man and old men tend to indulge themselves where they can. You, my lad, are merely an indulgence. If I did not expect payment I would never have agreed." He chuckled and ambled toward the door. Slowly he bent over the wheel and turned it. It creaked and whined and the door rose. "Well, off with you, then. Scheme away. We mustn't keep the Tower waiting, must we?"

Mad. That's what he was. But as long as he was also fit to make the material, I had no qualms. We strode under his door and when we were all on the other side, he pointed down to a ladder and instructed us to leave by that device. We thanked him and he went back into his lair and closed his portcullis. In the dark again, we climbed down his rickety ladder and left by the front door.

Walter grumbled. "I fear you condemn us by your trusting nature, Oswald. I suspect that man was only humoring you."

"If that is the case, then at least we got out of it alive."

"But when you must return to collect the Greek Fire, will it be there for you or will the king's sheriffs be ready to snap you up?"

"I could see it in his eyes, Walter. The very same I saw in your eyes when first I met you."

"Don't be so sure. I wasn't all that enamored of you on first sight."

"Aw, Walter." I slapped his back. "But you love me well now, do you not? And see how that turned out?"

He snorted. We walked down the dark streets, me and Walter side by side with Geoff trailing behind. I inhaled the inviting smells of cooking fires on the breeze.

"I tell you, Walter. That portcullis door of his got me to thinking. We had a hell of a time lifting it. I've come to the unfortunate conclusion that we could use a man with strength. And I could use another craftsmen for my devices. I'm thinking of asking the help of a blacksmith."

Walter spun. "No! Absolutely not. We cannot let anyone else know what we are about in this. It's bad enough you asked this absolute stranger to share our secrets. Do you realize the danger?"

"I know it all too well, Walter, and I tell you, I cannot do this with just you and Geoff. It's going to require special skills and strength. We're going to need a blacksmith."

"Can't *you* do the smithing?"

"No, I can't. I don't use the same materials and in not enough quantities. And I need *strength*! You saw the door."

Walter nibbled on a nail of one of his slender fingers. He turned back to the lane and trudged onward. "Whom can we trust?" he asked in a small voice.

I shook my head. That was the trouble, right enough. Who *could* we trust? No one who knew me, that was certain. "I'll go to the Tun and see about the blacksmiths there."

The Tun. A large stone building in the heart of London, much like a round turret that held water. There were cisterns all over London, but this was closest to us. One could see folk straining under bougets, swelled with water, making their slow progress down Cornhill after taking their share from the Tun.

It was only up the lane from the Tun that the blacksmith shops lined the streets. The clang of hammers and the belch of smoke grayed the lane. The smell of hot coals heavy in the lungs made it unmistakable. I confess that I loved the smell myself, having my own little forge but usually doing far more delicate work.

Walter protested all the rest of the night, but when I finally sent him home drunk and pliant, I had not changed my mind. We needed strength. There were going to be ropes to pull and guards to keep at bay. And much more work to be done at the forge. We needed a blacksmith!

———— ◆ ————

THE NEXT DAY I dragged Geoff with me, for as empty-headed as he was, he was King Solomon's equal when it came to judging a man's character, better even than m'self.

The first blacksmith we stopped at gave me the squint eye and Geoff shook his head. The second was not much better. I like to watch a man at work, see how he fares with his apprentice, just to get a feel for the man. If a man doesn't like my watching, then what secret thing is he doing?

I tugged Geoff along to the next shop and the next.

How exactly was one to ask a man to commit treason and not get hanged for it himself, I ask you?

I looked at Geoff and he seemed to sense my troubles. "Geoff, is it possible to trust a man you just met? How can I ask any man to do what we need doing?"

He scratched his head and peered deep into his thoughts. "Well, if it was me, Oz, and you asked me to commit treason — and I didn't know you, that is — I would have to have a mighty incentive for it."

"A mighty incentive? Isn't that what the crown jewels are?"

"Maybe these men have never seen crown jewels. Come to think of it, neither have I."

"You think I have?"

"You've broken into a score of houses, Oz. You've seen a lot."

"But I've never seen any sarding crown jewels. Maybe a ring or two, or a jeweled necklace, but nothing like this."

"Well," he said, gesturing awkwardly. "There you are."

The lad was right. How could you promise a man something he could scarce imagine? "I don't want a greedy man, Geoff. That's dangerous."

"We don't need a greedy man. Only one who is in it for the fun of the thing. Like me."

"Aw Geoff. Where am I going to find another man as empty-headed as you?" And I ruffled his hair when I said it, just so he wouldn't take offense, even though he seldom did.

Geoff chuckled. "There's men in London town like that, Oz. I know there is. You just pick out the blacksmith and I'll tell you if he's a worthy man."

I shrugged. We were where we were before. But to be sure, I'd raise a different banner on it. Before us was another blacksmith. Ah how I wish one of them owed me money! But alas.

When we entered, the smith, a tall fellow, was leaning over his forge. Stocky and solid, he had bulging arms sweating from the fire. He heard us at the door and only half-turned. His eyes were gray and didn't seem to be filled with suspicion, not like the others had been. His short-cropped hair, brown and spiked, sparkled from sweat and he had a burn scar on one cheek. His face was blunt with a wide, square jaw, and his teeth were horsy, but he said nothing before he turned back to his forge.

Geoff stood off to one side and stared like I'd never seen him do before. He fell silent and shy. I elbowed him. "Geoff," I whispered. "Eh?"

But he kept looking hard at the blacksmith sidelong before he dropped his eyes, repeating his curious gambol again and again. A bit curious myself, I approached the smith and cleared my throat. "I beg your mercy, Master."

He shoved the rod of iron deep into the bright coals, pulled on the bellows rope above his head and gave the fire a good breath of air, once, twice, and then smacked his hands on his leather apron before turning to me again. He looked me over from toe to hood and then he glanced at Geoff. Something in his face changed and he gave Geoff a long, slow look while Geoff shuffled and wrung his tunic and wouldn't look up no more. The smith raised his chin at me as if asking me to speak.

"Good Master, I am in need of a blacksmith. A good strong man." His arms bulged with strength, so there was no lying about that. "An honest man to do a curious job. A somewhat dangerous job, truth be told." I glanced over my shoulder once before I leaned in and said quietly, "It's a difficult thing to ponder, I know. But I'll wager it will prove to be the most exciting thing you have ever done. An adventure, as the minstrels might say. A poet could put it into better words than I, but you get my meaning, do you not? An adventure, man. Something to tell the grandchildren about someday. That you were there. That it was you — your strength and your courage that won the day!" Saint Dafydd, my own florid words sounded right good to me, too!

"Geoff here," and I grabbed his shoulders and gave them a hard pat (though he seemed to have swallowed his tongue). "He's an honest son of the Church, a godly man, is Geoff. And he chooses the path of adventure. True, he is a man short of his wits, but he's a good lad and loyal and that is what I'm after. If you can be a man who wants a bit of a quest, if you can follow orders, then we must talk further. If you are a man who cannot keep a secret thing secret then I will say good day to you and no harm done. So, what will it be?"

The man stood for a long time, just breathing. A long trickle of sweat rolled silently off his nose. Those gray eyes scoured me again but there was little change to his expression, one way or the other. It was the damnedest thing I ever saw.

"A secret?" he growled, low and deep.

"Well, it's not that I can tell the world about it. But it is something that a man can make a fair bit of coin at. Some men are not good with secrets."

He turned his gaze on Geoff again, lifted his arm, and with it, a hand the size of a ham and pointed it at Geoff. "*He* does as you bid? Keeps secrets?" he asked in his deep voice, a voice that sounded like it was dragged long over a stony road.

I put my arm around Geoff who still seemed as shy as when we'd entered. "Oh, aye. Geoff and me, we're like brothers."

"And do you often break the law…on your adventures?"

"Well…er…" By the saints, this one was no fool. "It's not that we…that is to say…I'm a tinker by trade, but we sometimes…you know…sometimes we must needs do…er…"

He waved his hand at me and motioned for us to sit. A bench up against the wall next to the shop doorway served us well and I pulled Geoff back and sat beside him.

The blacksmith took up a cloth and scrubbed his face. His stubbly beard did not seem the cleaner for it, but he tossed the cloth aside. He took a stool in that wide hand of his and plunked it down before us, then he lowered himself. It squeaked under his weight.

"What then?"

I looked at Geoff but he was still studying his feet. What was wrong with him? "I must have you swear an oath, sir, that you will not tell a living soul what I am about to tell you. There are certain quests that must remain secret until they have been achieved."

He becrossed himself but said no more.

"Very well. You've made your oath to God and no mistaking." I was giving him a fair chance to back out. But the stoic man merely waited for me to go on. I leaned over my knees toward him. "You've guessed it, right enough. It is a plot somewhat outside the law, as it were. It's a scheme to—now you've given your oath. It's only Hell for a man who breaks his oath to God." His gaze did not waver from mine. I licked my lips. My voice fell to a whisper. "We mean to break into the Tower of London and take the king's jewels."

Stoic is not the word, for he did not bat a lash or break a sweat. He sighed, flicked his eyes toward Geoff, but said nothing.

"Did you hear me, man? I said—"

"I heard what you said. Can you do it?"

"Aye. I think I can. With the help of a man like you."

"And him?" he thumbed toward Geoff.

I patted Geoff's shoulder. "I wouldn't do it without him. I trust him with my life. I have for nigh on five years. And I reckon he's the best lock pick in all London, maybe all England."

"Good enough." He rose and shuffled back to his forge.

"W-wait, good Master, I haven't told you —"

"It's good enough for him, it's good enough for me. Tell me when to meet you."

"Oh...well. I'm up Cornhill, tinker's stall next to the wool merchant."

"Long-faced fellow?"

"Aye, that's the one. Walter Pomfret. He's part of the scheme, too. And I'm Oswald the Welshman."

"I know who you are."

"Oh." And still he'd do business with us? The world was a constant surprise to me. "Well, this here is Geoff."

He half-turned and nodded. "I'm Trevor."

"Well now!" I was all smiles. "A right proper Welsh name is that. I'm very pleased to meet you, Trev. Come to my shop tomorrow morning bright and early and we will share an ale and I'll tell you what I can and why the hell I'm doing it. It's only fair you know all."

He nodded again, never turning round, and with a leather scrap to cover his hand, jostled the white-hot rods amongst the coals as if we had never interrupted him.

Satisfied, I left his shop, a spring in my step. Geoff kept looking back and I finally grabbed his arm. "Oi! Geoff. What ails you? You know that man?"

"No. Never seen him before, Oz." But Geoff was not his cheerful self. He seemed subdued somehow.

"Is he honest?"

"Oh aye. I think so."

"What are you keeping from me, Geoff? I've a right to know. I took you in and all."

"I swear, Oz. It's nothing. Truly."

I let it lie. If Geoff wanted to keep something for his own then I'd let him. Trev agreed easily enough. Perhaps I should have questioned that but that lunatic of an alchemist seemed easily convinced as well, and so I could see little wrong with it. I was merrier than I had been in a long time. I had my company. And I was forming a plan. And there was fabulous wealth to be had if we all didn't hang. What could be better?

This called for a celebration, so instead of returning to my shop, I steered Geoff about and we marched to the Cockerel and Bullock to down some fine ale and so I could look my fill at the fair Alison.

We turned the corner at Birchin Lane and followed it to the alehouse. I could almost taste that ale as I pushed open the doors.

Instead, I froze in place, taking in the scene before us.

Tables lay overturned. Stools and benches smashed. Two men had Alison each by an arm and they were leering at her. My heart gave a lurch when I seen the bruise on her cheek and the blood at her mouth, and one of the men cocked back his arm to deliver yet another blow.

I didn't stop to think. I leapt.

CHAPTER ELEVEN

I SAILED RIGHT through the air. God Almighty Himself gave me wings, to be sure, and I wrenched that cruel arm away from Alison, hoping in the struggle that I broke it.

The knave was surprised. Alison took advantage and wriggled away from him, delivering a solid kick to his shin. *Next time, higher!* I wanted to tell her, but I was busy slamming my fist into the first knave's face. But he recovered too quickly and stopped my fist with his hand and squeezed. He shoved it back at me and I ended up smacking my own nose. God blind me, that hurt! The hot rush of blood poured down my chin and I tasted metal.

Geoff threw himself into the fray and he hung on to the leg of the second man who was going after Alison. He took that man's calf in his jaws and bit down and the man howled and twisted, trying to kick at Geoff. I wanted to help him but I had my own problems. My man had pulled his dagger, which was unfair for I did not carry one. But I did have my hammer, and I pulled old Saint Joseph from his sheath and brandished it.

The man looked at it and gave a hearty laugh. True, it was a small hammer and I used it for the most delicate of work, but laughing at a man's weapon. That's tantamount to questioning the size of his pintle.

"Arsehole!" I cried and heaved it at his chest.

It bounced off him harmlessly and clanged to the ground. His laughter died and he sneered. His knife carved the air with a whoosh and I ducked. It came again and I hit the floor and rolled between his legs, snatching up my hammer along the way. I closed my eyes, swung old Saint Joseph upward, and connected with his bollocks. His chest might be like steel but there wasn't a man alive who had iron oysters.

He dropped to his knees with nary a sound and fell forward. I reckoned he was down for good. Spinning Saint Joe in my hand once, I kissed it and brandished him again. Now I was free to help Geoff, but there was my lad, holding on with teeth bared to the man's leg and there was Alison astride his shoulders like she was subduing a jackass—which by all rights she was! She beat on his head with her fists and he yelled like a demon and twisted and twirled, trying to fling them both off of him.

I swung Saint Joseph at his forehead and, cross-eyed, he plunged backwards, arms flailing. Alison leapt off his back in time and Geoff finally let him go. He landed in a heap amidst the rubble of a broken tables and vessels. I jolted forward and raised my hammer again when it was suddenly plucked out of my hand. I spun.

That first knave grimaced at me, Saint Joseph now in *his* hand. Not down for good after all. He winced and staggered with an unnatural gait. "I'm going to kill you," he said, and I had every expectation that he would do just that. I cringed back and mouthed a prayer.

Alison charged forward, a fire iron in her hands. "Let him go!"

He grinned at her. He had my tunic wadded in his fist and Saint Joseph in the other. He was going to pummel me to death with my own hammer! The indignity of it.

"Let him go *now*!"

He chuckled and squeezed my tunic tighter. My throat constricted. I was all for swooning. That way, I would be senseless when he beat me to a pulp.

She raised the rod again and with a jeer he flung me back. I tumbled to the floor just as the second knave, moaning and holding his head, rose from the disorder. He stood unsteadily over me. "What happened?" he asked.

The first knave ignored him. "Madam Hale. Have done with this. You know we are in the right."

"Attacking a dear lass?" I cried, my heart throbbing in my chest like it was bound to burst through it. "Are you mad?"

He looked at my hammer in his hand and tossed it to the floor. I moved to grab it but his dagger was quicker. "Hold, lad," he said, waving it toward my face. "I have the upper hand, make no mistake. She knows what I am talking about."

The other man shook out his head and limped forward, glaring at Geoff who still had a hank of the man's stocking stuck in his teeth.

"We will leave you now," the man said and sheathed his dagger. The hammer was on the floor between us but he knew it was too far for me to grab it. I *itched* to dive for it. "But we'll be back in a fortnight and you had best have the coin by then."

He kicked broken drinking vessels out of his way and made an ungainly saunter toward the door. I was proud of that at least. His henchman followed him but his bleeding leg made his saunter more of a stumble.

Once the door snicked closed, Alison sunk to the floor, sobbing.

I stood where I was, looking out over the room that had been a friendly and warm alehouse. Now it was a pile of sticks and kindling, broken bowls and cracked horn beakers. Even the fire stuttered indignantly, sending sparks into the room. I kicked the embers back into the hearth and crouched beside her. I didn't care if she would accept it or no. I curved my arm around her shoulders and let her weep into my shirt.

"There, there, lass. It's over now."

"No. They'll be back and they'll be taking my hide next."

"What did they want?"

She sat up and used her arm to swipe her hair over her creased forehead. She was bruised and bloodied and I longed to take her aside and gently bathe her face. She looked up at me with bright eyes, tears still clinging to her dark lashes. Ach! Those eyes laid me low. I couldn't have moved if the Four Horsemen themselves swept through.

"My husband, *requiescat in pacem*" –we all crossed ourselves – "borrowed money from those thieves. He borrowed a great deal. But we couldn't pay it back, not right away. And then he died. And he left me with his debt. I tried to explain to them that business had been bad and that the mice had eaten the grain and some of my batches had soured, but they wouldn't have it."

Lice-eating money lenders. The bane of a decent man's life. No good Christian would sink to usury and all the Jews had been driven out of England almost a decade back, but there were still men, foreigners mostly, who loaned money at interest. Fie on them!

"Can you pay them at all?" I asked.

She sniffed and the tears frozen in her lashes splashed to her cheek, tracking downward. "No. I haven't any money. I work my fingers to the bone just to keep the doors open."

Geoff settled down beside me and we all fell silent. My mind worked like a water wheel in a storm. "Mistress Alison, will you let me help you?"

"We can clean up this rubble but what good will it do? In a fortnight it will all be theirs."

"I didn't mean this place – though Geoff and I will gladly do so – I meant with your problem. You can earn the money you owe. I can help there."

Her face, once open in its innocence and dejection, soured. She pushed me back. "I'm not that sort of lass!"

"No! Madam, bless me! I didn't mean *that*. Heaven forbid! No, I mean to say that I have an opportunity...though it *is* outside the law."

Her glare did not cease but it did soften. She pushed herself to her feet and sighed, looking around. "Outside the law, eh? What sort? What sort of man are you Master...er..."

I scrambled to my feet and gave her a bow. "Oswald of Harlech, lass. Some call me Oswald the Welshman. But...you can call me Oz."

Geoff followed suit with a bow as well, only not as smoothly. "And Geoff...of London." He grinned.

She couldn't help but offer a small smile back, Geoff was just that way. "I'm afraid to ask."

"As you should. But I will tell you nonetheless. I am a tinker. But sometimes...only sometimes, mind...I also do a bit on the side."

"A bit outside the law?"

"Aye. I never hurt nobody and I never steal from a man what can't spare it."

"You're a thief?"

"Er...aye. That I am."

"Saint Luke preserve me," she sighed. "A thief." She laughed, but it wasn't a light sound. More of an hysterical one. She dabbed at her bleeding lip with her apron as the laughter subsided. "This is how the good lord answers my prayers? It only makes sense then that the only help I'd get was from a thief."

I felt just a wee bit affronted. "Now lass, it's not as bad as all that. Geoff and I do well enough."

"I'm certain you do. Well then." She crossed her arms over her chest. "Go on. Tell me. What thing must I steal to save my hide? From a rich man, I hope."

"Oh indeed. Well, it's like this. My company and I have been charged with stealing the king's treasure from the Tower of London." How easily those words seem to slip over my lips of late. First the alchemist, then the blacksmith, and now Alison. Walter was going to skin me alive.

Not a sound did she make. But she whirled on her heel and spat over her shoulder, "Get out."

"No, truly!" I grabbed her wrist and spun her. She stumbled and I righted her with a hand to her waist. It was a fine, slim waist. She was close now and I was not drunk as I was the night when we met. She was as lovely as I recalled. As sleek and as pretty as an ermine, with skin smooth and pale like cream. I wanted to push back that wimple, to see her black hair, to run my fingers through it. Her rounded eyes were brown, like a rich brew. I saw them study me, searching over my face. I could tell that a war waged inside her. She wanted to doubt me and yet she didn't, for I offered the hope of redemption. And yet, the thing that we had to do would give any sane person pause.

"You're mad."

I nodded. "Aye, most likely. But I'm in a bit of a bind, too. It is something I am charged with doing. But we will make a tidy sum for our endeavors. Enough to live well to the end of our days, no doubt."

"How do you hope to get away with it?"

"I have my ways," I lied, for I did not yet know just how we *were* to get away with the theft. But I hoped that de Mandeville would not make the same mistake those other thieves had made and not try to dispose of the wealth in London where its suspicious citizens gave up the culprits.

She looked down at her wrist, the wrist I still held fast to and I let her go. "You're mad," she whispered again.

"But persistent." I smiled. It wasn't every lass that could deny that smile but she had proved resistant before. Now she looked on me kindly and the bloody edge of her mouth even flickered upward a bit.

"You have a plan, I take it?"

"Oh aye. A good one." Well...

"And it can be done?"

Er... "I give you my word."

"The word of a thief?"

"Greater men than I have taken it as God's truth."

"Oswald of Harlech, you said?"

"And Geoff of London," piped Geoff.

"Well Oswald of Harlech and Geoff of London," she said a little wearily. "I suppose after all is said and done, I truly have little choice but to join you thieves...to beat the other thieves."

———— • ————

IT WAS BUSY in my little shop the next morning. Walter did not take the news well that a woman was now joined to our company.

"You *what*!"

"I had no choice, Walter. If you had been there, you'd have done the same."

"No, I would not have! I would have *run*."

"And left the poor lass to shift for herself with those knaves? Why, who knows what they would have done to a woman alone if we had not intervened?"

Walter scrubbed his face with his hands and shook his head, muttering to himself. Well, that was Walter.

I kept my shutters closed that morning, knowing that we had plots to lay. Trev was the first to arrive. I opened the door for him and Geoff got all silent as he did before. Trev cast a glance at him before he settled on a stool with his back to the hearth. He looked at my little brazier beside him and chuckled.

I poured him a bowl of ale and he took it with a nod. He said not a word.

We waited and drank a bit, no one speaking, until a knock banged on the door. We all stilled for a moment before I rose and answered it.

Her cheeks were pink from the sharp morning and her hair was now covered by a short linen veil that barely reached her shoulders rather than the wimple I had seen on her before. She wore a blue gown with a serviceable surcote of brushed brown wool.

I must have frozen for a moment, for she was looking at me oddly and I finally shook it off, poured ale into a wooden bowl, and handed it to her. She took it gratefully and Geoff got up and offered her a chair.

I rested my own bowl on the table. "Well now. Here we all are! My lads, this is Widow Alison. And here, you know Geoff. This is Walter Pomfret, wool merchant."

"Charmed," he said, barely looking at her, his chin on his hand.

I motioned to Trev. "And this brawny fellow is also new to our company. This is Trev the Blacksmith."

Trev blinked but said naught.

Alison nodded to him. "Masters," she said and sipped her ale with trembling hands.

"We have one more. An alchemist by the name of Benet Chigwell, but he will not be visiting us this morn. He's working on his own, so to speak. And so. We are here to discuss the problem of the Tower."

"How do we know where the jewels are?" asked Alison, her voice unsteady. She kept biting her lip, making it redder. I had to tear my eyes away.

"I've been inside. I was shown where they lie by the Keeper of the Wardrobe himself. It is he who has charged me with obtaining them. He wishes to take the king's gold out of greed and vengeance, and who am I to argue the point?"

Alison canted forward. "But why would you agree to do something so plainly dim-witted?"

"Because I'm afraid my lord insisted."

"He caught Oz burglaring him," said Geoff.

"What?"

"Aye," said Geoff with a proud grin. "Oz and I get up to lots of burglaries, don't we Oz? And other games, too. Some with dice, some with walnut shells, some with—"

"Ha, Geoff. No need to bestir the lass with our entire history."

"But Oz. She must know about our games." He looked around the room at me, then Walter who had dropped his face in his hand, then at Trev before Geoff's cheeks reddened and he faced Alison again. "One time we sold saint's bones. Only they was in truth pullet's bones."

A smile crept over her mouth. "Eh?"

"Erm…" I said. I felt my face grow unaccountably warm. "That hasn't got much to do with the Tower, Geoff. The fact that it must be done is…well, a fact. Let me tell you what I saw and what I saw last night when I went to look again."

And here I told them. How each gate had a portcullis and how there were three drawbridges and that the walls were forty feet high and twelve feet thick. How Water Gate was not accessible to the wharf. How there was a bell tower in the inner ward and how the Garden Tower opened to the Constable's Garden. That it was warren of dividing walls and low buildings inside the inner ward with the chapel of St. Peter ad Vincula situated at the northwest corner; how there were buildings for the servants and such along the south outer walls and then Geoff interrupted and told about the moat all around. And then I told them about the White Tower, how it stood on its mound and that there was one way in on the south face; how the chapel of St. John was above and the jewels below, a lone stairwell with a lone guard that reached it. Then I told them about the pit and the other trap, the which we knew not what, and then the two doors with dual locks.

I told them that I went again last night to look at the Tower in the darkness, and that there was a cresset burning on Lanthorn Tower.

It seemed that I spoke a long time and no one said a word throughout. At last, I fell silent and sipped my ale. I gauged their faces. None looked happy.

"Well," said Walter, taking a deep breath. "I think it is safe to say that we are all doomed."

Alison, who had been looking deeply into her bowl for the whole of my talk, raised her bruised chin. "If God has ordained it, then we are. But I do not believe that God dooms us."

Walter stared down his considerable nose at her. "You speak of God, young woman, as if he would bless this sinful enterprise. Do you forget that we are conspiring a burglary?"

"No, Master, I do not forget it. I am a godly woman and have run an honest alehouse. Bad fortune has followed me since I married my husband, God rest his soul. But I will not see all that I have worked so hard for fall into the hands of rogues. I will not! So if I must sin and steal to keep it, well. I have no choice in the matter." She downed her bowl and set it roughly aside.

Ach! A spirited lass! And good solid flesh that a man could put his hands around! I liked Widow Alison well.

But Walter, ever the dreamer, said to me, "I still do not see what this woman has to do with it."

"Well," I said, "you never know when a woman can come in handy."

"For who? You?"

My cheeks warmed again and I took a swallow of my ale to hide it. I needed to think, to wrap my mind around it. I knew some of what was needed but the rest eluded me.

"What of undermining the walls, Oswald?" asked Walter finally.

"Too far and it would take too long. We only have a fortnight."

"A fortnight?"

"Oh, did I forget to mention? Lord de Mandeville said the king will return by then so it must be now."

Walter grumbled under his breath but I ignored it as usual. "Walter, can you get your men to run some sheep up on Tower Hill to spy on the Keep?"

Walter snapped to. He wasn't much of master himself but if he saw a decent plan, he would follow its course, right enough. "Yes, of course," he said. "I shall inform them to do so immediately."

"Good. We need them to watch the guards and any regular activity that they might be able to spy. In the meantime, there are some things I need Trev to create for me. I'll sketch it out. You have iron, do you not? I'll need rods of steel made thin but strong. And a few other things. And we need rope. Lots of rope. And sacks."

"I have many empty sacks," said Alison. "The grain. I get supplies all the time."

"Good then. Does anyone have a horse or mule?"

No one spoke. I knew right well that Walter owned a horse and a mule but his lips were shut up tight except to drink my ale.

"Right, then. Walter. You are my cart man."

He opened his mouth to speak but seemed to think better of it and dipped his sour expression into his ale.

"And what about me, Oz?"

Geoff smiled, his eyes eager. "Geoff. You're my lock man. You'll have the devil's own time springing them locks. There's nothing else I need you to do, is there?"

Geoff seemed satisfied and a bit swollen with pride. His eyes darted once toward the blacksmith before he lowered them again.

I faced everyone and ticked it off on me fingers. "So here are the problems. The height of the walls, the drawbridges, which will be closed at night with the portcullises down, the cresset in Lanthorn Tower, and no way in from the moat. If we can be clever and get in, we still have the problem of getting across the mazes to the White Tower. If we aren't sliced in two before we get there and manage to get inside, there is one guard at the stairwell and that's the only way down to the vaults, but the Keeper has said he will make certain to absent that guard the night we break in. If we can surmount all of that, then it's an easy thing to get over the pit, manage the other trap, and get through the doors. But then we have the same problem getting the sacks of treasure out of the Keep, across the greensward, over the walls, and back to Cornhill. Any ideas?"

Alison's mouth had fallen open and her pale face had gotten paler. "I have an idea. Why don't we throw ourselves on the mercy of the king right now? It would be better than suffering in his clutches when we're caught!" She jerked to her feet and headed toward the door. "I must be a fool twenty times twenty to fall in with such a half-wit scheme."

"Wait!" I leapt up and slid across the floor, throwing my arm before the entry. "Alison. It might *sound* impossible now —"

"Because it *is* impossible!"

"No. Hear me out. I've got a Plan."

"God help us!" cried Walter. "Oswald has a plan. Oswald always has a plan. And they always seem to fail."

"Fail? Fail? When have my plans ever failed, Walter, eh? When?"

"Oh let's think. There was last year when you had a plan to resell the same wool to different merchants and it was found out. Mostly because you tried to sew the fleeces *back on the poor sheep!*"

"Now that would have worked if they hadn't —"

"And then there was the plan only a few months ago that entailed the rich widow when you tried to persuade her you were her long-lost son."

"How did I know he would show himself at last?"

"And then there was —"

"Enough, Walter!" I gestured to Alison who was by this time breathing hard. "You're scaring the lass."

"I'm already scared. Of you, of this…but, God help me, of those money lenders." She sagged against the door and tears blossomed in her eyes. "St. Margaret help us all. We are lost, all of us. At the mercy of men who force their will on us." She eyed Walter. "What's your excuse? You don't seem to like any of Oswald's schemes. Why do you help?"

Walter shuffled in his seat and made to drink his ale but discovered his cup was empty. He lowered it to the table and slowly spun the bowl. "I...I have known Oswald almost since he came to London. He was only a lad and as full of himself then as now. He...he helped me at a time when I needed it. My business does not stand on its own. We must occasionally join forces to...to...find other means of compensation. And so, though I might have to point out from time to time how foolish are his endeavors, I will always—reluctantly, mind—stand beside him. Even as dangerous and as foolhardy as this might be. So. Oswald has my unwavering, if hesitant, support."

He fiddled with his bowl before suddenly grasping the jug and pouring more.

I blinked hard. That was as fine a speech as I had ever heard from old Walter. He never said as much to me before. I gave him a grin but he would not look at me.

Alison shook her head. She turned to Geoff. "And you?"

Geoff swung his head this way and that, as if surprised it was him she was addressing. "Me? Oh. Oz is my friend. He's like a brother. He takes care of me and I take care of him. In truth, that's the whole of it."

"I see. And you, Blacksmith? What is your reason for getting yourself hanged with these men?"

He raised his eyes to her. He seemed too big for the stool he was sitting on. His wide shoulders rested against the wall and his ham-sized hands covered his knees with their dirty fingernails and singed hair on the back of his knuckles.

He shrugged.

A man of few words, was Trev.

"And this mysterious alchemist," she said. "Why does he trust you?"

I spread my hands. "I don't know. He seemed a bit mad to me, truth to tell. But a man willing to take a risk."

Alison sighed. "I must be as mad as the rest of you. It's no secret that I'm desperate. Oswald and Geoff saw that for themselves last night. And I am grateful they stepped forward to help me, as I was in sore need of it. But the Tower. Blind me. It's madness."

"But it's also an adventure, lass. When was the last time you had a genuine minstrel-sung adventure?"

"I reckon I never have."

"Then isn't it time?"

She blew a strand of dark hair off her forehead. "I'm not the adventurous sort. But I am forced to help you because of my situation. So I'd best quit my whinging." She straightened and seemed to gird herself. "What do you see me doing, Oswald? Walter is your cart man and Geoff your lock man. Trevor is the brawn and your alchemist is doing, I assume, his alchemy. What great talent do I have to offer?"

Bless me, but the possibilities ran rampant through my head before I calmed m'self down.

"Erm…well. For now, you might be a right good distraction."

"Eh?"

"You know. A distraction. To keep the guards' eyes away from the rest of us breaking in. You'd make a fine distraction. In fact, first thing tomorrow morning, you will take Walter's horse and cart, load up some of your finest ale, and offer free drink for the folk in the Tower."

"Eh?" She folded her arms hard over that ample chest.

"You will beg to enter the gates and get in as far as you can, offering free ale."

"And why in the Devil's name would I be giving it away?"

"Because. You…er…you wish to sell your ale to the Tower and you want to prove what a fine brew it is. And you will be cheerful and sweet and smile. Often."

"And get in as far as I can?"

"And the next day you'll do the same. And the next and the next. And I'll wager my last farthing that you will be granted access into the inner bailey by week's end."

"How can you be so sure?" she asked.

All a man need do was take one look at her and they'd sell their cows, pawn their jewelry, and grant her the deed to their estate. But it would not do to tell her that. I merely smiled. "Trust me."

Her eyes said she wasn't entirely convinced but she slowly moved away from the door and seated herself again.

"So Oz," said Geoff. "What are we to do? We can't get in from the moat and we can't undermine the walls."

I watched the hearth and the logs upon it, etched with cracks, perfectly formed, breaking into squares of coals. The edges grayed with red embers beneath. An ember cut loose and rose into the air, soaring on a cushion of heat waves. I watched it for a bit, fascinated. Something whirred in my head, taking the thought and spinning upward with it. So light, that ember. Winging on a wave of heat.

"How do you feel about...flying?"

CHAPTER TWELVE

I DROPPED THE coins into Geoff's waiting hand. "I need you to buy a crossbow, you ken?"

"A crossbow? Why would we be needing that for?"

"It's all about flying." His already perplexed expression deepened. "Geoff, just get it and be slick about it, eh? We can't afford questions. It should be a right sturdy one. Off with you now. I've got to see a man about a boat."

I made my way up the misty street just past the Tun and found him at his forge. With a bit of charcoal, I sketched what I wanted from him on a piece of bark. He looked it over, grunted, and then nodded his head. I felt dismissed when he turned away from me. He started gathering what was needed without exchanging a word.

It was time to head to the wharf and seek out Tim. I was glad that it was a good foggy morning. Especially since the mist seemed to hug the Thames like they were long-lost lovers. Tim had a basket of fish before him and he was quarrelling with a man who I took to be a fishmonger. Tim was trying to get the best price while the fishmonger was trying to get *his* best price. And this is the main problem with an honest day's wage. Be it employer or worker, no one is ever satisfied with the results.

I waited until they came to an agreement—and a handshake sealed the bargain—before I approached Tim. Like he always did when I greeted him, he put a hand on his money pouch.

"Oi, Tim. God's blessings on you!"

"And you, Oz. Still looking for that wench in the Tower?"

"Eh? Oh aye!" Almost forgot my lie! "And truth to tell, I was hoping you and your boat would allow me to take a closer look."

The life seemed to drain away from his face. "What do you mean, Oswald?"

"Well, love can't wait, can it? I need you to take me to the Water Gate and…"

"And what? Oz, no lass is worth the risk. I think you should forget this girl."

"Ah but I can't! She's the most beautiful thing. And I can't wait to get my hands—I mean, my arms around her. Come, Tim. You wouldn't stand in the way of true love? It's like a minstrel song."

"You and your minstrel songs." Tim gave the wharf a look over. "Half an hour. That's all I'll give you."

"That's all I'll need. Thank goodness for the fog, eh?"

He rubbed the back of his neck.

"Come, man. Love's dart has already smitten me. You can't stand in the way of it."

He grumbled some oaths and untied his boat. "Get in, you miserable pintle."

I got in his small boat and he pushed off from the wharf. It skimmed the water and he took up his oars and rowed us to St. Thomas' Tower. I looked up the tower but the battlements disappeared into the mist. Perfect.

I began to strip.

"Oswald!" he whispered harshly. "What by Jesus' toes are you doing?"

"I'm testing the waters, Tim." I kicked off my shoes and untied my stockings from my braies. Then I shucked my tunic and shivered. "Christ! It's cold." I grabbed the edge of the boat and slid into the freezing water.

"Oswald!"

"Just keep the boat here, Tim. I'll be right back."

He called my name again as I slipped below the surface. God blind me, but it was cold! I'd never see my bollocks again. I stayed close to the wall and swam deep. The blue-green water swallowed up around me, getting heavier on my body the deeper I went. I felt the ticklish sway of water plants and perhaps a nose of a curious eel—though I tried to ignore that—and though I could no longer see it, I touched bottom before I pushed off and broke the water's surface again, trying not to think about the privies hard by on the shores of the Thames.

I took another deep breath and sank again, this time walking my hands down the portcullis of the entry arch, down, down. It went nearly to the bottom but left a small gap, enough for a man to wriggle under. I experimented, feeling the slimy bottom of the Thames cradle my back. And there I was on the other side of the portcullis. I looked up but couldn't see the surface far above me though I knew it was there. It was in shadow and a dark thing. I pushed off and I let m'self glide upward until my nose just split the surface. I inhaled and looked up through the water. Stone steps leading upward into another arch. Looked like Wakefield Tower. No guard, either.

I bobbed in the frigid water for another few moments looking about and was not disturbed. I took another deep breath and dove, counting my heartbeats as I went until I hit the bottom and slithered under the sharp teeth of the portcullis. I counted to twelve before I was free of it and continued counting till I broke through the waves at last.

I shivered and pulled myself halfway into the boat before Tim grabbed my arm and yanked me the rest of the way.

"What are you doing a fool thing like that for? You could have drowned and you didn't even get in."

"I didn't want to get in. I just wanted to see how deep it was." I used my cloak like a flannel and toweled myself briskly before I donned my clothes with trembling fingers. "Jesus, that's a cold swim. I hope my bollocks drop again sometime soon."

"No doubt."

That was Tim's way of saying that I was more foolhardy than smart. I slapped him on the back. "Tim, my lad. What say you to lending your boat to me some fine evening?"

THE PLAN WAS coming together. Nothing made me as satisfied as that!

After sitting by Tim's brazier for a while to warm up, I gave him my farewells and headed to the Cockerel and Bullock to warm my insides. A glimpse of fair Alison could do that almost as well as a beaker of her fine ale.

But just as I turned the corner for Birchin Lane, I spied the sheriffs standing in the middle of the street. I spun, trying to make my escape but not fast enough for them both to point and shout at me. Before I could put heel to ground, I was nabbed by the collar.

The sheriffs' serjeant Robert had a tight hold of me. "Now Oswald," he said. "Best come quietly."

The crowds on the streets had stopped whatever they were doing to gawk. My face burned as I was dragged by the taller man to where the sheriffs were standing out in front of everyone.

"Ah, Oswald," said Sheriff Nigellus. He had the look of a ginger-haired mastiff, face all pushed in. "We've been looking for you."

"Yes," said Sheriff Nicholas. He was the taller of the two and had long black hair curled just so at the ends. He looked like a more successful version of Walter. "We would speak with you." He looked about and spied the Cockerel and Bullock. "Let us repair to this establishment."

Saint Dafydd's bollocks! What would Alison think of that? At least it wasn't Newgate. I tried to shrink back but Robert the serjeant was having none of it, and he grabbed my arm tight and pulled me forth.

I shook him off. "There's no need for that," I chided.

The night before, we helped her clean up what we could. The place was shy some tables and benches, but I made do by sitting on the raised stone of her hearth for I was still chilled through, no mistaking. Some who were sitting near us hastily dropped their coins on the table and hurried out the door, keeping their faces away from the sheriffs.

Sheriff Nick clasped his hands and rested them on the table. "Now Oswald. Something has come to our attention that I think we need to discuss."

"Yes," said Sheriff Nigel, leaning forward. He snuck a peek over his shoulder. "It seems there was a burglary at Lord Percy de Mandeville's house only two nights ago."

"Yes," Sheriff Nick cut in. "And that was the very same night the steward's son was found killed."

They waited, looking at me expectantly.

Were they waiting for a confession? They'd wait till Doomsday, then. I merely glared at them, using my most neutral face.

Sheriff Nick slid his glance toward Sheriff Nigel and tried another tack. "There was a servant girl by the name of Margaret who said you...*entertained* her that night."

Margaret! That was the wench's name. I'd remember it right well now when I cursed her to the Devil!

"Whatever do you mean, my lord?"

Sheriff Nigel tipped closer. "Don't be coy, man. You were there the night the boy was killed. And for all we know *you* were the thief!"

Just then, Alison appeared over his shoulder. Her face barely betrayed her when she spotted me. I cringed back. Surely this looked as if I was conspiring. She'd think me a traitor before anything was begun. I tried to convey with my eyes my innocence, but she quickly turned away from me when Sheriff Nick ordered ale.

Damn. I didn't suppose there was any hope with the lass now!

But I sobered again when Sheriff Nick and Sheriff Nigel both leaned in, glaring at me, their last words ringing in my ears.

"For all you know I wasn't!" I cried.

"Why did you come to Newgate the other day?"

"I, er, had wondered if, erm, the...the..." Christ's teeth! I was so befuddled I couldn't even come up with a credible lie!

Suddenly an arm slipped around my shoulders. Sheriff Nigel wore a smile, and with his pushed-in face it was rather frightening. "Your soul wants you to confess, Oswald. It wants you to reconcile with God. Why not tell us what happened that night? You'll see that all will be well. Justice will be done."

Around my neck, you mean! I wanted to shrug him off of me but I did not think that wise. "Good my lord," I said quietly, "I...I wish I could tell you what you want to know. But I cannot."

Into my ear he said, "*Can*not or *will* not?"

I swallowed hard. They had been fair to me for the brief months I had known them. But I did not know their hearts or what forces were behind their query. I recalled my mother's words: "Go carefully with a full cup."

"My lords...I...cannot."

The arm slid away from me and they both sat back just as the ale arrived. Tight-lipped, Alison said nothing and did not look at me. I felt like sinking low on my place at the hearth. As warm as the fire was, I felt cold all over.

They each took a silent quaff from their cups and then fastened their eyes on me. "Be very careful, Oswald," said Sheriff Nick. "London is a dangerous place filled with dangerous men. It would be a pity for an innocent man to pay the ultimate price for the devilry of another."

My jaw fell open. They *knew*! They knew *something* but they couldn't say any more than I could. Oh curse de Mandeville and his manipulations!

They knew right well I didn't kill that man. But it wouldn't stop them from hanging me for it just the same. But what else were they trying to tell me? Did they know about the Tower plot? *Ach-y-fi*! If they knew about that then all would be lost!

"My lords." I fiddled with my tunic hem. I had to concentrate and say this just right. "There is more afoot than you can know. Sometimes a man is forced to do that which he has no control over, being the kind of man he is... No, that's not coming out right. I mean, sometimes a man who is of low rank cannot be of his own mind. A...a soldier follows the orders of a general, does he not? And does not have his own mind on the matter. That is what I mean. Should he...should he hang for that?"

Sheriff Nigel smiled sadly. "A soldier comes in many forms, Oswald. And in many ranks. Soldiers follow orders. Sometimes that order might involve hanging an innocent man."

I sucked in my breath. They were both looking at me with kind melancholy.

"But," said Sheriff Nick, "if an enterprising fellow should keep us informed of these matters, it might go better for him than he supposed."

I slowly nodded. Well, he was doing his best. But there was so little I could say. I truly didn't know how he could help me. So maybe I had to help myself. *I* had to prove that de Mandeville killed that boy. I just didn't know how.

All at once they rose and I scrambled to my feet. They added no more words to what they had said, gave me a nod, and left without a backwards glance in my direction. I stood, watching them depart until my legs gave out and I thumped down to the hearth seat again.

When I looked up, Alison stood over me.

She said nothing, just stared at me accusingly with a hard sadness in her eyes.

I had to tell her the truth, all of it.

Reaching forward to take her hands, she shied back. "Don't."

"But Alison, I must tell you what just transpired."

"I *know* what transpired. You just sold the lot of us to the sheriffs."

"No, I didn't. I swear!"

She sneered. "Oswald, I know what I saw. You can't even lie decently."

"Because I'm not lying. Please, Alison. Sit with me."

She grasped her arms so tight she'd surely snap them off. But after a long scowl directed toward me and a loud sigh, she sat beside me. "So talk."

"Aye. Talk. Well. I wasn't giving anything away to the sheriffs, if that is what you were thinking. No indeed. For what would I tell them? That it was me burglarizing Lord de Mandeville just two nights ago? That is was me who found the…the dead man at the foot of the master's window?"

She was shocked right well. Her jaw slid open and not a sound came forth.

I nodded. "Aye. A dead man. Percy de Mandeville wishes to blame that death on me but all along it was him that done it and I've got to prove it to save my own neck. Those sheriffs, they're good sorts they are. They have no cause to side with me but they all but told me they don't think me guilty of it—and I'm not!"

"Then all is well."

"They also all but told me that they might have to hang me for it anyway."

"Oh." Her fingers curled over her bottom lip. "That's a hard place to be, Oswald."

"That's no jest."

We sat, she and me. No words needed to be said between us. What could be said, after all? But anon, I did ask her after I'd taken up the cup Sheriff Nigel left and took a dose. "And so. How goes it here at the Cockerel and Bullock?"

"I have patrons but for how much longer?"

I couldn't help but notice that her thigh almost touched mine. I tried to wriggle a mite closer but she looked up then. "And you? Are you...does it..." She shook her head. "I don't even know how to ask you."

"Best not to ask. This other will all come together soon enough. It must, at any rate, if we are to accomplish it before the king returns."

She shivered and crushed her arms to her. "I don't like it."

"Truth be told, neither do I. But, once resolved to it, I must admit, I've rather warmed to the idea."

"But then again, you are a thief. Whereas I am not."

True, I have been a thief for almost all m'life. But the way the word spat off her tongue gave me a twinge in my gut I never felt before. I didn't much like it. So I drank another dose of ale to quell the feeling. "Well, we all have our place," I said quietly.

I drank but I could feel her eyes on me. How I had wanted her to look at me before! But now her gaze seemed to weigh down my heart. Her face was kind and so very beautiful. I've bedded many women, some rough, some fresh, some old, some almost too young. But her. She wasn't the sort of woman a man could lay with and then cast off. Some women were the permanent sort. The kind men married. What sort of woman was she, I wondered? Before I could stop m'self, I asked, "Do you have any children, Alison?"

She sighed deeply and dropped her chapped hands to her lap. Her reddened fingers toyed with one another. "No, alas. Though I don't know if I'd be in better stead with a babe to care for and no husband."

"Was he a good man?"

"Rolf? He was…a man, is all. He was older. Much older. He and my father were friends for many years. I learned brewing from my sire. Rolf was a brewer as well. When Father died Rolf offered to marry me. It was kind of him. There were no other prospects. I had no brothers to continue the business. I would have starved. Rolf got whatever was left of my father's estate and it wasn't much. But we were building a life, or so I thought. He gambled away so much and then borrowed from those money lenders, though little did I know of that."

"Surely you can marry again."

"In a fortnight? Who would have me and my debt? But that's over for me. I'd not bring in another man to ruin the life I built for myself. I have no love of that, Oswald."

I stared hard into the dancing fire, watching the flames gambol and swirl. The warmth somehow did not reach me, at least not all the way through. It was the lonely sound of her words, I reckon. It plucked a chord inside me, echoing with an elusive feeling. Aye, sometimes I craved a household, with a wife and a babe. But other times, I knew it was easier on my own with little obligations. Though alone, I was only half a man, this I knew. Didn't God make Adam and Eve so they would be together, toiling in this workaday world? "Home is home, however poor it may be."

It was worse for a woman alone, but a widow had the dowry of her husband's business and estates and could make much of her life. Though in the end, it seemed that Rolf Hale had left his wife with very little but anger in her belly. And who could blame her? A man was supposed to care for his kin. He shouldn't be gambling it away… Of course now a surge of guilt washed over me, for did I not make fine sport of those fools that lost to my games of crooked dice? And I thought right well that they deserved it and it might be so. But it scarce made me think of the wife and babes at home that might go hungry because of my own greed.

God's teeth and bones! This is what comes of *talking* to women.

She made to rise and I touched her hand, stopping her.

"Wait, Alison." She looked at me, a sad, lost spirit in her eyes. What I was going to say to her seemed to dry up on my tongue. Instead, I offered, "Your luck will change. I know it will."

"It had better. For the only luck I have known thus far is bad."

I let her go this time, watching her weave her way back to the buttery. I wanted to keep that spark in her eyes. I knew nothing of the man she had married and less of her feelings about him, but I suddenly had a burning desire warming my chest like hot coals, to be the man who changed her luck. If I could be that kind of man, then I knew I could make her eyes shine again.

But hold! What kind of fool was I? I would have slapped m'self if I was alone. Falling for a sad eye and a pretty face? Ach, Oswald! For shame, man. Women were fit for a tumble and nothing else! If I fell into that trap I'd be as empty-headed as Geoff. It was only her body I wanted, not her heart. She was a shapely lass, no mistaking. To warm m'self between her hams was my only purpose.

When I looked again, she was staring at me from across the room, a curious expression on her brow, and she was cocking her head as if trying to understand a puzzle.

I left the jug behind and slipped out of the tavern quick as I could. I wasn't warmed through yet but I had to get out. I breathed the air of London, the hay-sweet smell of fresh horse dung sharp in the air. At least I wasn't closed in by walls and obligations.

I had almost turned the corner to Cornhill when I spotted Geoff. But he wasn't alone. Some men, lordly men, two of them, had him surrounded and Geoff got that cowed look about him, as if he done something wrong. I crept closer so that none would see me. I grabbed old Saint Joseph, ready to draw him out, though I didn't know what I could do to lordly men. That would be the death of me on the street, right enough. They both had swords as well as daggers and I was no gentleman. But Geoff was in trouble. There had to be something I could do! Reluctantly, I sheathed my hammer. They talked low and cruel to him and I crept up and hid behind a cart laden with sticks. I peered through the twigs, watching helplessly and thinking hard. Christ, how I wish I could *hear* them!

And then I recalled that I had seen them both once before — no, *twice* before — and a deep chill quivered my soul.

One man, a thin fellow all in dark blue, pointed to the bruise on Geoff's face.

Geoff cowered as they talked low to him. When they were done, they shoved him hard and Geoff nearly stumbled almost dropping his parcel. He bowed to the men and hastened away.

I waited until they had gone around the corner before I emerged from my hiding place. My first instinct was to run to catch up to Geoff and demand to know what was afoot. But the better part of me, the cautious part, told me to hold. It was difficult for Geoff to understand how the world worked. He knew I was here to protect him but his addled brain could only do so much.

I recalled those men. They had lingered on Cornhill before, staring at me. And when next I saw them, they were in the Tower, taking measure of me again. What were they up to?

I hastened back and found Geoff laying the parcel carefully on his bed. He startled when I entered and guiltily whipped around. "Oh! Oz. Didn't see you there."

I made my expression flat and casual. "Greetings, Geoff."

"Is...er...all well, Oz?"

"Aye, Geoff. All's well. Anything to tell me?"

"Me? Oh no, Oz. Not a thing. Not a thing."

"You certain, lad? Because you know I won't get angry with you."

Geoff dropped his gaze and fumbled with his tunic hem. "No, Oz. I've nothing to say."

So it was that way, was it?

As if it weren't all complicated enough, it had just got worse.

CHAPTER THIRTEEN

IT WAS WORSE than I thought. Geoff had begun sneaking out in the midst of the night and I'd catch him returning before the cock crowed. God's teeth! If I couldn't trust Geoff, then I couldn't trust nobody!

I went in search of Walter, for he had a level head if any man had one. He might give me some sorely needed advice.

I waited at his door until Sibbe deigned to open it. And then — that exasperating woman! — she stood and stared at me with nary a word spoken. Finally, I'd had enough.

"Woman, I'm at my wit's end. Tell your master I wish to see him!"

"Can't."

"And why, by all the saints, can't you?"

"Because he is not at home." She grinned, a toothless smug sort of grimace.

"But it's not yet Prime!" Walter was always home. Where else would he go, and so early in the day?

"He's not been home many a morn, lately," she said, haughty as you please. "And before you ask me, I don't know where he goes. And even if I did know I wouldn't tell you. It started with all your secret doings. I don't like it, Oswald. I don't like your meddling in Master Walter's affairs. You are a bad influence on him!" With that, she slammed the door in my face.

No doubt Walter was up to the tasks I had set him, but it was frustrating when I needed to speak with him about Geoff. Maybe I was being a fool. Maybe there was nothing to it. Just the same, I kept my plans to m'self, telling each companion only that which they needed to know. That way they couldn't slip and tell Geoff. But the plan had to go forth. There was Lord de Mandeville to worry over and Geoff. His safety was foremost. And Alison. She was depending on me.

I took my worry with me to the fields and copses above London where I practiced with the crossbow. Geoff hounded me to know what it was to be used for, but I kept my lips shut up tight. "Only when you need to know," I told him. And it was true. Not a moment before.

The crossbow helped keep my mind off my troubles and it didn't hurt that it was a weapon neither! I satisfied myself with shooting at trees. There was no one there but me and sheep. Might have been Walter's sheep at that, but no. I had him run them up on Tower Hill to keep watch. And de Mandeville had newly sent me the map which gave me a much better idea as to how to form my plans. It would work. I knew it would.

I cranked the crossbow's windlass again and placed the quarrel in place. It was a simple thing to aim and pull the lever. Clever, truly. Wish I'd invented it. But I'd invented many such devices and it was time to see if some of them would come to bear fruit.

The quarrel left the bow and shot away fairly straight and far. It needed to go at least a hundred and twenty feet, by my reckoning, or it would be all for naught. At least that's what it looked like from the map de Mandeville provided. If Trevor completed those other things I needed, then we'd see.

I fixed my own special quarrel to the crossbow, aimed it high, and shot. Saint Margaret! It was a disaster! The wrong place, not far enough, and a lot of wasted hours. But I calmed m'self down and looked at it critically. Oh I see. Aye. I did that wrong. And what if this were thinner? Would it still work? I fiddled and toiled, sitting on my bum on that cold field in Islington, filing away with a rasp, until I could try again.

Again and again. I broke out in a sweat, tinkering and bending and hammering.

Again. And this time, it worked. Shot well over that one-hundred-and-twenty-foot mark. I stood with my jaw on me chest, just staring. A sheep had wandered up beside me and suddenly bleated, startling the devil out of me. "Aye, you're right," I told it. "That was a right good piece of work I done there!"

She bleated again and waddled away, swishing her shite-encrusted tail.

I wrapped up my belongings, tucked it under my arm, and made my way home.

And so it went. Day after day, I'd perfect my tasks and I became a friend to the sheep above London. I even dragged Walter with me one day for he had to be able to work the mechanics of it if others failed.

First, I made him try the crossbow.

"No, Walter, you can't close *both* eyes! You need at least one to see where the hell you're shooting."

He held it loosely in one hand, waving it precariously about. I ducked when it swung my way and grabbed his wrist. "You're a dangerous man, you know that? Keep this aimed away from anyone you don't want to shoot, you fool."

Walter looked stricken and aimed it at the ground...and promptly shot his foot.

"Arrgh!"

"Walter!"

He fell over and I was on the ground trying to reckon what to do. Blood started to seep around the quarrel in his shoe and before I thought it through, I yanked the arrow out. He screamed again and shook the offended foot in the air as he rolled over and over. I pulled off his shoe and scrambled to his side and the whole time he yowled in my ear. I pushed up his cotehardie and attacked the laces of his stocking, struggling to untie it from his braies while he rolled and hollered. I had just pulled his stocking down to his knee when the shepherd broke through the underbrush with his crook.

Walter and me both froze, me with my hand on his naked thigh between Walter's legs, and Walter with his bunched cotehardie clutched over his belly.

The shepherd blinked. He gave each of us a studied glare before shaking his finger at us and moving on, saying not a word.

I finished pulling off his stocking and looked at his foot, expecting the worst, but he had made a lucky shot and had only grazed the skin between his toes.

"Look there, Walter. I think you'll live."

"No thanks to you!" He snatched his stocking from my hand and made himself modest again by pushing down his cotehardie to cover his cod. "Look at that!" He gestured toward his foot. "I'm maimed!"

"You're not maimed exactly. Look here. Wiggle your toes." I reached for his foot but he slapped my hand.

"Stop touching me." He struggled to his feet and picked up his discarded shoe. "I'm going home."

"Walter. It was just a little accident. Could have happened to anyone."

"No. These little accidents only happen when *you* are around. I'm going home." He limped away, muttered oaths and curses and I could do nothing but gather our things into a sack and quietly follow him back.

When we neared Cornhill, I spied them two knights again. I tried to ignore them but my mind was on spies and danger.

But the Plan. The Plan had to come first before any other worry. So that meant it was time to check on the blacksmith.

———— ◆ ————

"OI, TREV!" I called, turning the corner into his shop. A chair toppled over just as I caught a glimpse of a shadow disappearing out the back entrance. Trev was standing by his forge — the man never seemed to leave it — and merely watched the shadow disappear while it dislodged a basket and a jug from a shelf in its haste to depart. The jug shattered on the hard floor.

"Trev?" I ran to the back and cast open the door but I saw nothing but an empty alley and a hen pecking at the mud.

Not a robber, for Trev seemed unconcerned like always.

Someone talking to him, then. But who? Who needed to escape as quick as a wink?

He looked me up and down before turning away, paying no heed to the shards of pottery on the floor. He dipped his hands into his bucket and sluiced his face. He whipped his head, shaking the water off him like a dog. His short hair glistened.

"What was that, Trev? A thief?"

A thief, trying to steal my Plan?

"It was nobody," he said in that rough voice of his.

"Nobody? That's bollocks. I saw someone."

"Nobody important."

Christ Almighty. Was *Trev* a spy? He did agree to treason right quick. Did he have his own plans to turn us in for a reward?

I rubbed my chin and leaned against the wall. I needed Trev. There were no two ways about it. But if *he* should give me up, we were more than cooked. We were hanged for sure.

"I...er...came to see about those pieces I would have you make."

He pulled out the pieces and showed them to me, my spring-loaded *tegans*, only bigger. They worked just as I devised them to. "Are they strong enough?"

He grunted and shrugged.

"They need to be strong, Trev, or it's all for naught."

"They're strong."

"And the other things?"

He pulled them out from under his work bench. He was a fast worker, I'll give him that. They looked good. It was going to work. We just needed a few more days.

If he wasn't a spy, that is.

Someone skittered into the doorway and I thought it might be that shadow again but it was Walter, out of breath. He clutched the jamb and panted, waving his hand before his face as if that would supply him with enough air.

"Oswald," he gasped. "I have news from my shepherds. They tell me that they have discovered the king is returning. Sooner than expected."

Saint Dafydd's bollocks!

———————◆———————

THERE WAS THE fact that we weren't ready, a dead man's murderer to reveal, and the king was returning early. Christ save us!

I assembled everyone that evening at my shop and closed all the shutters. They were all staring at me as I paced, waiting for the answers I didn't have.

"We have to call it off," said Walter. He sat with his bandaged foot on a stool and he was toying with one of my block and tackles, making the wheel squeak. I'd have to oil that.

I yanked it out of his hand. "No one's calling anything off."

"But we must! We have no time to complete our tasks."

"And speaking of that," said Alison, plucking the wheeled block out of my fingers. "What is the plan exactly? I've gone to the Tower every sarding day like you told me, getting farther and farther inside. But you've only told me a speck of what's supposed to happen. I want to know all of it."

"Yes," said Walter. "I, too, would like to know what is such a dark secret about all this. Since it's to be cancelled then—"

"No one's said anything about it being cancelled! Now just calm yourself."

"Calm myself?" Walter looked at each person in turn in amazement. "Calm myself? I will not be calm. This is definitely not the time to be calm!" He slammed his hurt foot on the floor and everyone winced at his wail of pain. He took a deep breath. "You have strung us all along like an ox with a nose ring," he went on, "and I refuse to be party to it any longer unless you divulge your so-called plans." He crossed his arms before him and raised his nose in the air.

Alison cocked her thumb at him. "What he said. I want to know, too."

It was mutiny, is what it was. I gestured to Trev. "Well? Got anything to add?"

Trev, like the bullock he resembled, only swayed his head from side to side. I glanced at Geoff and he shrunk on his stool. I noted that he never looked at Trev at all no more.

I felt affronted. That they didn't trust me. Well! Wasn't *that* a pastie all crimped and browned!

A knock on the door startled us all and Alison even yelped. We all turned toward it and I wondered who it could possibly be.

Don't open the door, Walter mouthed.

But it was no use. "The sow has gone through the shop," as my mother would have said. Ah well. I opened the door.

Benet Chigwell pushed his way in and stood in the middle of my floor. He was brandishing a flask and suddenly realized that there was a host of us.

"Well, well, well. It seems I have come at an opportune time to meet the other traitors."

"For God's sake!" cried Walter. "Keep your voice down."

Benet pressed his fingers to his mouth in mock humility. His eyes positively sparkled. "Oh. Don't *they* know they are committing treason?"

I grabbed his arm. "Ben, I am glad to see you but please have a care. These folk are not as mad as you are."

He cackled and settled himself on a stool. "Mad indeed," he chuckled. "I think the question of sanity has long ago left this cottage." He gestured with his jar and then hugged it to himself again. "I have your Greek Fire, Master Thief. Since all the conspirators are gathered it looks as if you were about to tell them the plot. I should like to hear it myself."

"How soon is the king supposed to return?" I asked Walter.

"My sources say three days."

"Trev, can you get those things done in two?"

He thought a moment, scratching that unkempt beard of his, and slowly nodded.

"Very well, then. I'll explain it all as I see it. We've all got to have the courage. It's got to be done by all of us, for if any one of us is caught, the others have got to be able to get away. So harken to me carefully."

They all sat again and our faces were hidden in shadows as the firelight jumped up the walls behind us. "Alison, you have been taking Walter's cart and a cask of ale to the Tower, have you not?"

"Every day, just like you told me."

"And do they let you in further each day."

"Aye, they do. I think on the morrow I shall be in the inner bailey."

"God be praised. That's a right good job. That's just where I want you the next few days, so they get used to seeing you. And I want you to stay later and later. Even after sunset."

"What about my alehouse? I have only the one lad to run it and he's a thieving dog."

"Just a few more days, Alison. They have to be so used to you that they take no heed. And with free ale, they are pleased to see you, eh?"

"Too pleased," she said, rubbing her backside.

Were those guards taking liberties? I punched down a spike of jealousy.

"Aye, well. You'll need to leave the cart in some lost corner, so they will not think of it sitting there all night."

"And why must it sit there all night?" she asked.

"Because. That is how we are to get the king's booty out of the Keep. One of your barrels will be empty when you bring it in. Well, that is to say, empty of ale, but Geoff will be inside."

"I will?"

I patted Geoff's knee. "Aye. You will. It will be a snug fit, Geoff, but you'll manage. You can sleep in it if you like."

"Oh! Aye, Oz. I can do that."

"And you'll have your lock picks with you. And Alison will make herself scarce as night falls. You can sleep by the cart, too, or pretend to, Alison. Just stay out of sight of the men-at-arms. It will be a new moon in three days and a fog will help our course. When it is midnight, you are to take the jar of Greek Fire that our Master Chigwell has made for us and, as stealthy as you can and as far away from the White Tower and your cart as can be, and set the Greek fire aflame."

"What? You want me to start a fire?"

"Aye. That's the distraction, lass. De Mandeville has already assured me that he will keep a guard away from the vault stairs, for that is our one big obstacle, but the other men will be called to the fire to extinguish it and find that they cannot, it being Greek Fire."

Her puzzled expression spurred on Walter who could not help himself. "Greek Fire," he explained, "is derived from materials that will not extinguish with water. In fact, the more water that is put to it, the greater the flames become. It is used for sieges against castles."

She stared at him and then at Chigwell. "Such a devilish thing."

Ben grinned like a jackal and stroked the jar cradled under his arm.

"And so," I went on. "They will be engaged with putting out an unquenchable fire. And they will not notice Trev and me coming in from the sky."

"The *sky*?" As one, they said it and I wanted to laugh, but their expressions were so serious I set to explaining.

"First things first. Trev and me will take a boat to the Water Gate and with our tools and devices, we will swim under the portcullis and get into the grounds. With my crossbow, I will shoot a grappling hook up the wall and we shall climb up a rope. Once we have breached the wall, I will use another bolt with a rope attached to shoot at the shutter of one of the windows of St. John's chapel in the White Tower." I picked up one of the wheel and blocks and showed them. "We fit these on the rope, which is aiming downward, mind, and slide over everyone's head to the White Tower. Once there, we get inside and await Alison

159

and Geoff and let you in. And then, we all go down to the vault where Trev has devised an expanding ladder to go across the pit so's that Geoff and I can get to the doors. Once inside the treasure trove, we fill up the bags and make our way to the cart where they are loaded into the empty barrel. Trev, Geoff, and me will leave as we came, up and over the walls and under the portcullis and Alison—brave Alison, will leave in the morning with her ale barrels and none will be the wiser."

There was dead silence. It went on a long time. So long, in fact, that I thought I had gone deaf until Walter dropped his face in his hands and shook his head from side to side.

"*This* is your plan?" he said at last, voice muffled under his fingers.

"Well, aye." I was proud of it. The angels couldn't have done better.

"That is insane! I won't be a party to it!"

I sighed at him. Walter never wanted to be "a party" to anything I ever thought of. Nothing was different now. Except that Alison was bearing down on me as well.

"I don't see how it will honestly work. It's never been done."

"Of course it's never been done!" I told them. "Because no one has ever thought of something this brilliant before. Trust me."

Chigwell was nodding wildly and grinning again.

"And yet, you waited this long to tell us," she said scornfully, "so it would be too late for the rest of us to come up with something better."

"Whose got a better idea? Anyone?" I waited, looking at each in turn. Not a one had anything to say. I gave the lass an "I told you so" nod. "And it will work," I went on. "The new moon will help it work. Alison, Walter. Please! We must. Don't you remember Lord de Mandeville's threat?"

Walter stood. "Well, if we are speaking of absolute trust, none of us actually heard Percy de Mandeville threaten you, Oswald. It was by your word alone that we came together on this."

"Aye," said Alison. "Answer that!"

Hold! Now the suspicions were being turned on me? *Me*? Well…truth be told, they had a point.

"Now just hold, all of you. I swear to Almighty God, that Percy de Mandeville did threaten me. He did. And he forced my hand. I can't help it if I came up with this Plan. It's all we got."

Alison turned away. I saw her raise her hand to her eyes. Was she weeping? Aw, for the love of —

"Alison." I rested my hands gently on her shoulders. "I know that you must do this, too. It is your only choice."

She wriggled away from my touch. "My only choice, is it? So you say."

"So you know. You said so yourself. No one wanted you in this scheme. I'm the one that let you — "

"*Let* me? You practically *begged* me!"

"*Stop!*"

We all froze and stared at Geoff. Tears were flowing freely down his face and he hugged himself for comfort.

"Just stop," he said, wiping the snot from his nose with a sleeve. "Look at all of you. We were a fine company before. Oz made a fine plan, a brilliant plan. A plan the angels would have devised. We trusted him before. Why wouldn't we trust him now?" He turned to me. "I trust you, Oz. I've always trusted you."

Oh, it made my heart hurt. For could I trust Geoff? And I wanted to with all my heart. Him talking to them knights and agreeing to…something. But all of my heart wasn't in it. Aw Geoff. What have you gotten us all into? But that settled it. If I had to tie a leash to the lad, I could not let him out of my sight for the next three days. It wouldn't do his going off and telling them knights about our Plan. Even if he had no idea he was betraying us.

They all fell silent again. Walter was slumped on his chair, staring at the table. Trev had not moved from his place by the fire. His brawny arms hung at his sides and his face lay smooth and impassive. Geoff looked from one to the other of us, his eyes shining and wet. Chigwell was still smiling his inane smile. Alison's gaze was on the floor before she spun away, threw open the door, and stalked out.

I don't know what I was thinking, but my feet did the thinking first. I tramped off after her and grabbed her arm. She wrestled me for a bit but not too hard and I dragged her to the warmth of my neighbor's brazier just under the eave of his shop.

"Alison." Truly, I did not know what to say to the wench. Whenever I was in her presence, I lost my mind. "Alison. I swear, it will work. I'm just…as scared as you are. Maybe more so."

She would not look me in the eye, and I wanted it. The light was golden on her features, warming the globes of her cheeks. Her lashes hid her eyes in shadow and she hugged her cloak about her. She huffed an impatient breath and muttered "Oswald" like a curse. It wouldn't be the first time it was used thus.

"I'll tell you a secret," I said to her. She dragged it out of me. Women. Eve coaxed Adam to eat of the Forbidden Fruit, after all, and Alison wrenched a deep truth from me. "It isn't only to save *my* skin, for God knows that skin isn't worth saving. But de Mandeville." I edged closer, being as quiet as I could. "He threatened Geoff."

She looked up at that.

"He knew I'd been before the sheriffs more times than a man can count and did not fear it. But he saw how I cared for Geoff and he threatened to send him away, take him to the sheriffs, and because Geoff is…how he is…they would just as soon hang him as anything else. Geoff don't deserve that." My eyes were blurry and I wiped at them hastily. "That whoreson, threatening Geoff like that. He's as innocent as a lamb, is Geoff. No man should have the power to do that. But there it is. That's why I need you, Alison. That's why I need all of you. But don't tell the others. I can't let Geoff find out."

She held her cloak tight, fingers digging into her forearms. Her gaze never left mine. "What kind of man are you, Oswald? You're not like anyone I have ever met."

It was on the tip of my tongue to say something light and jesting. But, for some reason, I held my peace. I could see her eyes now. They were wide and bright. Like a doe peering through the underbrush. "I...I'm just a man. Like any other, I reckon."

"No, you're not. You are..." She sighed and shook her head, leaning against the wall. The mist rolled up the street from the Thames, shrouding the lane like a woman's veil. The candles in windows became the small glow of intimate lights, of families gathering round hearths and paternosters. I strained to see, but shutters were being closed and the light was shut away. All that was left was mist, the dying flames of the brazier, and the steadily growing light in Alison's eyes.

"A thief," I supplied softly. For I knew she wanted to say it. But I could not abide hearing the word on her lips any longer.

A faint smile curved her mouth and formed a dimple just there, at the edge of her lips. "I wasn't going to say that. As true as it might be. No, what I meant to say was that you are like Robin Goodfellow. Like some forest sprite. Always slipping free of capture without ever a scratch. Something in a tale rather than a flesh and blood man."

"Eh?"

She shook her head, maybe loosening the fancies that had taken hold. "You don't seem to be just a farthing thief and gambler, for I *have* seen you at your shell games."

Embarrassed again. How did she manage to do that to me?

"You seem...more than that."

"Well, it's a poor excuse for a man who does not want to better himself."

"If you had only wanted that, you could have married some lass with a fat dowry who had a father with a good business. And you could have charmed your way into it. You *are* charming..."

Oh lass!

"...in a clumsy sort of way."

Oi!

Wait.

I felt a smile growing on my face. "You think I'm charming?"

"Oh look at him. There he goes. That's the least of what I was saying." She sighed. "You seem to want to better yourself in spectacular ways. Ways that any sane man would never approach. Ways well above your station. Everyone has their place, Oswald. Why can't you find yours?"

"I have." I spread my hands out and encompassed London. "This is my place. Some call me a tinker, for I am so. And some call me a thief, and I am that, too. And I am both and more." It was my turn to sigh. "I'm a Welshman in London, Alison, and I came a long way to get here. Do I love England? I don't know. Wales gave me life but London gave me a home. And I have my fun at what I do."

"You can't do it forever. One day they'll catch you and hang you."

"That may be so. But that's not today. Or three days hence, if I can help it. So what say you? Are you still in? Truth to tell, Alison, we need you. But it will be difficult. Aye. Like nothing you'd ever done before. But riches like these, they take a bit of work to get a hold of, don't they?"

She was looking at me kindly and we inched closer. "And doing it for a good cause, too. For Geoff," she said, shaking her head. "You have the Devil's own tongue, don't you?"

"Maybe." With my finger, I lifted a curled lock of her hair that had escaped her wimple. It was an intimacy she seemed to allow. "But I think that you want it. I think that a Robin Goodfellow in your life is just what you might be after."

"And you," she said, batting her hair from my fingers, "want little more than quim."

"That is not true, lass. *Partially* true, but not all true." A brilliant smile. That's what I gave her. It worked so many times before.

But not on her.

She stepped back into shadow. "Very well, Oswald. I'll help you in your scheme. And I'll say nothing about Geoff. But when we are done and those money lenders are out of my life...so shall you be."

She gave me a pointed look before turning and stepping into the mist.

CHAPTER FOURTEEN

I WATCHED THE blacksmith at his art while I sat on a stool in the corner of his shop. There was strength in that man's arm, to be sure. I could never do it. Mind you, I have strength. I am a man, after all. But I'm not the tallest or brawniest man in London and my true strength lies in using my mind for clever tricks. There's no man cleverer than I.

But Trev. Ach! The man could swing a hammer and make the iron sing! He brought out the white-hot rods and beat them on his anvil, stretching and hammering them over a template until they were thin, hollow things, but strong. I had to modify my plans because Trev would not have enough time otherwise and truth be told, this was better. Far better.

I listened to the music of hammer clanging against metal, the hiss of the water bath, the whoosh of the bellows. In Trev's shop, I was warm for the first time that day.

Aye, he had skill enough, but what of the man himself, for I knew little of him but that he agreed to be part of my company. And just why had he agreed? Well, a man cannot turn away coin, certainly. But why was Geoff so uneasy around him? Like he knew something about him. If something were amiss with Trev, he never showed it. Never showed anything about himself. Never rubbed two words together. I could sit all day with him and he'd say nothing at all.

"So Trev," I said, trying to draw him out. "Was your sire a blacksmith?"

He slowed his hammering but never stopped. Clang. Clang. "No."

"Oh. What *did* he do, then?"

Clang. Clang. "Died."

"Before that, man!"

Clang. Clang. Shrug.

What did I tell you? Few words.

I stood and hovered, watching close up what he was about. The hammer's rhythm never wavered. But when it did, when the hammer slipped a bit off the end of the anvil, I looked up and spied Geoff in the doorway.

"Oh," he said, twisting his tunic till the wrinkles became permanent. "I didn't know where you was, Oz"

"What is it you need, Geoff?"

"Nothing. I was just looking for you."

"Well, come in. Trev won't bite."

But Geoff hesitated. Perhaps he knew something I didn't. Did those lordly knights tell him something about Trev? The thought of it roiled a hot stone in my belly. I thought of dragging Geoff inside, demanding to know, but that was not fair to Geoff. The lad can't help it.

"Go on home, Geoff. I'll be there anon."

He brightened. "Shall I start cooking?"

"Aye, Geoff. You do that. It will be good to come home to food on the fire."

"Right, Oz. We've got a fresh pullet. I'll go now." And just like a child, he scampered home to do his work.

Hammering again in rhythm, Trev watched me before a mysterious smile curved his mouth. I don't mind telling you, it sent a bad shiver down my spine.

———•———

AND SO. ALL was finally ready. The new moon was the next day and it also looked as if a fog would cover our doings. Well, I couldn't ask the saints to do any better than that.

Anxious, I stood outside over my brazier, thawing my hands. My cloak was warm over my shoulders and I was feeling content but a bit edgy. The sky had not brightened yet, though I detected a mere blush at the horizon. Geoff soon joined me and the two of us silently watched the flames, saying nothing.

Finally, Geoff looked up at me. "Tomorrow night, eh, Oz?"

"Tomorrow night, Geoff. Er…there isn't anything you need to tell me, is there? I mean, something truly important that you perhaps shouldn't keep from old Oz?"

His eyes were bright with tears and I regretted saying it the moment it escaped my mouth.

Very slowly, he ground it out. "You know I'd tell you…if I could, Oz."

"*If* you could? Well, if you find you can't, will it make a difference? What I mean is, will something happen to you…or me?"

Geoff chewed on his lips. He thought long and hard on it when he finally raised his head. "I don't know," he whispered.

A little voice in my head told me to abandon the scheme, that it was too risky, that Geoff — bless his heart — couldn't be trusted, not truly, even if it wasn't his fault. All my nerves were telling me to do that very thing. My skin tingled with it.

But even with such good advice — which might very well be my own mother scolding me from Heaven — I couldn't do it. I couldn't abandon it. Oh, it wasn't because of the gold and jewels, the likes of which I had never seen before. And it wasn't for the coin to be earned from selling it all. Although, I confess, that I would be pleased to see it with my own eyes.

No, all in all, it wasn't all that. What it was, was the idea of doing the thing, that it hadn't been done, that it was *me* that was going to be achieving it. Me, a lad from a little village in Wales, who never did a thing of note in his life. Should a lowly man aspire to be something great? Perhaps it is in the heart of a man to want to try. For a knight will take up the lance and go to war and he will march with the king to distant places to protect a castle or the Church or some such ideal. He will lay down his life for it.

But me? I am not such a man. There are so many of us who live on ordinary streets in London town and we sow and spin and do our allotted tasks. And if ever we were conscripted to take up arms for our king, we should be proud to do it, like any other man. But can we not also find that same wonder in doing some other daring thing? And if that must needs be outside the law, then so be it.

Well...listen to me. That was a speech fit for any alehouse or battlefield. Aye. Tomorrow was our battlefield.

I slipped my arm around Geoff's shaking shoulders to show him I had no hard feelings one way or the other.

Geoff was no Judas and I was certainly no Jesus.

———◆———

IT WAS AT midday that I heard about the funeral for Hugh Aubrey. Some fellows were talking about it in the square where Cornhill crossed Three Needles and Lombard. It was to be in a church near the de Mandeville manor off St. Clement's.

I had a lot to do, a lot to occupy my mind. But I knew I couldn't do none of it till I saw Hugh planted proper in the ground.

With my hood up for the rain, I hastened down the streets and alleys and made it to the churchyard as the priest from the house chapel presided over his linen-wrapped corpse. Hugh had shrunk down again and had a smell about him. I caught a whiff even as far back as I was behind the other servants who knew him well and what I thought was the grieving steward and his wife. Four men wrestled him down into the moist earth while the drizzle made all gray.

The priest said his words and men with spades shoveled the dirt over him as Madam Aubrey wailed and fell into her husband's shoulder.

I didn't see any sign of Lord de Mandeville.

The people started to disperse, but I hung back behind a large stone cross, half behind its mossy carvings. The priest noticed and stepped carefully over the wet grass to join me. "Young friend," he said.

"My lord." I bowed.

"And so young Hugh is laid to rest at last."

I crossed m'self. "God rest him."

"So wretched a thing to snuff out a young life." Then them sheriffs must have decided it was murder and Hugh could have his Christian burial.

The priest stared down at the top of my head for a good long time. "You know, I don't recall seeing you in the household before."

"Oh. Well, I was in the scullery. Didn't get out much."

"I see." He breathed deeply. All I could smell was wet and the dirt of a graveyard. I itched to leave.

"I fear his soul lingers, waiting until his blood can find justice. That his killer be found."

"Aye." I said quietly, not truly thinking. I just stared at the little mound of naked earth. "Justice will be done."

"I do hope so. Anyone who knows a kernel of truth on the matter is morally obligated to step forward, else *his* soul is surely in peril."

I swallowed hard. "What is your meaning, my lord?"

"Well, any man who has evidence to a crime such as this and does not step forward, it is as if he were a party to it. Both before God and the king's justice."

"But that isn't fair! Perhaps the man has his reasons for not stepping forward."

"Selfish, sinful reasons, no doubt. Only a man of low character would remain obscure."

"Forgive me, Father, er, Father – ?"

"Father Simon."

"Father Simon." I bowed. "But there is more you do not understand. It's not always a situation of low character. For a man could have very good, important reasons. Reasons out of his control."

It was then I turned to face him and his dark eyes studied me intently. "You make a very strong argument…for a man who knows little of these affairs."

Er…

Before I could answer he shifted away from me and raised his face to the rain, squinting at the drops pelting his square face. "Should let up by late afternoon."

Relieved at the change in direction of his thoughts, I opened my mouth to answer, but I was stopped by distant movement.

Deep in the churchyard I spied two men. Those same two sarding knights, whispering close together. They raised their shadowy faces and looked right at me.

I took a backwards step and then another.

It wasn't until I had made it home, panting and gasping in my doorway, that I realized I had not bid Father Simon farewell.

I TOOK MY thoughts with me late into the next morning, folded them up tight, and concentrated on the difficult hours ahead.

When evening fell, we were ready. Walter was our lookout and he had gone on ahead, limping and muttering. With any luck, Alison was already within the gate, for her task had been to ply the guards with her ale in order to persuade them to buy a barrel or two from her. She had Walter's cart and inside one of the empty barrels was Geoff with his lock picks. Geoff had the final tasks. We'd see the signal that was to let us know to proceed once we were inside the walls.

I gathered Trev and our devices together, and Christ, they were heavier than I thought they'd be.

I was no longer afraid. Just excited to be doing it at last.

We made our way to the wharf as silent as we could, but even wrapped in the sacks Alison supplied, the devices jostled, clinking against one another. The new moon made all dark, and just as was predicted, the mist had risen and all was shrouded in fog. My heart swelled at the sight.

We spotted the boat and got in. Tim had left the oar locks wrapped in rags like I asked him to and we skimmed over the placid Thames, Trev and me. The tide was down so the walls seemed even higher, but I knew it wouldn't matter once inside.

I watched Trev's face, as much of it as I could see in the darkness and the dim light from the distant cresset burning on top of the turret of Lanthorn Tower. His expression was neither fearful nor excited. He looked as he always looked. What manner of man was he? I wanted to ask but I doubted I would get a fitting answer.

He was doing this thing with me. Could he still be a spy and put himself under the threat like that? We'd soon see.

We came upon the Water Gate. Trev held the boat against the stone wall. My eyes darted here and there, looking for movement and saw none. How relieved I was that the king's guards couldn't be arsed to be at every tower. But perhaps Alison was enchanting them with ale as I instructed. With a sudden pang in my chest, I hoped that this was all she enchanted them with. I didn't think I could stand it if she were giving them undeserved kisses, for she was surely already giving them false smiles and cheer. A great jealous beast suddenly reared inside me, but I tamped it down. No use. And no time to ponder it. I had my job to do.

Besides, she should be feigning sleep about now by that cart.

Trev and I both began to strip. Cold! There went my bollocks again! We knelt in the rocking boat and pushed our clothes into oiled sacks and tied them up tight. We took the boat as close to the tower wall as we could, tied ropes to the devices, and lowered them down into the water till they hit bottom. I looked up at Trev but all I could see was a vague outline of his hulking body. I let the coils of ropes go and kept hold of the other end, watching as they floated for a bit before they sank.

Looking up, I could not see the top of the tower except for the faint glow of the cresset in the lantern tower. The light was scattered by the fog. And that meant that they could not see us either.

"Shall I go first?" I asked Trev. I began to wonder if I had miscalculated. Would he really be able to slip his bulk under the portcullis? Too late to worry over it now. We'd see very shortly.

He motioned for me to go first, the first sign of emotion. After all, I had made the trip before, not him. He'd follow me in, then. Into the dark depth of the unforgiving water. I hoped he could see me. If he drowned, we'd all be sunk.

I made certain one of us had our sack of clothes. We both leaned into the water when I heard "*Oswald!*" as a hissed whisper from the fog.

Christ! What was that? God Himself telling me to give it up?

The Lanthorn Tower's vague light flickered over the waves and against the light mist, I saw a shadow of a man approaching in another boat. "Oswald! It's Walter."

Walter? What by Christ did *he* want?

"I can't talk, Walter. I'm going in."

"Oswald, no! I just discovered something about—!"

I couldn't hear the rest of his words as the frigid water closed over my head. Did he say a name? No matter now. I grasped Trev's beefy wrist, making sure I still held the end of the rope with my other, and we dove.

CHAPTER FIFTEEN

BRIEFLY, I WORRIED over what it is that Walter wanted to tell me, but it couldn't be helped. We were too far in. And Alison and Geoff were already within the inner bailey. I wouldn't leave them there in any case and so we had to proceed. Whatever it was would have to wait.

I concentrated instead on holding my breath and keeping a hold of Trev. We sank like stones. I couldn't see a thing and began to wonder if this was the smartest notion I ever had. But I had a keen sense of things, and I found the wall quickly enough, grateful when I touched slimy stone with my fingertips. I walked with my hands down the wall till we reached the portcullis. I pushed Trev first, for if he couldn't fit below it, we'd have to re-plan. Down he went. I felt him struggle, felt the waves from him kicking his way, but I soon felt his hand on the other side giving me the signal. I slipped under it in haste, for my breath was almost gone. I slid under easily, Trev having made a nice trough for me, and just like that we were on the other side. I found Trev's hand and pushed up from the bottom and tried to swim up, but Trev was like a dead weight. He wasn't drowned for I could feel him thrashing beside me but we weren't rising. And my breath was just about done. I smacked him on the side of the head and took his hand roughly and began kicking my feet. He did so, too, and we slowly rose, my lungs screaming for relief.

As soon as we broke the surface I gasped and glared at him. "What by the saints' feet is the matter with you?"

Trev still splashed about, his head bobbing in and out of the waves, and to keep it all quiet I had to tug him quick across the moat to the stone steps.

"You can't swim, can you? Why didn't you tell me?"

"You never asked," he grunted.

Lackwits, all of them.

I dragged him up the steps, and as wet as we were it was like trying to wrestle a greased swine. But he got his breath and his strength back and stood up. He emptied the sack with our clothes, which were only a bit damp, and we shrugged into them, shivering madly.

Once dressed, I let him haul up the devices, which was a sore thing them being made of iron and now at the bottom of the Thames. I tucked the oiled sack between the rope and the dock, and Trev put his weight into it. It was a good thing he was here for I didn't think I would have been capable.

I helped him pull them to the surface and we scrambled trying to pull them in and keep it quiet. We paused and listened.

Nothing. Good.

I wondered how Alison was fairing. If she was caught then so would we be. I only hoped that the men-at-arms might be a bit drunk by now. That would also help our cause.

We were in the inner walls but not yet the inner bailey. It was time to get started.

Out of the bundles I took my crossbow. This was not the crossbow I had started with. The one Geoff bought had only served as my model. I had taken it apart and tooled my own, for it had to be stronger and send the quarrel farther than the original. And instead of an ordinary quarrel—a dart-like arrow—I fixed my own special quarrel in place. This one had a shaft holding a grappling hook on one end and a rope on the other. A special hook, that was folded flat until it caught, where it would spring open, just like the ones I used for the alchemist's house. I must say, I was proud of that particular devising.

I aimed toward the top of the Garden Tower for we needed all the height we could get. I said a quick prayer and pulled the trigger.

The hook made a whirring noise as it winged into the dim mist. The rope whined as it unrolled. I heard a faint clang somewhere above me and I waited, listening for any guards. All was well. I tugged on it and it must have skidded a few feet till it stuck fast between the crenellations. I yanked, pulled my whole weight on it and it never moved again. Well now!

I signaled to Trev. We loaded our bundles on our backs. Ach! The bastards were heavy. But I went first, grabbing the rope and walking up the wall, the pack and the crossbow slapping my back as I went. It was hard work and dangerous. If a guard should come all he need do was cut the rope and we'd be broken-boned at the bottom of a forty-foot wall. Each labored step I took was a paternoster and I prayed good and hard as I had not done since at my mother's knee.

Once I was up halfway, I felt the rope strain and Trev was up behind me, his bundle clanking softly.

I was sustained by how well we were doing so far, for I don't mind telling you, I was already sore tired. The cold can take your strength and the frigid Thames did that by the cartload. And then climbing up a wall with forty pounds of iron on your back! Oh, but I thought mightily how that load would feel when it was gold and coin and jewels. It would be light as a feather then! I was already plotting how I would cheat that bastard de Mandeville.

I surprised myself when I broke through the mist and was at the top of the wall. I grabbed the stone and pulled myself through, huffing and panting like a fat man. I laid the bundle down as carefully as I could and made sure the hook was secure. I couldn't see Trev but I heard him puffing and straining and I could see the rope, taut and straight, quivering downward.

I'm not a patient man and I could barely stand to wait for him. What was taking so long? But Trev was three times my weight, I'll wager, and something simple for me was three times as hard for him. And blind me, that got me thinking about the next part. Would it work for him? I should have tested it but there had been no time. I becrossed m'self and looked heavenward. *You got me this far, Lord. The rest of the way, if you please?*

Wheezing like a bellows, Trev finally cleared the crest of the wall, and I leaned over and hauled him forth, taking the bundle from his shoulder so that he could roll over the edge and topple to the floor. He breathed uneasily for a bit while I untied the one bundle and set to preparing it.

A set of interlocking tubes, it was a sort of three-legged grappling hook. I fixed it to the crenellations looking out over the inner bailey, as much of it as I could see. The fog was thick but I could make out the White Tower. Below me were the walls to the Constable's Garden and some buildings. I could see braziers burning beneath me with the aint shadows of clusters of men. I was relying on Alison now, for surely she had distributed her daily allotment of ale to the men. Her task now was to sneak away to a far place in the northwest corner by St. Peter ad Vincula with the Greek Fire and set it off. And when would it happen?

Just as I began to wonder it, a burst of light billowed up from the northwest corner. It did not take long for the shouts of men to reach my ears. I looked at Trev. It was now!

The saints were with me for God had provided cover with his thick fog, but I had not counted on the fact that it would be difficult for me to aim at the right window! I could barely see the White Tower rising like a ghost through the mist. The windows were dark smudges on an already smudged looking apparition. Well, there was nothing for it.

I readied my crossbow and aimed toward what appeared to be the lowest window of St. John's Chapel. But I didn't account for the narrow angle for there was a tall building below and to my right. And the fortified entrance to the White Tower jutted out leaving a very narrow way indeed.

I studied the problem. I had only one window I could now aim for and even if I did hit it, Trev or me might run into the building's eave.

I shook out my head like a horse. No. Concentrate.

I leaned against the battlement, steadying the crossbow, and slowly squeezed the trigger. It fired and the rope spun away into the night but I had the awful feeling it fell short. Something clanged against stone and when I tugged on the rope my fears were all confirmed. God's teeth! I'd have to try again.

I hauled it back all the way. Trev huffed a breath over my shoulder and I stiffened. A fine time for me to recall that he might be a spy!

I dropped the thought like a hot coal. I couldn't think that way, not now. I readied my quarrel again and steadied myself on the wall. Just as I was about to pull the trigger, feet running below me stopped me dead. I looked down. All eyes were toward the glow and not, thank God, upward where me and Trev stood high on the turret. Taking a breath, I held it, took aim with the one eye, closed the other, and shot.

The rope whistled away, spinning and spiraling. Distantly I heard a sharp thud. The window's shutter! It sounded solid. I pulled and it didn't budge. Thank Christ!

Trev hitched the last bundle over his shoulder nice and secure. I gave him his block and wheel and I fitted mine to the rope.

It's a simple device, the block and wheel. You understand, surely, how a pulley works? A block of wood called the shell holds a strap with a hook atop or below. Inside the shell there is a wheel or sheave with a groove on its outer edge that fits a rope. The hook attaches to a loft in a stable or upper floor in a shop. The rope fits through the breech in the shell and over the wheel. One end of the rope attaches to your bale or what have you, and the other end is what you or the horse holds on to. Pulling the rope lifts up your heavy burden making all easier. The heavier the thing, the more block and tackle you need to make the job slick.

But we weren't going to be lifting anything so there was no hook. We were fitting our blocks all by themselves on the rope. The rope was secured at the one end when the quarrel struck the wooden shutter where it was stuck fast. The other end, the higher end, mind, was up on the Garden Tower with me and Trev and further attached to the three-legged device I'd set up earlier. Get it?

Imagine this: A long rope, taut and straight, with a nice angle aiming down to the lower window of the White Tower. I'd already attached ropes to the blocks and Trev and me would slide quick as a swallow down the rope over the heads of the guards and right to the very spot we wanted to be. Like dark angels.

I went first. I fitted my hands into the ropes secured to the block, tightened my fists around them, and pushed off from the battlement.

It was like sailing into the darkness of Hell itself. The cold air whooshed around me, flailing my hair back away from my face. My arm muscles were taut and stiff, bent as they were. It seemed so far and I seemed to fall for ages. I could hear the block above my head spinning wildly and I even smelled the burning as it whizzed over the rope. God help me, but I was terrified and thrilled at the same time.

My shoulder grazed the corner cornice of that jutting building and I spun helplessly on the rope for a moment, slowing my progress. *Ach-y-fi*! It hurt like a whoreson, but I didn't lose my grip. What I worried about more was the block slipping off the rope and me falling to my death — and now I couldn't get the image of young Hugh out of my mind. But worse! If I slowed too much, I may not slide all the way to freedom. I'd be dangling above like a coney hanging in a butcher's stall.

I rocked forward with my feet. Forth and back, coaxing the block on. Slowly, I picked up speed again, and headed toward my destination with a prayer of thanks on my cold lips.

My feet were stretched out ahead of me and it was a good thing for I thumped hard against the shutter to stop myself. Trev was to count to twenty slow so I could get the shutter open and out of his way, but I couldn't see no way to get the damned thing to open. And hanging as I was from the block left me little room to maneuver. I struggled for a bit, trying to think my way through it, when I heard it.

A whirring noise.

I only had time to turn and look behind when Trev himself—all bulk and iron bundles—crashed into me, cracking the shutters wide open. With a stifled yell we clattered through the window and fell, arse over ear. I landed on the floor first with him landing hard atop me.

"Christ Almighty!" I tried to say, but the breath had been stamped out of me like a bagpipe under an ox's hoof.

Trev rolled away with a grunt and I lay for a bit, gasping and dizzy from the pain. My backside! Ach. My bum was flattened right good.

We both lay on the broken wood and glass and listened, for we had made the Devil's own noise. But de Mandeville, that bastard, had done his part well, for there were no guards to come running.

All at once, a bell pealed and, petrified, we stared at the other. Then it dawned on me right quick that this alarm was for the fire, not us.

We scrambled down the chapel's nave and to the door. I opened the door slowly, expecting the guard to be there at the spiral stair but he was not. The door to the Tower itself was flung open and no one was there.

I made my way forth and peered out the White Tower door and down the steps to the misty courtyard. Where the hell were Geoff and Alison? They could have been caught starting the fire. My stomach plummeted. If they were caught... Hark! I heard a sound of feet running softly over the turf. It changed to shoes over stone and I spied two cloaked figures approaching.

God be praised! Geoff scrambled up the steps and I enclosed him in a hug. "Geoff, you *gadeling*! I'm sore happy to see you!"

"And you, too, Oz. Saints be praised."

Alison rumbled up behind him and before I had a chance to think on it, I grabbed her too, so relieved was I. I hugged her tight, scarce realizing the soft roundness pressed against me...until I did. I pushed her back slowly. We were nose to nose and I stared into soft eyes. So close, I could feel her breath pelting my mouth. I could smell the sweet scent of her, of woman and spilled ale and hay. My blood was ablaze, not only from the excitement of being in the Tower where we longed to be, but because of being so close to her, to feel her warmth, to almost taste her breath. I leaned in. I wanted a taste of those lips, forgetting all else.

A shove hard to my chest awoke me and I stumbled back. Alison's face was red and she stepped away, wiping down her surcote for no reason. "W-what's next?" she asked breathlessly.

If only I had a bucket of the freezing Thames now. But I shook m'self and gave her a nod. "Aye." I cleared my throat. "Well, then. It's down this staircase."

I grabbed the oil lamp on its shelf in the stairwell and trotted down the stairs, leaning my shoulder against the smooth stone wall. My little lamp's flame flickered. When I reached the bottom step, I held the lamp aloft so that the others could see.

The vault was as dark as the inside of a cloak. My little light painted a ghostly glow against the fat round pillars of the vault. It was quiet, too, like a tomb, though that was not what I wanted on my mind just then.

The pillars upheld the vaulted arches and marched away into the gloom where I knew lay the door, and behind that door, treasure. When I was a child, I heard tales of vast treasures and the dragons that guarded them. I knew a pit lay before us and for all I knew, a dragon lived at the bottom of that pit. But there was also a trap beyond the likes of which we knew not what. And it was a feeble excuse Lord de Mandeville gave to me that he did not know the nature of this trap. Was he not the Keeper of the Wardrobe?

I led the way with the cautious steps of the others behind me. My mouth was dry. How I wish Alison had brought some of her fine ale to me. I could have used something bracing.

I slowed and slid my foot forward, for it was so dark I could not tell just exactly where the pit was. My toes skimmed the surface, searching, until they dipped ahead of me and the ball of my foot teetered on the edge of nothingness.

I swallowed and pulled back. "No one move," I whispered, and that sound trickled back to me in a thousand echoes. "Trev," I rasped over my shoulder, "we need the ladder."

His bundle clunked hard on the stone and I heard him unwrap. I couldn't take my eyes from the pit, for even though I raised the light, I could not see to the bottom of it. My eyes looked beyond and I could barely make out the large oaken door with its bands and locks.

Metal tubes sliding one inside the other. Trev had worked his magic well, for all ran smooth without a burr to stop its easy slide. He came up alongside me and I handed Geoff the lamp, but his hands were shaking so much I took it from him and handed it to Alison. She stood at the precipice and the flames never wavered. A cool-blooded lass was she. I stole a glance at her. The soft light from the lamp made her features almost painfully beautiful.

Ach, Oswald! Now was not the time!

I tore my gaze away and helped Trev. We steadied the catwalk against our thighs once it was stretched to its utmost and slowly lowered it like a drawbridge. When it clanged on the other side, we both breathed a sigh. I shook it and it seemed sturdy.

"Now my friends, I'll go first and Geoff will follow, eh Geoff?"

I realized I hadn't heard a squeak from Geoff since we arrived and I turned to him. The light shone him pale with eyes large with worry. "Don't fret, Geoff. It will be fine. Easier than walking across the lane. I'll go first with the light, eh?"

He nodded and licked his lips.

The ladder, catwalk, whatever you would call it, was made of thin tubes of steel and it had many rungs like a ladder only closer together. Trev tried to make it as light as he could while still keeping it usable as a bridge. But in my state, there was no way in hell I'd be walking across it. For that maw below me beckoned like the gates of Hell itself and I did not want to tempt it to help me in. So it was a crawl for me, made more difficult for the lamp in my hand.

I was going to take it slow. No need to rush, for I could still hear, muffled and distant, the sounds of men rushing to put out the fire that would not be quenched. *Take your time, Oswald.* I knelt and leaned forward. With the empty sacks over my shoulders like a bouget, and the lamp tight in my fingers, I inched along the steel. It was cold beneath my palms and still smelled of the forge. It was a comforting smell and I took courage from it until the ground fell away before me.

Now I'm not one to have fears. There are men who cannot abide high places and some who would never enter a house in the dark. They are full of superstitions and unholy thoughts. Me, I fear nothing. But crawling under my own power across vast nothingness even gave *my* heart pause...before it started to beat madly against my chest. I swear, there was nothing below me! I do not know the makers of this pit but they surely must have bargained with the Devil himself to create such a thing. How could a pit like that exist in London, one that leads to the Devil's own backdoor?

I was only halfway across when I felt a breath of wind come up from the pit. My sweaty hand began to lose its grip on the lamp. I fisted the little clay pot. There was little I could do for I could not wipe my hand. The flame flickered and I froze, staring at it. I think we must have all held our breaths, praying every prayer we knew to every saint there was. God blind me! I even prayed to my mother, for she, too, was a saint in my mind.

The little flame steadied and with a short breath I eased along the steel again. My knees were feeling the ache of the slim metal digging furrows into my flesh but I was almost there. Almost… almost… and then the lamp touched solid ground. I pushed it onto the stone away from the edge and used both my hands to pull me all the way. I rolled onto the stone and lay on my back, just breathing.

"Oz! Oz, are you well?"

Geoff was frightened and we couldn't have that. I lifted an arm and waved it and then I chuckled. "Right as rain, Geoff. Right as rain. And now it's your turn. It's sure to be easier without holding a lamp."

I swung up into a sitting position and brushed up against something, like a fine cord that snapped in two. A cord? I've got fine solid instincts and it was a good thing, for the blade came swinging down like Death's scythe and I froze on the spot staring at it as it headed right for my neck.

CHAPTER SIXTEEN

I FLATTENED TO the floor in a blink, feeling the blade swish by me. It missed by a hair. What the—?

The other trap!

I stayed flat as it swung by again. No. It was another one, coming from the *other* direction! Mother of God! I was helpless.

The others started screaming but there was no place for me to go. I could barely see it in the dim light but I could hear their relentless motion. It wanted to slice me and there was nothing I could do.

I could hear under the screams Trev climbing onto the ladder. "No, Trev! It won't hold your weight. You told me so yourself."

The metal groaned under him and he had the good sense to back up. The steel bent and shivered when he left it. And yet, the blades continued to swing above me, leaving me spread on the floor with my nose crushed flat against the stone. I didn't want to, God knows I didn't, but I had to roll over to see what I was up against. I waited till I could feel the breath of it pass over my neck hairs and I rolled. Now I was looking upward into blackness until a glint of a curved steel blade flew over me, one and then the other, not in any sort of easy pattern, neither. The air was suddenly thick with the smell of my own sweat and a bit of coppery blood. My nose had taken the brunt when I slammed back to the stone and I tasted a trickle on my lips.

I watched the blades come at me for many heartbeats, which were wild and fast indeed. "Saint Joseph preserve me," I muttered. And then, of course, he did. For I remembered my own trusty Saint Joseph at my hip!

I wriggled until I could grab it. Now if I misjudged, one of two things would happen. If I was too shallow, the hammer might get knocked out of my hand and fall into the pit, and if I aimed too high my hand would be sliced off at the wrist. Neither seemed the best option. It would have to be perfect, then.

I wiped my hand down my tunic, grasped the hammer, and lifted it into my hand. I watched the blades go by me two, three more times and then I counted. "One…two…God-help-me-three!"

I thrust it up just as the blades swung down together. One sharp blade sliced a sliver of skin from my knuckle and then locked solid on the hammer's head. Gritting me teeth, I forced my arm muscles to hold it steady and the whole mechanism vibrated in anger. Bits of oil and duff fell down around me as the pendulums strained to stop, and whatever gear it used, groaned and quaked with the force of my hammer holding it steady. At last, the noise weakened and fell to just echoes and I felt the strain slacken in my hand. Slowly I lowered the hammer and the blades did not move again.

I breathed again for the second time.

I kissed my hammer and slipped it back in its loop. "It's good," I gasped. "It's all well. You can come across now, Geoff. I swear on my mother's grave that it's safe," and I sat up to prove it, wincing, thinking that some other thing would come down like a Fury and smite me.

But nothing happened and I smiled at Geoff. "See?" I said, my voice weak. I stood, shimmying past the deadly blades. "Come now, Geoff. I've done the hard part."

But Geoff would not be moved. I could see the terror in his eyes. Saint Dafydd's bollocks! We'd come so far! There was only a little way now. I could *smell* the gold. I *could!* "Come, Geoff," I coaxed. "It's up to you now, lad."

But Geoff was a mule stuck at a mud hole. He would not move. And all my cajoling couldn't bestir him.

Just as I was beginning to think—and dread—that I would have to go back over that damned catwalk to get him, Trev leaned down toward him and whispered something in his ear. Geoff's eyes grew wide and he looked up at Trev. Trev nodded and Geoff, like nothing had troubled him, sank to his knees and began crawling across! What, by God's toes, did he tell the lad?

I sneered at Trev, thinking thoughts of spies and traitors. I saw his gaze look mildly back at me, not caring a whit what I thought.

Geoff approached, smiling. I crouched at the edge of the pit and coaxed him along. "Come on, Geoff. Just a little further." When he got close enough, I reached out and snatched his hand. He skittered the rest of the way and stood up, staring slack-jawed at the two blades that swayed gently with the breeze swelling up from the pit.

"Jesus mercy," he muttered and crossed himself.

"Aye." I showed him my sliced knuckle. "A close one, at that."

He grabbed my hand and squinted at it. "That was too close, Oz."

I slipped my hand from his and used it to gesture toward the doors before us. "This is it, Geoff. What think you?"

Geoff's gaze rose and rose, going up every inch of the door. It was banded with multiple stripes of iron and the whole of it was pocked with rivets. There were two locks, one atop the other.

"De Mandeville said they must be opened at the same time. Can it be done?"

Geoff finally turned a grin at me, as if to say "You fool, Oz. 'Course it can." I was satisfied and nodded my head. I stepped back and let the lad work his miracle. Out of the pouch at his belt, he withdrew his lock picking tools. Years ago, he had me fashion them for him. Just wires with little squiggles at one end, all different. I knew the theory right enough—how the pins needed to be manipulated in the lock to force it to release the bolt—and this was done with a key that had the right shape to it. But I was no good at it. Not like Geoff. The lad took to it like a duck to water. He had a sense about it, he had. Like I said, God took his wits but He gave him this instead.

Geoff approached the door and ran his hand up the dark oak. His stubby fingers teased over each raised rivet, each band of iron. They played over the lock and felt the keyhole as if it was speaking to him alone, and by Christ, it might have been doing so at that. For it was almost spiritual what Geoff could do with a lock. I was hoping for one of them holy moments now.

"Remember," I told him, "both locks must be opened at the same time."

"I remember, Oz."

He stared cross-eyed at each lock pick, then up at the lock, then changed his mind and picked another. I didn't want to hurry the lad but time was a-wastin'. At last! He chose two and reached up to the door again. Not a quiver was there in his hands now, and I glanced back at Trev through the gloom, trying to read the man who stood stiff as a stone wall, large hands hanging at his sides like hams in a pantry.

Geoff inserted the two picks into the key hole and moved them gently, listening with his head cocked toward it. His eyes seemed blurry to me as he stared at the lock, not truly looking at it. He gave it the kind of concentration I could only dream about getting from him about anything else. "Peel the turnips, Geoff." "Sweep the *whole* floor, Geoff." "Carry the water, Geoff." He drifted. He lost focus. He could never seem to complete a task. But this, *this* was what the man was born for.

I heard a click and Geoff smiled. But he left the picks within that lock and reached up to one high above it, one he could barely reach. He examined his lock picks again and carefully chose two. With his tongue pressed between his teeth, he worked the second lock and I heard a click again.

"Here's the tricky part," he said softly. "Now Oz, you work the bottom lock and I'll work the top and when I count to three you give it a half turn to the right."

"Aye, Geoff. Just tell me when." I took hold of the picks. There was no question my following his orders in this, for he was the master of this little kingdom. I trusted him as I would trust no other man.

Geoff reached up and grasped the picks. He licked his lips and said, "One...two...three!"

We turned. I was trying to be delicate, trying to be gentle. But I haven't the touch as he's got and so we had to do it again.

"Are you calm, Oz?" he asked, just as tranquil as pond water.

"Aye, I'm calm, *I'm calm!*"

Alison snorted from across the pit.

Geoff frowned and I took a breath. "Aye, Geoff. Let's do it. On your count."

"One...two...three!"

The beautiful noise of pins falling into place. Geoff pulled on the door ring and it swung to, with barely a whisper of hinge.

Of course, beyond the door was another just like it.

Geoff carefully removed the lock picks from both locks and waited for me to bring the lamp before he strolled forward.

The process was repeated, swifter this time. And when I heard the last pin drop, my heart started to flutter.

I licked my lips and rubbed my hands together. What a great feeling it was! To have slain the dragon and take the treasure! It didn't even matter that de Mandeville would get the lion's share. I just wanted to cast my eyes upon it.

I grasped the door ring and pulled. The door swung open and I grabbed the lamp.

Just before the little light cast its glow within the dark portal, a quiver rolled down my spine, making the neck hairs rise. I don't know why. But I seemed to know it before I saw it.

I turned this way and that with the little lamp, but no matter where I held it, I was shown the same.

Empty. There was not a crumb there.

CHAPTER SEVENTEEN

"OSWALD?" CRIED ALISON in an anxious voice. "What do you see?"

I was speechless — possibly for the first time in my life. I lifted the lamp and stalked into the room.

"Oz?" Geoff touched my sleeve. "Where's the treasure?"

I thrust the lamp into the dim corners, into the shadows, around pillars, and felt a growl scramble up from my gut.

"Oswald?" she called again.

"There's nothing here." I heard a crack in my voice and cleared my throat. "It's empty." That growl in my belly turned to an ache and I feared to get sick right there. I was thinking of what Walter tried to warn me of. "We've been deceived. We have to go. Now!"

There was no other explanation. That bastard of a man had somehow already stolen the jewels. All of it! And he hired me and mine to take the blame for him. Rage boiled my blood and I called to Trev to get his attention. "Oi!" I tossed him the lamp and it sailed with an arc of light over the chasm. Thank God he caught it. I motioned to Geoff to get across the bridge. "Make haste, Geoff. I don't know how much time we've got to get out."

Geoff dropped down and scrambled across. He had barely reached the other side when I started over, dropping the empty sacks into the pit. But by then I heard the voices. Jesus! Was it too late?

I hurried. I made it to the other side and Trev grabbed my wrist and hoisted me up to my toes. I grabbed Alison's arm and ran to the stairwell. There were voices right outside above us. God's hands! The men-at-arms had returned and they'd soon find the quarrel and the ropes.

I doused the light and we stared helplessly up the round stairwell and at the light shining down from it that spoke of freedom. I was a fool. I had condemned them all with my arrogance. *Saint Dafydd and Saint Joseph. Help your old friend Oswald out of it. I can't swear to you that I'll reform but I can swear that I'll be a good man, the best I can be.*

Well, it wasn't much, but there was no use in lying.

"We have to get to the roof," I rasped.

Alison was at my side and her voice hissed into my ear. "What about the cart?"

"Leave it. You're going with Trev and me."

"But—"

"Lass, there's no time to argue."

I slithered up the stairs on my belly like a worm and when my head poked out enough for me to see, I sized up the situation. Aye, there were men in the Tower now, but it was still dark and they were gathering away from the stairs. According to the map from de Mandeville — and Christ knew if it were a farce now — we'd have to get to the northeast turret and we could get there through to St. John's chapel, through a passage into what was called the Presence Chamber, and into the turret. It was a short distance into the chapel but with men milling about, it was an uncertain situation, though no more uncertain than it's been all along, I reckon.

I sat on the steps and gathered my company like goslings around a goose. "Now then. Get yourselves in the chapel and I'll lead you from there. It's only ten feet to the right. Alison, I want you to lead the way. Then Geoff, then Trev, then me. Got it?"

"B-but Oz..."

Geoff was all a-tremble.

"I know, Geoff. Just do what Alison says. I'll get you out safe and sound. That's a promise." One I couldn't necessarily keep.

Alison cooed softly to him and took his hand. I was liking that lass more and more.

I eased up the stairs once more on my belly and signaled to Alison. Up the stairs she crept with Geoff in tow and they trotted quickly to the chapel arch and disappeared inside. I breathed a little. I turned back toward Trev who was looking at me with stern eyes. I am not a man of violence, but if I discovered that he was a spy and had put Geoff in danger, well. There was a dark anger in me that could take up a dagger if I had to.

I wanted to say something but there was no time now. "Go!" I whispered.

He went. His bulk, like an ox's shadow, lumbered across the floor. I watched till it had disappeared into the chapel.

And now it was my turn. But the men-at-arms were coming closer. I suppose they were deciding at last to investigate down where the treasure was—or rather, *wasn't*, and not by our doing. All they need do was take me and all the innocent pleading in the world would not stop the noose from tightening around my neck.

My fingers curled on the stone step and I felt a pebble under my hand. It was the oldest trick there was, but it had to work for me now.

I picked up the pebble and hurled it some distance from me.

The conversation halted and the murmurs grew urgent. I heard swords being drawn and spears lowered. They trotted in that direction and as soon as they turned, I was up and out of the stairwell.

And then I came face to face with two guards who did *not* go with the others.

They looked at me and I looked at them.

They were no older than me, mere lads. And under different circumstances, we could have easily exchanged places.

But at the moment, it was them with weapons and me alone. And one of them was ready to shout out a warning to the others.

A hand came out of the darkness and closed over his face. It knocked his head into the other one with a sickening crack. They both went down as silent as a falling leaf. I looked up at Trev's dispassionate expression. He gestured with his head to come along.

Didn't need to ask me twice.

Shadowed figures with desperate eyes stood around me in the chapel. I said not a word and hastened to the side door. It was not as large as the Council Chamber we had just left. There were windows here, embedded deeply in the thick walls and the scattered light from the misty night offered just enough light for us to see. I ran for the stairwell and was thankful that Trev still had his bundle over his shoulder, spy or no spy.

I heard noise below. The other men-at-arms must have found the unconscious lads. No time to spare.

Up we went, higher and higher, passing arrow slits that sent cold fingers of night at us as we ascended. There was a barred door at the top and Trev helped me lift the beam. We emerged out into the chilled night.

On the outside of the entry, Trev wedged the bar at the door to prevent them from following us. Bright lad. Silent, but bright.

Oily smoke from the Greek Fire filled the air but the glow of it was gone. Instead, men moved about franticly below, with captains shouting orders. We had to be quick.

The lead-covered roof had two peaks and I led the way sideways across its surface. I heard a muffled shriek behind me and turned in time to see Alison slide down the east side. I motioned for Trev to continue to the westernmost turret and I went back for Alison. I slammed down on my belly at the spine of the roof. She was holding on to the slant of it, but just barely. I reached my hand down. "Take it, there's a lass."

She strained. "I can't reach."

"You can. Get a foothold."

"I çan't!"

"You can!" I inched down m'self. If I had to hang by my toes I would. My thighs were doing the gripping now. The roof was slick with mist and Alison was holding on with prayer. I stretched further and grasped her fingers. She climbed up my arm. I could feel my legs slipping. "Hurry, lass."

She used me like a ladder and there was a breast and then a thigh passing by my face though I could not enjoy it. She lay panting on the spine and then—heart of a lioness—she reached down to help *me*.

I took her hand, heaved m'self up and, at last, we were both on the spine. We hurried to the western turret.

Trev had already gotten out my crossbow and fitted it with a grappling hook. "This is the last," he said.

Naturally. And so my aim had to be true or we were dead.

Except I could not see the far wall! Not only was the mist still heavy but now the air was full of smoke from the fire. *Ach-y-fi!* Could it get worse?

Aye, it could. For below I could hear the shouts of the men. They had discovered our ropes in the chapel.

It's now, Oswald.

I rested my arm against the crenellated wall. *Saint Dafydd of Wales, hear my plea. Please let me hit my mark true!* I held my breath and aimed for the direction of the Record Tower, shut my eyes, and pulled the trigger.

The whirr of the rope spun away and I cracked my eyes open. Miracle of miracles, the rope was taut! It had struck something and stuck fast. I didn't suppose it mattered anymore what it was. We were on whatever course the saints had set for us.

Tentatively, I pulled at it. I shoved my hand in the almost empty bundle and pulled out two more blocks. "Trev, you take Geoff and I'll take Alison."

There was no mocking jaw from the lass. Her mouth was set in a sober line. This was as serious as a funeral mass. No one argued. We both fixed our blocks to the ropes. Trev never mentioned that the extra weight would probably bring down the whole affair and I was not going to offer the same. It would be what it would be.

I secured our end of the rope.

"Very well. Geoff, you and Trev go first. And God speed you to safely."

Geoff wrapped himself around Trev like a squirrel clasps a tree. Trev waited till he was secure and then pushed off from the battlement. I saw the rope sag but it stayed mostly downhill. They disappeared far away.

I turned to her. "Come, Alison."

She hesitated before folding herself around me. At any other time, it would have made my blood sing, for indeed, her warmth was giving me inappropriate notions. She smelled of smoke and ale and a touch of what could only be "Alison" herself. She twined her arms around my neck and looked me in the eye. Ach, there was so much in them. Fear, aye. But disappointment and with that more fear. All was lost for her. If we escaped from the clutches of the Tower, what was she returning to? The hope that had been in her eyes was now shattered like a clay pot. I wanted to kiss her. Not only for the obvious reasons but to tell her how sorry I was.

Instead, we merely looked at one another, she clutching me and me clutching the block's hand-holds. "Ready?" I whispered.

She nodded and tucked her face into my neck. I think I died a little at the gentle feel of her.

It was then that someone tried to open the door to the tower. We heard the shouting and someone beating on it. Distantly, I saw the beam wedged at the door move.

I girded m'self, tightened my grip on the handles, and pushed off.

We flew but then the rope began to sag even more and to my horror we began to slow and finally stop...right over the inner bailey.

"Bollocks!" I swung my legs to urge us on but there was no use. The rope was no longer at a downward angle. We were lodged in a dip of the rope and stuck between Heaven and Hell.

And the bastards broke through the door. They shouted and I looked back. Hands pointed in our direction and a line of men were trying to make their way over the top of the roof.

Alison's terrified eyes gave me a helpless look. "Alison, I have to let go of the block."

"No! We'll fall to our death!"

"I have no intention of falling, lass. But I've got to hand over hand it down the rest of the way. Now, can you hold on to me nice and tight?"

"I'm too heavy for you to do that. Let me hold on to the rope."

"No. I've done this before. You won't be able to do it."

"But I can try!"

"There isn't any trying about it now, Alison. It's do or don't and don't means..." I gazed down meaningfully.

Her expression warred with it. In the end, she settled for clutching me so tight I could barely breathe. With one hand, I released the grip I had of the block and grasped the rope. Carefully, I released the other and now we were on our own.

Alison was shorter than me but she was a shapely thing and therefore no light burden. Oh, she would have been light indeed had I been carrying her to a bedchamber or hoisting her into my lap for a bit of play, but having her hang onto my neck like a millstone was no easy thing and with me, holding on for dear life to a sagging rope where I still could not predict the ending. I'd not wish that on anyone.

Hand over hand I went. I no longer cared how much noise I made huffing and puffing. I couldn't be quiet about it if I tried. And there was noise enough below and behind to muffle it in any case. More torches were being brought out and men were now furiously on the alert for intruders.

But I couldn't worry over it. All my concentration was on putting one hand over the other and to keep going no matter what.

Oh how my arms and hands ached! How I longed to stop and rest. But I couldn't. Hand over hand. That was the world I knew. It was as if it was the only world I had *ever* known. Was this what Hell was like? Laboring at an undoable task for all eternity? That was a clever God who would devise that. What better punishment could there be for a sinner like me?

The rope suddenly shook with a mighty force. I looked back and the men had reached the grappling hook. I saw the flash of a blade and I almost wet my braies when I recognized that they were sawing it through.

I hurried. But their shaking the rope made it that much harder. We had to get across for if they cut through and we didn't…

All moot. I don't exactly know the moment I realized the rope was cut but the world gave a great jolt and suddenly we were both screaming and sailing right toward a wall coming up fast. I braced myself for the impact. My feet took the brunt of it and I was lucky not to break a leg. When I opened my eyes we were still hanging from the rope and now it was time to climb. I tried. But my sore hands and Alison's weight was too much for me. And we were so close.

Suddenly, we were yanked upward. What the devil—?

Trev. His strong hands gripped the rope and he pulled, urged on by a softly chanting Geoff. We jerked upward with each pull of his arms. Slowly, slowly.

A whisper in my ear. Was it an angel? "We're almost there, Oswald. Hold on. Just a little farther."

But it was Alison and her soft breath.

Trev reached out and with his two hands, lifted us both and set us on the wall. I couldn't feel my arms and my hands were slashed from the rough texture of the rope.

Alison kissed my cheek and there was gratitude in her eyes, a brief respite from all the other aches I saw there.

That kiss was renewing. I felt a thousand times better. Better than better!

I assessed where we were. God be praised, right where we needed to be. But there was more climbing. Down more ropes. I shook out my hands. Had they been cut down to the bone I'd still have to do it.

"Only a little farther, my friends." I peered over the battlement and our hook was still there, its rope dangling on its own down the wall.

"Trev, go first, then Alison, then Geoff."

"You'll be last?" asked Geoff.

"Aye. The captain is the last to leave his ship. And so you, my crew, must leave first. Trev, watch out for Alison. And hurry. Our pursuers will be gaining more help."

He nodded and climbed over the side. One by one they left me. I was worried. I heard more calls to arms and more feet running our way.

I looked over the battlement and Geoff was almost to the middle. Time for me.

Something whizzed past my head. It was too late in the night for a bird. When another flew passed, I knew it was an arrow.

God blind me!

I leapt over the side. "Hurry, Geoff," I called below, for I was moving at double time.

I hit the ground running. There was no time to strip. "Into the water!" I hoped they followed. I worried over Alison but I saw her skirt billow beside me in the green waters. I pointed. We all dove deep.

Two at a time I shoved them under the portcullis. I saw Alison's skirt fly past as she soared upward like a strange bird. Again, I was the last. Cold, lungs aching for breath, I shimmied under and caught my tunic on the iron point of the portcullis. I tugged and ripped the thing and pushed off as hard as I could.

My face broke the surface and I gasped before I swam toward the boats. Walter was sitting in his, helping a soaking Alison into it. I was surprised to see him. With all the commotion in the Tower I would have expected him to retreat and leave us to our fate.

"Walter?" I said with chattering teeth.

He arched a brow at me. "What?"

"I... I'm just glad to see you."

He snorted. "I'm a fool for staying." He noticed that there were no bags of treasure and his eyes rounded. "An even greater fool, I see."

"Aye, Walter. It was all for nothing."

"That was what I was trying to tell you." He looked sharply at Trev before he turned back to me. "Lord de Mandeville is *not* the Keeper of the Wardrobe!"

CHAPTER EIGHTEEN

"WE COULDN'T HAVE found that out a fortnight ago?" All of us were wrapped in blankets in front of Walter's fire, a concession since he seldom allowed either me or Geoff in his house. Sibbe was nowhere to be seen. Alison had wrapped my sore and bleeding hands in linen and they throbbed and stung.

Walter shook his head, his face buried in his hands.

"So what is he, then?"

Walter raised his long face. "He is *deputy* to the Keeper of the Wardrobe...who is Thomas Bek, the Bishop of Lincoln!"

"Good Christ! It was all a jape from the beginning."

"What did he hope to gain?" asked Alison, her voice downhearted through chattering teeth.

"Dupes. Us. And we fell for it."

"He threatened you," said Walter. "So you said."

"Aye, he did. I'm not afraid of the sheriffs. But I do not think it will come to that. Instead, he will use us as shields. If he is suspected then he will make certain that eyes will be turned toward us." I dropped my head in my bandaged hands. "What have I done to you all? Especially you, Alison. I've done nothing to change your fortunes except for the worse!"

Her hand fell gently on my shoulder. "Now Oswald. You asked and I answered yea. I could have said no. Perhaps I should have. But I took a chance just like the rest of you." She sighed deeply. "Serves us right for committing a sin. It's God's will, then, to make a pauper of me. I'll soon have no home to go to. Walter…might you need another maid in your service?"

He looked aghast.

"I take that as a no," she said quietly.

"Alison lass, we'll think of something."

But we didn't. We simply sat around the fire till there was no excuse to continue to do so. Alison was the first to rise. She thanked Walter for the use of his blanket, gave me a sorrowful glance, and walked out.

Then it was Trev. He folded the blanket and left it on his stool. He looked to each of us, with a long look at Geoff, and then he was gone.

I lifted Geoff and put an arm around him. "Let's go home, too, Geoff."

Geoff said nothing and we shuffled next door and locked the world behind us. We both climbed out of our damp clothes and hung them before the hearth. I knelt there in nothing but my braies and stoked it, poking the ashes and placing more peat on the fire. We climbed into our beds, but sleep would not come to me. I stared at the ceiling and up into the rafters where I could hear the cooing of sleepy doves. I must admit, I had never been that low. Even in our little village when I was a child and I was taunted by the other children for being a bastard and an Englishman's bastard at that. I was saddened that the world I thought I knew could be cruel and how a man can be beaten down to a stain. "I was wise once: when I was born, I cried ", my mother used to tell me.

There had to be a way to help Alison, for I could not stand the fact that her whole life was about to tumble around her. The Wheel of Fortune was about to turn and turn for the worse. It is ever thus. The people sin and the crops wither and die. Then the people starve. They cry out to God and His saints and Heaven closes its ears until we have learned our proper lesson. And so we plow and sow and tend again. God Almighty is a stern taskmaster. And now the flail has fallen and Alison has been struck down. That did not sit well with me. For a woman is a feeble thing in the world. She is servant to her father and then her husband, but her father and her husband are supposed to be gentle overlords. They are to feed and clothe their kin.

What had Rolf Hale done to his innocent wife?

It made me angry all over again. I cursed his bones. I cursed his father for siring him. I cursed his gambling…and then I cursed m'self. For I was to blame as well.

It was a selfish rage that bubbled inside of me. I had wanted to be her hero, Saint George slaying her dragons. I wanted to be…something…to her. And I didn't know why. Women I had aplenty and cast them off just as quickly. But I couldn't cast her off from my mind or my h— Foolish. *Foolish!* I rolled over, facing the wall. It was done. The chance was gone. We had no gold.

And Lord de Mandeville. I didn't want to surrender my anger toward him for his foul deception. I cursed him for good measure. A murderer, too! If I put my mind to it, there ought to be a way to get my revenge on him, even though he was a lord. I curled my blanket around me and plotted late into the night.

But even as the night wore on and I was far from sleep, so also, it seemed, was Geoff. For I heard, as stealthy as the lad was capable, him rising and dragging his clothes from the place they hung and steamed before the flames. I almost turned over to say something— "Get back into bed, you miserable half-wit"—but I said nothing. There was still this mystery to contend with. Aye. Someone needed a blade stuffed between their ribs for their mischief. And since Geoff by virtue of his mind was blameless, it had to be another. Another he had gone to meet this very hour, as he did almost every night. Them two knights, is who. De Mandeville's lackeys, no doubt. And here Geoff, telling them every step we were to take and all the while, de Mandeville was slowly robbing the king of all his wealth and holy crowns.

I waited silently in my bed as he made his way out the door. As soon as I was certain, I scrambled up from my cot and dressed fast as I could. I left the warmth of my hearth and peered out the door. A slim silhouette shuffled up Cornhill and I kept to the shadows following him. *That's right, my lad. Go to your spy. Let me see his cursed features before I send him back to his Creator.*

Geoff seemed only mindful of the Watch, being careful not to be spotted. It was a fine or gaol to be found after curfew. But that was the only stealthy thing about him. Geoff was all feet and he paid no attention to where he was half the time. Oh, for that vile cur to have used a sweet soul like Geoff!

Saint Dafydd and Saint Joseph, I will ask you to turn your faces away so that you will not see your son commit a grave act, for surely I cannot spare the whoreson who would use Geoff so dishonorably.

We passed the Tun and turned up the street of blacksmiths and I began to get an awful ache in my heart. For it was looking more and more that I had been right about Trev, that *he* had been the eyes of those knights.

And there it was. He slipped through the blacksmith's entry and I followed soon after, peering in through the slit in the door. Trev was a big man capable of snapping my spine in two without a second thought. I had to plan this carefully.

Trev was at his forge, turning the coals in his fire one over another with a spade, scooping up ash and covering it.

Geoff just stood there, saying nothing, and Trev glanced over and without a word—no surprise there—continued to finish his work. Finally, he turned to his bucket and cleaned his face and hands. He turned to Geoff then, who was standing as stiff as the statues in St. Margaret's Church, and approached the lad. Water sparkled in his short hair and dripped off the scrub on his chin. He strode right up to little Geoff, who looked like a child compared to the mountain that was Trev. Trev stood toe to toe with him and looked down at him curiously before he raised his hands and covered Geoff's cheeks.

What the hell? What's he doing?

And before I could blink again, he leaned over and planted his lips hard on Geoff's! And it was no hasty kiss, neither. And not the kiss of peace from one monk to another or of a lord to his vassal. It was instead the tenderest kiss I ever laid eyes on. A kiss a man might give a maid.

And what was Geoff doing? Was he pushing the oaf off him with a "Here!" No! God help me, but his arms twined upward and grasped the blacksmith's neck and he clung to him tight like a vine on a garden wall, kissing back with all his vigor.

And it didn't much look like the first time they ever done it either.

My jaw sat long on my chest before I finally awakened. I shoved the door open. "Oi!"

They broke apart and Geoff jumped back.

"Oi!" I said again. "Good Christ! What the hell are you doing, Geoff? And what the hell are *you* doing?" I jabbed a finger at Trev.

The pintle just looked at me.

"It isn't his fault," said Geoff, wringing his tunic. "It's me as much as him."

"Geoff, you don't know what you're doing. I know that. It's him leading you to sin."

Just then, a large hand landed on my shoulder. "Oz," said Trev. "I think you'd best leave."

"Oh I shall, Blacksmith. And I'm taking Geoff with me."

The hand on my shoulder tightened. "No."

"I'm not asking."

"Geoff stays."

"I'll not have you hurting him."

Finally, the steely hand left my shoulder. Trev shuffled over to his stool and sunk to it. He shook his head. "I'd never hurt Geoff," he said to his feet.

"Oz," said Geoff softly. "I...I know I'm a half-wit. I know that I can't think good as you. But I know what is in my heart. And my heart says that Trev is...is for me. I've never blinked twice at a lass. You know that well, Oz. But Trev. He looks at me like you look at wenches, it's just that he only looks at *me* that way, not lots of other lads. And I like it."

"You don't know what you're saying."

"But I do. My heart works just fine, Oz."

I realized several things in that instant. One, that Trev was not a spy. And two, that I knew less about Geoff than I thought I did.

And then I started thinking. Every time I found Geoff on his own, he had his arm around a young lad or a lad had his arm around Geoff, with lots of secret smiles and shy looks. How the hell had I missed that?

Ach-a-fi. The Church frowned on such things but they mostly turned the other way. God knows their own monks got up to mischief often enough. And as for the king, he got up to the same with the earl of Cornwall, Piers Gaveston. England's own king cavorts openly with a man, forsaking his wife even on his wedding day, so they say. Of course, to be fair, she was a maid of twelve.

Was it the fashion now for men to become the lovers of men?

My Geoff. My mind filled with such images I suddenly didn't want to have. But Geoff looked happier than I'd ever seen him. There seemed to be nothing I could do.

I ran my fingers through my hair. "Saint Dafydd's bollocks," I muttered. "Well I..." They both looked at me anxiously. I threw my hands in the air. "I didn't know. I couldn't have guessed, now could I?" I shuffled my feet. "It's still a sin," I muttered.

I stood in the silence a bit longer before I turned toward the door. "Is this what you got up to night after night, Geoff?"

Geoff had the decency to lower his face.

"I thought...Geoff, I thought you were sneaking off to them knights. I saw you with them. I thought...Trev was a spy."

There was genuine shock on his face and then he shook his head. "No, Oz. Oh them lords wanted me to spy, but not on us. On Lord de Mandeville."

"What?"

"They said they thought he was up to no good."

"Geoff." My head was reeling. "Why didn't you tell me sooner?"

"They told me not to. Threatened to put you in gaol."

I laughed. A sorry lot were we. Me protecting Geoff and Geoff protecting me! But then I sobered. "So, Lord de Mandeville is already suspect."

"Aye, that's what they said."

I waited another heartbeat or two. I expected Geoff to come home with me, but that was now foolish, under the present circumstances.

Trev was still standing there and Geoff...Christ. Geoff wanted to stay. Like he stayed for many a night before this.

"Well, hmm. Erm...if it's good enough for the king...I reckon...I guess I'll...see you in the morning, Geoff."

Geoff put his hand on my arm. "I'll be back anon, Oz. Tonight. Like always."

I nodded and slipped out into the cold night. I wrapped my cloak about me and ducked my head into the darkness, trudging back down Cornhill. There was a lot of thinking to do. Saint Dafydd. I felt like I'd been dunked down a well. First Geoff and now this other. So there had been no spy? All that suspicious nonsense had been his sneaking about meeting Trev. And that shadow that escaped Trev's shop with all the grace of an ox must have been Geoff sneaking away, broken crockery in his wake. Even now I tried not to think of it. Such vile things were said of King Edward behind whispers. I would not have the same done about Geoff. But when had I ever seen the man as happy as all that?

I'd say nothing. There was no need for Walter to know. No need for anyone to know. All would be the same and Geoff could go on and...*meet*...with Trev as he would. God help him.

God help us all.

CHAPTER NINETEEN

SOMETIMES YOU CAN patch a pot with a simple weld. And sometimes you have to do a bit more. I reckon a cracked kettle is a little like life. It happens so unexpectedly and turns your world upside down. There is nothing more vexing to a wife than to lose her best cooking pot. She can't boil no water. She can't make her husband his stew. She can't feed her children. All is disaster. And it takes money to set it right. As it always does.

Now I'm a mender of pots. You might say I save these little lives, like a guardian angel. For I patch the cracks, straighten crooked spoons, and sharpen knives. What I do makes life simpler for all. And I'm right good at it, if I do say so myself.

But for some reason, today, I could not get my mind on such things. I had heard nothing from de Mandeville and frankly, I never expected to hear from him again until the ax fell. The murdering swine. We were coneys in a snare. And there was nothing we could do. The only thing we had in our favor was that we were as poor now as we were before. No great purchases were we making. Oh no indeed! We were lucky enough to get a sheep shank for the cooking pot and a few fish on Friday for our supper. I didn't think that any of the guards in the Tower could identify us. It was too dark.

But then there was Alison.

For the men in the Tower had seen her day after day. And they might put two and two together for we had to leave the cart and horse behind. That sent Walter into fits but there was nothing we could do. I was fairly sure they could not identify the cart or the horse as Walter was such a miser he never used either to any degree. But losing it was a sorry thing and I felt bad about it. Likewise, I knew, even if all had gone well, that we would be leaving Trev's and my handiwork behind. There was no way to save the hooks and such. It was a loss we thought we could bear for all the riches to come.

But alas.

And Master Chigwell. There was nothing with which to pay him and I was too sorrowful to make the journey to tell him myself. Let it wait another day or two.

So all were worse off because of me and my scheme. With the sword of doom dangling over our heads.

No wonder no one talked to me.

Oh, Geoff did. Course he did. He was my lad. And, well. He said that Trev had no hard feelings about it. He disappeared regular each night. I tried not to dwell on it. Geoff smiled a lot. I couldn't begrudge him.

I couldn't even get up the strength to play one of my games. My heart just wasn't in it.

And word had spread around London about some doing at the Tower. They couldn't hide the smell of smoke or the ruckus. Truth be told, I thought it best to keep my head low.

But I couldn't watch Walter pace at my door hour by hour. I pushed the door open and stood in the entry. "Walter."

"I'm not talking to you."

I kicked at a stone, rolling it back and forth under the sole of my boot. "Aye, I know it. But I do have a question to ask."

"Go ahead. I may or may not answer as I am no longer talking to you."

Huffing a sigh, I rested my hands on my belt. "There was many a time you disappeared in the morning. Where did you go?"

His lip curled in a familiar sneer. "I see. So this suspicious activity naturally leads you to believe I was up to no good? After all the years we've known one another?"

"I was just curious, Walter. I didn't mean anything by it. Aw, I'm a poor excuse for a man."

"Indeed you are. And if you must know, I had gone to meet my shepherds on Tower Hill to get the latest news for *you*. I hope that makes you properly contrite." He folded his arms and thrust his big nose in the air.

Contrite was not the word. "Walter, you are a true friend. I pray I shall be worthy of you from now on."

"Hmpf." He paused and finally turned toward me. "Well, perhaps a cup of ale can go a long way to repair that breach."

I grinned and bowed, stepping out of the way to let him in.

"I'm still not speaking to you. Yet," he said, taking his usual place.

At least Walter, Geoff, and Trev had forgiven me.

But it was Alison who weighed heavy on my mind. Two days after our disastrous burglary, I found m'self haunting the Cockerel and Bullock. At first, I merely shuffled outside, leaning against the opposite wall just looking at the place. Until an old wife shooed me away from her wall with a broom.

Then I took to peering into the windows and watching her patrons partake, little knowing that all was not well. She would serve them to the last, I reckon. Why not? Take any last scrap she could.

Once or twice, I thought she spotted me but I ducked in time. I ended up sitting outside on a bit of stone and watched London walk by from Birchin Lane. That would teach me. Getting big ideas, ideas too big for the likes of me. But it was to save Geoff. Maybe him and Trev was a good thing after all. Maybe I could convince Trev to take him in. He'd be safer away from me now. It would take a lot, though. Geoff was nothing if not loyal. The lackwit.

"What are *you* doing here?"

I scrambled to my feet and ran a sleeve under my nose. "Alison."

Her arms were crossed over her chest and she leaned against the doorframe. "You have your nerve."

"I...I beg your mercy. I'm sorry. I'll go."

I took two strides and she grabbed my arm. I stopped but I didn't turn to her. I was too mortified. So she came around to face me. "You meant well. I can see that."

"I did, lass. I swear I did. I did it for Geoff. At first. But you well know that I did it for greed, too, plain and simple. And I ruined you. And I will do whatever I can—"

She waved her hand and looked up at the gray sky, breathing in deep. "I should be angrier with you. But I find I can't be. Why is that?"

I gave a half-hearted smile. "Because I'm charming?"

She smiled back, a little sadly. "Aye, that must be it. I've never been... charmed...before."

I stepped closer. "Well, I can't say I believe that."

"Believe what you will. But I've had a husband and no one else."

"Alison, I…"

It began to drizzle. Tiny drops dappled my face and cooled my cheek. I swallowed what I wanted to say. It would have been some frivolous jest. Some flirting comment designed to entice. But as deep as her gaze was, I knew that the time for such games was past. Nothing that I said would be good enough for the likes of her. Smile fading, my heart ached. "You deserve a good husband, Alison. One who treats you well. God keep you." And that was that. I said no more and I walked away. Because for once in my life, my golden tongue could not talk its way out of or into it. She did deserve better. Better than a meaningless swive with the likes of me.

She didn't call me back and I'm glad for it. I don't know whether I would have been strong enough to keep going. But I didn't look back, didn't give m'self over to it. Instead, I just trudged up Birchin Lane with a heavy heart, thinking to go back to my work and my brazier, my honest work…when I saw Benet Chigwell heading toward me. I straightened. I had to face him eventually.

He stood on the lane looking at me with one narrowed eye. "Well?"

I sighed. I'd been doing that a lot lately. "You might as well hear the bad tidings."

"Oh?" He stepped closer. "When I didn't hear from you, I thought that you meant to cheat me. But that was not the impression I had of you. So then I thought you had been captured. But I see that is also not the case. And yet I heard of strange goings on at the Tower."

I kicked at the ground and stuffed my thumbs in my belt. "Aw, Ben. I wouldn't have cheated you. My word is my oath. And I meant for it to go well. But that son of a whore Percy de Mandeville was the one who cheated. He used me as a shield. He stole all the treasure well ahead of time and hoped we'd get caught for it instead. So there *is* no treasure. But I swear to you, if I don't get hanged and I can scrape up the money, I shall pay you for services and your faith in me."

Ben was thoughtful and he watched me steadily, ignoring the bustling traffic from cart and man around us. "You were deceived."

"More than that, I fear. For I am certain as Death that de Mandeville is also the culprit who killed his own steward's son," I said for our ears alone. "And he would blame me for that, too. That was why he coerced me into this fool scheme."

"Oh ho! Extortion! So de Mandeville hopes to get away with theft *and* murder? Hmm."

"There's nothing to be done. I'm just waiting for the ax to fall."

"Are you? That's not the Oswald I have come to know. The man who broke into my house and conquered my traps and defiled the very Tower itself would not seem the sort of man to roll over and die."

"Saint Dafydd's bollocks, man! I done what no other man had done. And there's a good reason for it. It's mad. And men hang for it. And surely I will." And Geoff and Walter and Trev and dear Alison. My eyes stung suddenly. It was the icy drizzle, of course.

"No," Ben persisted, standing his ground. "The Oswald I know would make a scheme of his own to exact revenge. A clever revenge. One that would not only teach Lord de Mandeville a lesson, but also make certain that this lesson was learned by all who would make you their fool. That is the Oswald I have heard talk of in London. The clever Welshman. The trickster. Are you not he?"

I stared at him, at his wild, white hair and his winking gray eyes. A true sorcerer, was he, getting into a man's head.

Well!" he said suddenly. "I will leave you to it. You know your business better than I. I have no doubt you will fulfill your agreement and pay me what you owe. Before you hang, of course." There was a tinkle of laughter as he marched up the lane, gown trailing after him.

Curse that sly devil for he got me to thinking, just like he wanted. It wasn't like me to give up. Not at all. What did he know about it, after all? He'd only known me a few days. But he was right. I always got out of it. Always slipped the noose before. The only way to do it this time was to make de Mandeville pay and not in a small way. In the biggest way possible. I had to prove and prove right well to the sheriffs that it was him that killed that boy. I needed proof and a reason why.

Aye. I'd get the proof and see *him* hang! And just as I had that daring thought out in the open of a London street, someone hissed at me.

A man in the shadows gesturing. Now what? I neared and then I recognized Arno. A goldsmith. "Greetings, Arno. It's nice to see you but I haven't got time just now. I have…something to plot."

He did not reply and would not come out of the shadows so, not wishing to be rude, I reckoned it was my lot to join him. I stood impatiently watching the rain and inhaled the sweet damp of wet hay, wet earth, and wet wool.

Just as I was about to bid farewell, he said, voice low and hoarse, "Oswald, I was hoping to find you somewhere on the streets."

"On the streets? Why didn't you just go to my shop?"

"Oh no. I can't be seen there. Not now."

"Why not now?"

"I pray you, meet me at my shop at sunset and make certain you are not seen."

"What? Arno, I don't have time—"

"Just meet me." He pulled his cloak about him and kept to the sides of the houses, avoiding the puddles under the eaves.

I watched him go, perplexed. But I'd get no answers, I reckoned, until that evening.

———————◆———————

IT WAS HARD to tell when the sun set for the rain had continued in an even drizzle, behaving like other Aprils before it. But when it seemed darker, I set out for Aldgate Ward.

If Arno was being mysterious then there had to be a good reason for it, for he was a practical man and did not take to dreaming. His shop was shut up tight, earlier than his neighbors' shops. I kept my hood low over my brow and knocked lightly on his door.

I heard a shuffle within and then a whispered, "Oswald?"

"Aye. Let me in, man!"

The scrape of wood on wood and the grating of the lock and then the door opened. A hand emerged and snatched me by the collar, dragging me inside.

He turned the key in the lock and dropped the beam back over the door. "Oswald," he said, eyes wide and white, looking me over as if not believing what he beheld.

"Arno. What is it? You look as if you'd seen a ghost."

"I have. My own, perhaps. Come. Let me show you."

He jostled behind a table where he drew a covering from a collection of iron-clad boxes and coffers. He took a key from the ample key ring at his belt and turned it in a lock of one such box. He removed the key but kept his hand on the lid. I don't mind telling you, that when I'm usually in his shop, he keeps a tight lock on all his coffers on account of the fact that he can't trust me, and the place *is* reeking with gold, and its true enough. For I'd be happy to *inhale* a fortune if I could.

But this time, he was actually opening a coffer for me. All thoughts of de Mandeville and my new plot fled from my head.

"Now," he said, panting a little, "I'll open this but there are only so many questions I can answer. Some I cannot, no matter how you beg me."

I was getting very anxious. My palms were sweating!

"Have done, Arno. Get to it!"

He opened the lid and there, lying on top of a bed of velvets, shining just as pure and as beauteous as the sun, lay a jewel-encrusted crown.

CHAPTER TWENTY

"WHAT—?" I SPUTTERED. But I knew exactly what it was and where it came from. He snapped the lid closed once more and locked it smartly. The sheet was back covering them and he stood up and fell back, looking at me expectantly.

"Sarding hell, Arno. That's the crown jewels!"

"Shush!" He made mad motions with his hands and then wrung them, pacing the floor. "I know it is. I'm not a fool. Who but the king has crowns and scepters? And I knew that *you* would know it is, too!"

My heart was in my throat. "Why do you think that?"

He stopped. "Oswald, it is all over London. Someone broke into the Tower of London two days ago but no one is saying anything of the jewels. And then these show up. Of course I thought of *you!*"

"But Arno! I never—!"

"Oh do stop lying to me, Oswald. I need your help."

"*My* help?" Sarding nerve. He just accused me of stealing the crown jewels. And I was going to come to him first when I had them in my hands. A fine thing!

"A gentlemen brought them here wanting to exchange them for coins. I told him I am no moneylender but he insisted in the most belligerent of terms. I feared for my person. So I told him it would take me time to collect that many coins and he agreed to return at a later date. Oswald, I know that these belong to the king. What am I to do with them?"

"'Render unto Caesar what is Caesar's.'"

"I can't do that! They'll accuse *me*!"

"So you want *me* to do it? No thank you!"

"But Oswald. *You* know, and *I* know, and *all* of London knows, it had to be you!"

There went my heart in my mouth again. "*All* of London? Well, what about James the Hairlip? Or Rodney of Devon? They're the roughest thieves in London town."

"But they're not clever. No, it took a clever man to do this deed and that means you."

Here I was getting all the blame and none of the advantages.

I pulled my fingers through my hair. "So who brought them in?"

"I can't tell you that."

"Was it Lord Percy de Mandeville?"

His cheeks sucked in and his lips screwed up tight. A hit.

"That bastard!" I cried. "I had a beautiful Plan and he went and pulled the rug out from under me. That's gratitude."

Arno still wore his sour-sucking face.

I threw up my hands. "What would you have me do? Take them back to the king for you? Tell him 'I'm sorry for the theft' — which I did not do, by the way — 'but here are your royal decorations, sir'? And what do you think they'd do to me, eh? I'd have a noose slapped around my neck so fast I'll be able to watch my own execution. No thank you!"

I turned to leave, but he grabbed my wrist. "Oswald, you can't leave me with these."

Curiosity was getting the better of me. "Just how much of it do you have?"

"All of it," he said, whimpering. "I'm certain. These coffers," he said gesturing, "are full of scepters, crowns, and jewels. *Jesu* mercy!"

And no one in all London knew it...but me.

I closed my mouth and turned to him. "Well now, maybe there *is* something I can do for you, Arno."

"I don't like that look, Oswald. I didn't tell you this so that you can take them to some money changer. They need to be returned. They belong to the king. As an Englishman I have a sworn duty to protect them."

"I'm no Englishman."

"That I know. But you are a most honest thief, if such things are possible. You must find a way to dispose of them back to the king without getting either of us involved."

Aw Christ. I wish he hadn't put it like that. Holy Virgin! I heard my mother's voice again in the back of my head: "Repay evil with good, and Hell will not claim you."

A fortune ready for the taking and here the man was *trusting* me! Maybe I'll awaken.

"I..." But what was there to say? "I...need to think on it."

"You can't wait too long. Lord — er the man will return in three days-time for his payment. I am not equipped to do such transactions, Oswald."

"Three days-time you say? Well, I'll have your answer before then."

I took his hand and assured him and told him to hide the coffers and to keep his shop locked up. What a fool was de Mandeville. If it were me, I would have had the things on a ship and sailed to Calais. No one would question it there. But in London town, the merchants were loyal. At least the ones who wanted to keep their heads.

The rain had finally stopped but the night drew heavy over the city and I made my way slowly back to Cornhill. I hadn't been walking long down the lonely streets when I detected the sound of more footfalls behind me.

Surely all good folk were in their houses. Then that only left the thieves and rogues. I quickened my steps but my "shadows" quickened theirs as well. Ahead was a stable where I knew that one wall was patched with hay. I headed for it and slipped around the corner. I sank into the hay wall and listened to the lane from the other side.

Two pairs of footsteps without and I had an idea who they were.

I burst through the wall and, raising my hammer, told them, "Halt!"

They spun, them two knights who had been following me from the beginning. Them knights who beat on Geoff and admonished him to do their spying for them. I was angry as a man could be.

"You've been following me long enough. You tell me now, my lords, what this is about. This hammer of mine says he wants to know."

They looked at one another with a smirk passing between them. They approached though they stayed well away from my arm.

The one in blue said, "I am Thomas Cull and this is Henry Galthrop, knights of the king's household." He smiled. "Knave."

My mouth was suddenly dry. My hammer felt too heavy in my hand but I was loath to lower it once unsheathed. Yet what could I truly do with it?

In the end, I did lower it and clumsily bowed. "M-my lords." It wasn't a matter of pride, after all. It was a matter of my place. But I tried to keep my head high nonetheless. "I wish to know why you have been following me and mine."

Thomas Cull sauntered forward. He fingered the hilt of his dagger but did not draw it. Yet. I was thankful for that but didn't know for how long was my reprieve. "You are a saucy fellow, aren't you? Threatening the king's knights."

"Well…" I took a step back. "My lords, a man gets angry, does he not? Especially when he is protecting what is his."

Sir Thomas nodded, making like he was thinking about it. "And what, pray, is yours that needs protecting…knave?"

I took another step back. "Y-you spoke with a man, Geoff. He's a half-wit. He don't know naught. He's a good man. A god-fearing lad."

"And yet he consorts with thieves."

"But that isn't his fault. He just does what I tell him."

"And if you tell him to sin and break the law? Does that make him blameless?"

"Aye. Aye, it does!"

"Not in the sight of the law."

Panic. My limbs were heavy with it. "But good my lords—"

"First he accuses," said Sir Henry to his companion. "Now he begs."

I took another step back but found m'self up against the stable wall.

"I tell you what you must do, Master Oswald," said Thomas Cull, drawing not his dagger but using his finger just as dangerously. "You must be very careful whom you accuse and of what."

I was afraid, true, but I was also still simmering with anger. I girded m'self, thinking of Geoff. "Very well. But it does not explain why you were following me and why you had Geoff spy for you. I would know that, at least."

"The kitten has claws," chuckled Sir Henry.

"I think you know far too much for your own good, Master Oswald."

"That is true enough," I muttered. "But I would know anyway. Days have passed and we have not been arrested."

"Arrested?" Sir Thomas glanced at his companion. "Have you done something illegal?"

It was not I who was the kitten. No, I was the mouse and he the cat.

"You know very well! You know all! Now please. If beg I must then I will. Tell me. Are we to be arrested? Why did you stalk us?"

He seemed to consider but I already kenned his way of thinking. "No one is to be arrested. Not yet. Not if you cooperate."

Now to it. At last!

"And what would you have me do?"

"Why, nothing at all. Continue to do as you are doing. Whatever that is."

"But…but…"

Sir Henry reached for me and I cringed back…but it was only to pat my shoulder as he would pat his horse. They walked past me into the street and I'm not ashamed to admit that I was shaking. But I had to say it. God help me for the poor fool I am. "Lord de Mandeville. You had Geoff report to you on Lord de Mandeville."

Slowly, they turned back to me but their faces did not change. They approached as one and Sir Thomas leaned down close to my face. I smelled his wine breath, so close was he. "The less said about that the better, eh, Master Oswald?"

———◆———

I POKED MY fire for perhaps the hundredth time and still didn't remember doing it. Geoff finally took the iron out of my hand and set it aside. "What vexes you, Oz?"

I sighed. "Nothing for you to worry over, Geoff." But I looked him in the eye. "Geoff, if anything should happen to me, well. You've got Trev, haven't you?"

"What do you mean, Oz? What's going to happen to you?"

"Oh, you know. I might get struck by lightning in a field or fall down a well or…some such."

He laughed. "None of that's going to happen. You're jesting with me."

"I might be. But still, Geoff. If something *should* happen, Trev will take care of you, will he not?"

"I suppose. He's…quite fond of me." He had the grace to blush. "But nothing *will* happen to you so there's no sense in dwelling on it. And I like living here."

"No. You're right, of course." But I felt better knowing the words were out in the open, even if Geoff dismissed them.

First the sheriffs then these men. They all knew, and all waited for me to solve their problems for them. Or hang I will. In truth, either way, I was to be hanged. Not the best of options for old Oz.

It was later that day that Walter came to call. As if nothing had happened between us, he settled himself in his favorite chair, poured my ale into a horn beaker, and silently drank. I smiled to m'self. It was good to see him there.

He continued to drink while I worked on my kettles and ladles, fixing this one then that, while Geoff set to polishing them till they shined. And all the while I kept thinking of golden crowns and sparkling jewels. Poor Arno. I'm certain he was jumping at each shadow and creaking beam. That was no way to live, to be sure. And I wouldn't live that way neither. I might fear the future but I couldn't stop living for the day. It's all in God's hands in any case. If He feels you need punishment then that's what it will be. Reward? Then it's to be that.

My arm was getting tired from constant hammering — sometimes the delicate work is harder than the hard hammering — so I decided I would give m'self a rest. I set the hammer and pot aside and rolled my shoulders.

Without my asking, Walter poured me some ale and scooted the beaker toward me across the table.

"Thanks, Walter. That's thirsty work." I tipped it back and wiped my mouth on my sleeve.

"You're a fool, Oswald. You do know that."

"Aye, Walter." I sat and poured more. I did not tell him of my encounter with them knights and, looking at Geoff, I wondered if they vexed him anymore as well. I kept a good eye on Geoff and I thought that now that I knew about he and Trev, Geoff would tell me if he encountered them again. At least I hoped he would.

But Walter had gotten his hearth stoked. "Yes, you are a fool. And I am a fool for following you so blindly."

"Are you speaking to me again, Walter?"

He glared. "Of course I am!" He splayed his hands. "What do you think I am doing now?"

"Very well, Walter. Go on."

"As I was saying. You are a fool. I should have known there was something amiss about Lord de Mandeville. No one would speak of him. They are all afraid of him, no doubt. It took my examining some records at the Guildhall. Did you know that he, too, is a wool merchant? Percy de Mandeville has wealthy trappings but his income does not seem to exceed his expenses. He dotes on his wife. And if tales are true, there are many others who dote on his wife as well. Yet all this dotage does not prevent Lord Percy from a roving eye. It is said he dallies in bedchambers not his own."

"That's a fine pair they are," I said. "Whatever happened to marital fidelity?"

He rolled his eyes. "At any rate," he went on, "there was good reason for him to seek to fill his coffers."

"They looked full to me."

"Yes, well, perhaps because that was not *his* gold. There is a rumor he has been skimming gold off the top of the king's treasure for years."

"That bastard!"

"So they say. Down at the Guildhall, there is no good to be said of Percy de Mandeville."

"I've got a few choice epithets m'self."

"Did you also know," and he took a sip of ale, "that the last man to have stolen the crown jewels, Richard of Pudlicott, was also a wool merchant?"

"No, I didn't know all that."

"Of course you didn't. Because you're a fool."

I rolled *my* eyes. Walter was slurring now, so he could be excused.

"Well, if it please you, Walter, if I am captured, I shall tell them I was alone in it."

He snorted. "Don't be an idiot. So did Richard Pudlicott but no one believed him."

"Aye, Walter, so you told us." I drank my ale and sighed. "But it was a beautiful thing, wasn't it?"

"What was?"

"The Plan, Walter. You know I love life best when I've got a Plan."

"Your plans." He shook his head and slurped his ale. A spot of foam burbled on his shadowed upper lip. "Well, I concede that it had its merits."

"It all would have worked. If the gold had been there."

"God knows where it is now."

God and Oswald.

"Do you know what I would have done with those riches?" asked Walter dreamily. Aye, he was far gone in his cups now, for Walter never shared his secrets with nobody, least of all me. "I would have built a fine manor house in the heart of London. It would have had a gatehouse and footmen and a cistern and all the luxuries a man could want."

"What of your trade, Walter? What of the wool market?"

"Oh pfft!" He waved his hand in a careless gesture. "Who cares? I would have been wealthy beyond my wildest dreams. Who needs sheep?"

"I know what you mean. Know what I would have done?"

"Wasted it on wenches."

"Ah Walter. Money's never *wasted* on wenches. That's money well spent indeed! But I was thinking that I would have bought new clothes for Geoff and got him a horse. He is fond of animals."

We both glanced over at Geoff, head thrown back, softly snoring by the fire, the fork he was polishing forgot in his lap and slack hands.

"And then I would have got us a fine house and servants. And Geoff would have someone waiting on him for a change."

"He's not your pet, Oswald. Why do you treat him so?"

"I never treat him as a pet. I never! I care for Geoff." Perhaps not as much as Trev did, but still… "And he needs me. It's a man's duty to take care of others. It's as Jesus told us to do. 'Do unto others as you would have them do unto you', eh? And Geoff needs doing after, don't he?"

"You're a strange man, Oswald. That's one of the many reasons I am fool enough to like you." He belched, set his beaker aside, and rose unsteadily. "I'm going to bed." He made his way none too soundly out the door. There was a crash outside and Walter's voice crying, "All is well!"

I thought of putting Geoff to bed but when he awoke, he might have…well. His own plans. I tried not to think on it.

Before I could get m'self settled, the sound of horses trotting down the lane gave me pause. Naturally I listened, wondering which poor whoreson was getting an untimely visit at this hour.

And then they stopped before *my* door.

CHAPTER TWENTY-ONE

SHERIFF NICK PUSHED my door open. Geoff jolted awake and sat up. The light from the sheriff's torches splashed into the room and I stood there like a deer surrounded by hunters.

"Oswald of Harlech?" said the sheriff, well knowing who I was. This did not bode well.

I bowed. No sense in not maintaining the proprieties. "Aye."

"You are to come with me."

"No!" Geoff was out of his chair in a wink and pulling at my tunic, dragging me back. I put my hands over his and looked him in the eye.

"Geoff. That's a good lad. You're wanting to defend me is an honorable thing. But I must go with the sheriff." I leaned in close. "Once I'm gone," I whispered, "you high tail it to Trev's, you hear?"

"Oz, I..."

I gave him an expression that would brook no argument and he shut his mouth up tight, though his chin trembled.

I did not look back as I went with the sheriff. In fact, I'm certain Sheriff Nick was surprised at how compliant I was. They tied my hands together and tethered me to Serjeant Robert's horse and I stumbled after them on our way to Newgate.

The streets were quiet. Cold swept up the lanes with the smell of smoke from countless hearth fires. The sheriff and his serjeant stared straight ahead, the torch in Robert's hand casting fluttering light all about us. Nothing else was said to me as I followed the clomping of the horses' hooves down lane after lane. What was there to be said? If I made some sort of confession, perhaps Geoff would be free. Since there was no recourse for me, I might as well. It could be my last act on this earth. Pure. Aye. It might even help get me out of Purgatory all the sooner, though I began to wonder how long that would truly take. There was a lot to make up for, to be sure.

We turned the corner and the tall tower of Newgate loomed ahead of us in the darkness. I began to regret a few things. For one, I never kissed Alison and that thought suddenly took on great importance. I wanted to. And it seemed, sometimes, that she wanted it as well, but I might have imagined that.

They brought their horses to a stop outside the gate and Falkes came sleepily forward to take the reins. Robert untied me from the tether but kept my hands bound. He took my upper arm in a tight grip and followed Sheriff Nick through the gate and up the dark stairwell.

In his chamber, the serjeant released me and I found m'self standing before both sheriffs as the door was closed upon me. Not a cell, then?

I waited, looking at my feet. I'll be damned if I was going to confess first. Let them threaten me and *then* I'd do my spilling.

Sheriff Nick approached. I looked up. Was he going to strike me? I braced for it, even closed my eyes, coward that I am. But I snapped my eyes open when I felt him untying my hands.

"We don't need this," he said, tossing the bindings into the fire. I watched them sizzle with satisfaction.

He leaned back against the table and crossed his arms over his chest while his ginger companion stayed seated behind the table. They seemed to be waiting as well. *Till Doomsday, then*, I thought. We'd all be standing here when the Lord Himself came down out of the clouds for I was not going to talk first.

Sheriff Nigel leaned forward over his clasped hands. "It's late, Oswald. Very late. Isn't there something that needs the saying?"

"Maybe." I hated how my voice broke.

"Then perhaps this is the time for saying it."

"Perhaps. Or...perhaps not."

Sheriff Nigel stared at me for a moment before he thrust up from his chair with a frustrated sound. "You see? I knew he would be difficult."

Sheriff Nick had not stopped staring at me. "He is cautious. Wouldn't you be?"

They were talking to one another, not to me. That was all well. The longer they talked to each other the longer my torture was delayed. Don't get me wrong. They had every right to torture me. I was usually guilty but I also usually confessed far before any hot iron was presented. Which was why I fully intended to confess to murder. I just had to think of a logical reason for doing the deed.

But then both men suddenly turned toward me.

"Well?" said Sheriff Nigel.

"Well...what?" I said.

He sighed deeply and frowned. "Haven't you anything to tell us about the murder of the steward's son?"

"Oh. About that, Lord Sheriff. Aye, I did it."

Sheriff Nigel seemed taken aback. He exchanged a hasty glance with Nicholas. "You did?"

"Oh aye. I did. Killed him right good. Dead as a coffin nail."

"I see." He slowly walked to his sideboard and poured himself a goblet of wine. He offered one to Nick and then drank his own for a long time. I was getting a bit thirsty m'self but there was nothing for it.

Without turning round, Sheriff Nigel asked, "And why did you kill him?"

"Does it matter?" I wrung my hands. I was nervous, after all. I never confessed to murder before. "All that matters is that I did it alone without anyone's help." There. I hoped that kept Geoff's neck out of the noose. He'd be safe and sound with Trev. As much as I did not like to think of the two of them, I was at least satisfied that the lad would be in safekeeping... once I was...gone.

"No, I don't suppose it matters." He glanced at Sheriff Nick again. "Except for one minor point." He spun to face me. "You *didn't* do it!"

I startled back. He scowled at me and poured more wine, sloshing it over the rim of the goblet because he was staring at me instead of the jug. He swilled another dose and slammed the goblet down. "Oh we know that you were robbing the manor. That was plain to all. Too many witnesses for that. We also know that you escaped without managing to steal even an ounce of silver. So why, by all the saints, are you confessing to a murder you did not commit?"

I rounded on them, the bastards. "Because I thought you'd convict me anyway! My lord!"

"So who are you protecting?"

Now they both bore down on me. I felt like cringing into the floor.

"No one. Well, Geoff, but you know well he didn't do it. Wasn't even with me. He wouldn't harm a bed bug."

They waved that away. A known quantity. Interesting. I would have to think on that later, providing I had a "later."

"Then who are you shielding?"

"No one!"

"Do you know who the murderer is?"

"Aye, but you'd never believe me."

Sheriff Nigel grabbed his cup again but did not drink. He fisted it instead, gesturing with it like a scepter. "Try us."

I shook my head. "Never."

"Oswald. Need we remind you of your peril? You have confessed to murder. If we so desired, we could consider the matter over and you would hang. We also know that it was you who plotted the crown jewel theft. For that, you'd be drawn and quartered."

"What? No, I—"

"And so." The ever-moving goblet was set down again. It must have sighed in relief. "Why don't you give us the benefit of the doubt?"

I thought on it long and hard. I had nothing to lose at this point. My life was forfeit. My soul was in the palm of their hands.

"It...it was Lord Percy de Mandeville. He knew about it all along. Hugh Aubrey was killed in the solar. He was choked and then coshed on the head with a candlestick. You can see what was left of the blood on the rug. And then he was stashed on the treasure room stair under the trap door until nightfall. And then he was dragged down the corridor to the chamber beside de Mandeville's and tossed out the window to make it look like he jumped."

There now. Confession *was* good for the soul. I felt better already. Especially if I wasn't to hang for it.

They had their mouths open. A bit surprised, perhaps, at the extent of my knowledge. If I wasn't innocent, they might begin to suspect me.

"That's a...an interesting conclusion," said Sheriff Nick.

"I went back to the house, you see. To discover what became of the boy."

"You went back? After you had escaped?"

"Aye. I know it was foolhardy."

"Foolhardy is the least of it," said Sheriff Nigel.

I shrugged. What's done is done. But it only just then occurred to me that they might not have known all that.

"So you think it was Percy de Mandeville?"

"Aye. Who else could it be? It was his household. Who else had the run of it or knew about the trap door to the treasure room?"

"How did *you* know about it?"

"Found it, didn't I?"

Sheriff Nigel pushed Sheriff Nick out of the way. "But how did you know the body was hidden there?"

"I saw the blood drops on the stairs. I thought it was wine."

"I'm amazed at your logic, Oswald," said Sheriff Nigel, ginger brows high.

Sheriff Nick leaned back upon the table again. "But you've got it wrong."

"Eh?"

There they were exchanging glances again. It was Sheriff Nick who took the lead this time. "It was not Percy de Mandeville."

"Had to be. He threatened me, after all, knowing full well it was him and not me."

"No. It was not. De Mandeville was in the company of others for the whole of the day."

"He's lying! He's a lying bastard! For...for a lord."

"Greedy he may be, but he was not guilty of this murder."

"Whose company was he in, then, if I may ask, for they are liars, too!"

It came out sheepish for Sheriff Nick, a man so marked for his fierce rectitude. "Ours," he said.

CHAPTER TWENTY-TWO

I RETURNED TO Cornhill in a melancholy mood and pushed open my door. I nearly screamed when a demon came flying at me and crushed me in its embrace. But the "demon" was sobbing and I suddenly realized it was Geoff.

I pushed him back just as someone lit a candle.

I turned and saw Walter and Trev sitting in the dark beside the low glow of the hearth.

"Geoff, you dunderpate!" I hissed. "I told you to go to Trev."

"And I did, Oz." He wiped his dripping nose on his sleeve. "And I brought him back here in case you returned. I knew you'd come back." He gave me a wet smile and I couldn't help but be cheered by it. I ruffled his hair like he likes it. "Aw, Geoff. What am I to do with you?" I turned to them. I gave Trev a wary nod. "Walter, what are you doing here?"

"A man can't get a decent night's sleep with all the goings on right under his own roof!"

"I see. Well. I'm glad you're here. There is much to report."

It was time to confess to one and all that I hadn't been detained about the burglary but about a murder.

"Murder!" cried Geoff. Trev moved closer to him, but in Walter's presence he did not touch him.

"Aye. I didn't tell you, Geoff, 'cause I didn't want you to fret. When I was committing burglary at the de Mandeville manor, I found a dead body, the son of the household steward. Well, when his my lord paid me a call to get us to steal his jewels for him" –and Walter ran about madly shutting windows— "he also accused me of a murder he'd most likely committed himself. Them two knights who been sneaking about, Sir Henry and Sir Thomas, might know more than they are saying. It's possible they can vouchsafe for me, if we can get them to cooperate."

Walter, who had been worriedly peeking out the shutters, made a noise of exclamation. "And just who are *they*?"

And now I had to explain again how Geoff was accosted by them and what they wanted. It didn't put Walter at ease.

"Walter, you've got to find out about them knights. Why is it they would have Geoff spy for them? What has it to do with Lord de Mandeville?"

Walter nodded blearily. It was late. I shooed him to the door. "Get a good night's sleep, Walter."

"Too late," he muttered out the door.

I turned to my other guest. "Well, Trev. Thanks for coming. It was a right good thing you done."

Trev said nothing as usual, but he looked at Geoff like butter was melting off of him, and Geoff! The lad gazed back as if the sun would rise over the man's shoulder.

I puttered, tossing some sticks on my fire. "You two best get along if you don't want the Watch to catch you."

"See you in the morning, Oz," said Geoff dreamily.

I heard the door latch before I turned again and saw I was alone. Warming my back at the fire, I did some thinking. It had been a busy night. And more was to come. I noticed a hole in our company. I didn't expect Benet to come nigh, but Alison had not been here either. And now I began to think of my regrets and the one thing that stood out in my mind was that I had not kissed her. I did not want to die without that blessing.

It was foolish to dwell on it. If I was to ever kiss her it would have to be stolen, and though thief I am, that was one valuable I was not willing to steal.

I had to try to get some sleep. I blew out the candle on the table, covered the ashes on the hearth, and kicked off my shoes. My heart was still heavy on all that lingered about us like a stench. The death of that poor lad, them two knights, Lord de Mandeville, Alison, them cursed moneylenders...

I had tried to tell them sheriffs that Hugh Aubrey was dead long before they saw de Mandeville, but he had used them as much as he had used us just as he had used straw to wipe his bum. We were expendable in his eyes. And a man like that should not be free to walk the streets of London.

And then I worried over Alison yet again. She would not take my charity, that I knew. Walter could be convinced to take her in but she was too proud a thing to take it. What would become of her? Cursed moneylenders!

I dropped my clothes to the foot of the bed and slithered under the blankets. There was too much to think about for one simple tinker.

I closed my eyes, even though I knew sleep was long away. The puzzle danced in my head and I tried to ignore it but I should have known better than that. Alison, murder, moneylenders, cursed de Mandeville...

I sat bolt upright. I've been a fool! It was right there before my eyes, all laid out like a tapestry! And Benet Chigwell, God bless him, had put it there.

I tossed the blankets aside and dressed. I knew it was late and I'd already been all over the king's London, but what was one more trip? I threw on my cloak last before I shot out the door and into the night.

———— • ————

TRUTH TO TELL, I'm used to creeping down dark, deserted streets. Would seem to be what I do best. But it's always wise to keep a sharp eye skinned and listen with all ears. And so I made my way down Birchin Lane and stood before the silent, shuttered windows of the Cockerel and Bullock. There was a slim alley with a wattle fence on one side and a courtyard before a stable to the other side. Since the stable housed a sleepy horse, a few hens, and a not nearly deaf enough old dog, I opted for the other side and easily hopped over the short fence.

The narrow close was dim and the smell of moldy straw was harsh in my nostrils but I kept close to the wall until I reached the back garden, fragrant with rosemary and tansy. It was an easy thing to climb the exposed timbers to the first floor. My fingers gripped the sill and I pushed at the shutters.

Barred.

Hanging from one hand, I worked my eating knife from its sheath and poked it through the seam between the shutter doors and worked it up, up, until it raised the little latch within. With the blade, I pulled open one shutter, sheathed the knife, and peered in over the sill.

All was dark except for a faint glow coming from the direction of the hearth. My eyes were already adjusted and when I pulled m'self in and landed into a squat on the floor, I scanned the small room. The bed, with its posts and curtains, seemed an inviting bit of furniture, for the only other things included a heavy coffer, a table, and a chair.

Rising, I closed the shutter and without thinking, did not bar it. Years of experience taught me to allow for a hasty escape should the need arise.

My feet slid carefully over the floor. One never knew when a floorboard would creak. But whatever Master Hale was, he kept his house in good order. The actual structure, at any rate.

Once I stood beside the bed I listened carefully. A slow rise and fall of breath within. Parting the curtain, she lay before me and I could not help but stand and gaze at her in the darkness. I did not take Alison for the kind to curl like a kitten but she was. And like a child, her hand lay under a cheek while the other was coiled under her chin. Her lips, plump in repose, were slightly parted, and her lashes were twin feathers upon her cheeks, keeping her eyes shut tight. Ach. I could have stood there all night merely gazing…and, I confess it, with a fair bit of wanting. The lass made it clear, though, that there was little place in her life for the likes of me. Very well. I won't pretend it did not sting, but there were many other lasses to be seen to and far more willing. So it was wasted time indeed to sow in a rocky field.

I swallowed my pride and reached out, curling a lock of her hair around my finger. "Alison," I whispered. "Awake."

A furrow at the bridge of her nose was the first indication of wakefulness, and then her eyes fluttered. But when they stretched wide and her mouth parted, I slammed a hand over her scream. And scream she did! Thank Christ it was muffled.

"It's me, lass. It's Oswald."

A hand slapped my hand away and then a fist collided with the side of my head. I reeled, stars shimmering before my eyes as I staggered back.

She scrambled from her bed, but I was too dazed to appreciate her nakedness as a flash of pale zoomed by me, slumped into a shift, and commenced beating me over the head. I shielded myself the best I could with my arms.

"Alison! Stop! It's me, Oswald!"

She stopped only long enough to say, "I *know*!" and commenced wailing upon me again.

"Lass! *Lass!*" I grabbed her wrists and stretched them above her head. She twisted but it only served to topple the both of us upon her bed, me atop her. She squirmed beneath me, and I don't mind saying, it had a most profound effect…which made her stop when she noticed.

Her wild eyes stared up into mine. "I beg your mercy," I said, mere inches from her face. There are some things a man has no control of.

She panted, heaving that generous bosom and puffing her sweet breath against my mouth. All it would take was to bend a little and I would be kissing those delicious lips. I was so close.

"Get off," she said sternly.

My cod was pressed against her and I was loath to move. A garden of delights awaited below, I knew, beneath that thin shift. Her scent was in my nose and her pliant body was laid out before me like supper.

But my raging thoughts were stilled by her soft, "Please." Damp eyes, short, ragged breaths, stirred me at last and, very reluctantly, I lifted m'self away. Running a hand down the hot skin at the back of my neck helped not at all. A plunge in the Thames was the only cure.

She straightened her gown and sat on the edge of the bed. "What are you doing here? It is the middle of the night!"

I stepped back again and searched for something to distract me. A candle! I rushed to the hearth, took a straw, lit it, and lit a candle sitting in its holder on the table. A little more light and a little more distance. Aye.

She stared at me, her eyes strangely bright in the shadows of her bed curtains.

"I needed to talk to you." But now that I was there, looking at her, it dawned on me that this could surely have waited. "Erm…" I sank to the chair. "I…I got an idea. About making certain Lord de Mandeville pays his dues."

Her hand found her hip, the universal sign from all women everywhere that a man has said or done something stupid. "This couldn't have waited till morning?"

"Er…"

She leapt to her feet and began to pace. "Oswald, you are the most infuriating man I have ever had the displeasure to meet! What ails you, eh? What makes you think that you are better than any other man? That you can walk in here…"

The shutter flapped with a breeze and she stared at it with horror.

"*Break* in here," she amended, "and do what you will! Get out."

"Now, Alison."

"Get out or I'll scream murder."

"Please, Alison, just hear me. Let me speak. It is a truly brilliant Plan."

"Like the last one?"

"That was not my fault!"

"I'm counting. One…"

"Alison, please. I'm begging you. Lass." I dropped to my knees and opened my arms in supplication, like figures in a stained-glass window. The posture seemed to have mollified her and she stopped counting. Slumping, she stood before her bed, a drape of dark hair revealed a pale shoulder from a hastily donned shift. The glow from the hearth and the single candle did nothing for my own problem, for her face, now partly in shadow, seemed to grow soft. Her tiny feet were bare, and for some reason I could not fathom, the sight of their vulnerability endeared me with a ridiculous flip in my belly.

I made to rise but she raised a hand like a statue of the Holy Virgin. "Stay where you are. I somehow trust you better on your knees."

I licked my dry lips. "As you will," I said, rough-voiced. "De Mandeville has never seen you, has he?"

"No. What has that to do with anything?"

"Well, I'll tell you if you give me a chance. You meet him accidental, see. And you're friendly with him."

Those eyes narrowed again. "How friendly?"

"Not that friendly." The thought revolted me so much I shuddered. "But you have this bag of gold ingots and you show him—"

"And just where do I get gold ingots?"

"Now lass, you said you'd listen, did you not?"

And I explained it as best I could what she was to do.

CHAPTER TWENTY-THREE

THERE WAS STILL much plotting to be done but I swore to Alison that I would make it right, just as I swore to Hugh Aubrey. A man might argue that the dead can wait, but if a soul must linger because his blood is not satisfied, then all is not well. The dead cannot wait. And so I found myself, once more, loitering near the de Mandeville manor house the next morning. Aye, I was a fool. I had broken the thief's code, returning to the scene yet a third time.

I needed ironclad proof. There had to be something that would prove the whoreson's guilt. Perhaps young Hugh was dallying with his wife and the sin of jealousy reared its monstrous head. Or perhaps the wife trifled with an innocent Hugh. Either way, de Mandeville slew him. But I needed proof to take to the sheriffs. For if de Mandeville was with them, then the deed had to have been done earlier, as I tried right well to tell them.

I began to ponder just how many windows and walls I had used getting in and out of the house already when I saw a familiar figure walking away from me. Ach! I do recall that walk!

I crept past the guardhouse and sidled up to the wench. "Dear Margaret," I said close to her ear. She turned a broad smile on me until she recognized who I was.

"Oh. It's you. You've got the Devil's own bollocks showing your face here."

"That, I know," I said, steering her away from the guardhouse and into the shadows.

"Here! Unhand me!"

"Margaret, dearling. Please. I've been wasting away thinking about you."

She slapped my hand away. "What do you want this time? It *was* you stealing from the master, was it not?" A cold, hardness stole over her face. "They say it was you who killed our Hugh."

A stealthy look around told me we were still quite alone. "Margaret! How can you say such a thing? I'd never!"

She pouted, that plump bottom lip jutting forth. "You used me to get into the manor."

"I did not. Margaret, it was *you* I wanted. Still want." I gathered her in my arms and though she was stiff and unyielding at first, I felt her give way, and she angled her head into my shoulder. I kissed the top of her head. "Now lass. For shame that you should think that of me. But truth be told, I am vexed by that very thing. To think that others would hunt me down for killing such an innocent lad!"

"I didn't believe it," she said, voice muffled by my shirt. "Not when you are so gentle with me. And you did not know him."

"No, I did not. But tell me, lass. Who *could* have done such a thing?"

"Who can say?" She nuzzled my neck, making my thinking a bit foggy.

"Well…surely someone at the manor could." I pushed her back. "Look, lass. I cannot have the sheriffs coming after me for something I did not do."

She frowned and placed her hands at her hips. "So. It's *not* me you've come back for."

"Oh, but it is. *And* to find my innocence."

She made a rude forked gesture with her fingers and turned her back on me. I ran after her and grabbed her hand but she shook mine loose. "You're a liar, Oswald. And you've broken my heart. I should never believe a word you say."

The lass had a point.

And yet, I did need to get into the household. "Hate me if you must, but you know I should not hang for a crime I had nothing to do with. Please, Margaret. Help me talk to the other servants. Someone must have seen something! Servants always know what their masters are about."

"The coroner already asked us all."

"But he did not know what I know."

She squinted. "And what is it you know that the king's coroner does not?"

"More," I said. "Will you help me?"

Her scowl was deep and she sighed the whole weight of the world. But at last, she said, "Damn you, Oswald. I will help you, though even God's own angels have a hard time of it."

"That's the truth, right enough." But I thanked her and followed her through a garden gate.

She led me down a damp gravel path with the smell of rain-drenched herbs in the air and came to the kitchens. The cooks and scullions stared at me with surly faces as we walked through, out, and then down another small path to the house again. I allowed her to look first, just to make sure there were no men-at-arms about, for there would be no time explaining to them what I was doing there. I'd be piked, for certain.

She motioned me forth and I made my way, wondering where she was leading me. Down a corridor and down to a large door with ornate ironwork. It was only once she knocked and stepped back that I had some inkling where we might be. "No!" I hissed at her.

But it was too late. The door opened to a page, but I could clearly see Master Hamo Aubrey in the alcove as well. I gave her an angry look but she brushed it off with the up tilt of her nose.

Yet there was where she lost the thread, for she did not know how to announce me. Thinking quick, I stepped forward and bowed.

"Master," I said addressing the steward, and pushing past the page. "I am Oswald, come from the office of the Lord Sheriff. And I have but a few questions for you as concerns the tragic death of your son."

The man, of medium build and a square face, looked me over with surprise. His dark hair matched that of his erstwhile son and came to just below his ears in a soft curl. His long gown was embroidered with a pattern of crosses.

He wasn't quite certain what to make of me, whether by my looks I was to be invited in, or whether I was to stand in the entry. I wasn't in rags, but I wasn't in no fine velvets neither. Truth to tell, I didn't know either. His eyes lingered over the hammer hanging from my belt.

At last, he made up his mind and gestured me forth. I looked back at Margaret but she was already backing away. I girded my courage and walked in, pushing my hood off my head just as if I belonged there.

Master Aubrey faced away from me, staring at the fire. He stood a little unsteadily, and the closer I got I could detect fumes of spirits lifting off of him. And then the notion of the reason saddened me. He was drinking, aye, for sorrow over his lost son. And I hoped to God I could help him find his peace. "The coroner has already asked his questions," he said. "And so...Master Oswald, is it? What is it you have to ask of me that hasn't already been asked?"

I played with the loose flap of my belt that snaked through the buckle. I could not look the man in the face. "I beg your mercy for troubling you, good sir. But there are questions that need the asking, else I would not have vexed you."

"I understand," he said softly.

I licked my dry lips. I couldn't help but scan the room of its tapestries, candlesticks, and fine linens. But I kept my eyes on the dark blue of his gown instead and on the business at hand. "There is no doubt in the mind of the sheriffs that young Hugh met his fate at the hand of rogues. And so, Master, can you tell me, how long was the master here in the morning before he left for the day?"

"The morning? But my Hugh was found that night."

"We have reason to believe the deed was done that morning, not that night."

He turned to me, dark brows low over his eyes. "But then that thief. He could not have done it."

"No indeed!" I said heartily, stepping forward. "Absolutely not!"

He rubbed his chin and turned inward, staring at nothing. A gold ring on his smallest finger glimmered. "The morning, you say? The master was here well into late morning and left for Newgate near Terce. Or do you mean the others coming to the manor?"

"Others?"

"Sir Thomas Cull and Sir Henry Galthrop. I wonder who told you of them? Was it Lord de Mandeville? He is not fond of them and they are not fond of him and yet they must do their business together. Was it he that told you?"

"Er..." Those knaves. What *did* they have to do with this scheme?

"There are so little secrets in any such house as this, no matter what the masters think," he went on. Fisting his hand, he leaned with it against the stone wall near the hearth. His knuckles whitened. He looked back at me over his shoulder. "Shall I tell you all? You are the sheriff's man, are you not? Am I not obliged by the law to tell you, to expose corruption?"

"Erm..."

But the master had got his blood up. And Hugh lay dead in the ground and surely a man, a father, is permitted to vent his humors when he is faced with such deeds.

"Sir Thomas and Sir Henry." He said the names like spittle. "And my Lord de Mandeville. What a trio are they. For each in his own way is a thief, perhaps more so than that poor fool who found himself in this wretched household a fortnight ago."

He turned to me with a scowl. A scowl for the men he had named, not for old Oswald. Wasn't that a turn of events?

"Lord de Mandeville is supposed to keep watch of the king's treasure," he went on. "But I wouldn't be at all surprised if he was involved in the stealing of it. No, indeed. And the irony of it is, that Sir Thomas and Sir Henry are aware of his thievery and yet they, too, would steal. If they could have gotten there first, they would have." He lowered his arm and rubbed his face with his hand. "I am taking liberties," he slurred through his fingers. "But I have been a loyal steward in this household for twenty-five years. And now my son is dead. My only son." His mouth curved downward and trembled. He pushed away from the fireplace and paced. "If you think it was these men—how I would love to accuse them. But alas. They were not in the house that day. The master had a falling out with them recently and they were not permitted entry."

"Oh? Could they not have forced their way in?" For I would have loved to include them in murder as well.

"And the guards would have forced them out again. Perhaps you do not understand. Sir Thomas and Sir Henry had been stealing from the king's treasury for years. So my Lord de Mandeville said." He had the grace to blush when he added, "I overheard as much when they argued. It was then that those fair knights took to spying on my lord. And rightly so. For my lord plotted the same thing. God knows how he managed to do it so spectacularly."

I tamped down a flush of pride. "A servant hears many things, then."

He raised his head and his eyes betrayed his fear. For I have no doubt that he never meant to say so much. It was the wine that did it.

"But this is all speculation," he said, retreating. "Half-heard speeches mean nothing."

"That is true, my lord. Eavesdropping is a sin. Or so it should be, for one can never know what exactly one heard. On the other hand, much can be learned from people who do not know others are listening. No trouble shall befall you, if that is what you fear."

He offered a half-hearted grin. "You are a good lad. Much like my son. He was a good man. The household favored him for his fair face and kind heart. Yes, he was much admired for both qualities."

"Amongst the ladies of the household?"

Instead of the pride I expected the see, his face clouded. "Perhaps too much."

Some call me a fool, but others know that I have an eye for detail. And the detail I saw on the steward's face was the merest change when talking of his son and the women of the house. A particular woman, perhaps? "Did he dally much where he should not, Master?"

He searched the room with panicked eyes, much as I might do when looking for escape. "I...I have said too much."

Boldly, I stepped up and grasped his arm. "Master, how can too much be said when a murderer walks free and your son lies in the arms of the angels?"

A tear glistened in his eye. "This tragedy has made me forget myself, my responsibilities. I should never have spoken ill of my masters."

I stood beside him, letting him get control of himself again. Silently, I appraised the fine goods around us, wondering the value of this or that.

But as the silence wore on, I felt it was time to prod him again. "Master, you spoke of a woman."

He turned a glare on me. "No. It wasn't his fault. It was *her*. *She* tempted *him*."

Tread carefully, Oswald. I already knew the answer, and I'll wager you do, too. "This 'she', then. Someone in *this* household?"

He sighed, seemed resigned. But still he whispered it. "Yes. Lord de Mandeville's wife, Joan. She is a temptress. She beguiles my master and he fawns on her, but she is not faithful to him."

I recalled well the kiss she extracted from me before I could make my escape. A strange one was this Joan. Ah, the sins of Man and Woman are many.

"She causes all manner of inconveniences for she preys on everything male in this house."

"Then...it was a simple case of jealousy?" Oh how a man can turn to murder when his blood is up, especially over a woman! The creatures of Eden, tempting Man to sin. It was foul, indeed.

But he was suddenly staring at me. "Then that would mean—"

"Aye, it would."

"All for a woman. A sinful, despicable woman. I should kill her myself!" He charged for the door but I held him back.

"Now, now, good master! You would hang to no purpose."

He seemed to crumple in on himself. All his blood was expended. All that anger turned outward had diminished him somehow. He grasped a chair and leaned against it. "My son deserves justice."

"Aye, Master. Justice is important to me as well." Never more so now when my own neck was in the noose.

He had no more to say but it was enough.

I took my leave of Master Aubery and when the door closed him away, I stood in the quiet corridor and thought. I must find the man himself. Get a confession. It may not do for the sheriffs but it would do enough for my own purposes.

But where was the bastard?

I grabbed a passing page and asked him and he was a smart lad, for he told me he had just seen the master in the chapel.

The chapel, was it? And how was he able to walk through the doors of that holy place without the Lord setting him ablaze with his sins?

I ran down the corridor. Down each passage I went, upstairs, down. That guard again. I flipped my hood up over my head as I flew by him. When I looked back, he was looking at me suspiciously.

Out the garden door, I slid on the gravel and headed quick to the chapel. De Mandeville was there, right enough, talking to Father Simon. I waited several paces behind him, catching my breath, waiting for him to be left alone.

Luck was with me and as Father Simon left, I stepped away from my hiding place behind the pillar.

De Mandeville turned and spied me. "If it isn't the thief. How surprised I am to see you in my household. A place where you definitely should not be." How well I knew it. Three times now, by my reckoning.

"Aye, I'm here, right enough. I'm here catching a thief and a murderer."

A dark brow ticked upward. "Are you now?"

"Aye." I raised my chin and puffed out my chest. My hand fell to my hammer but I did not pull old Saint Joseph from his loop. Not yet. There was no one in the chapel save him and me. "Begging your mercy, my lord, but...but that would be you on both counts."

He looked surprised at first before his mouth curved into a smile and he shook his head. "My dear Master Oswald. Your enthusiasm is to be commended. But your conclusions leave much to be desired."

Eh?

"No." He smoothed down his robes and walked sedately toward the rood. Brazenly, I followed. He looked over his shoulder and seemed amused that I should.

"My lord, there isn't anyone else likely to have done it. And as far as the treasure, you made certain that a notorious thief would be caught for that crime. You stole all that yourself. Probably days or weeks before."

"Impertinent. I truly should have run you through with my dagger. Saved the sheriffs the trouble of hanging you…and your companions. As for murder, your audacity knows no bounds. What drew you to such an outrageous conclusion?"

He kept a steady stare at me which unnerved, for he seldom blinked and I felt my own eyes water in sympathy. "It is said that your wife has a roving eye."

There was no mistaking the anger in his eyes. "Such lies!" he rasped between his teeth. "Such lies that you would speak about a fine, devoted lady!"

"A fine devoted lady who begged a kiss from me before she'd let me escape out her bedchamber window?"

He struck. The flat of his hand marked my face for certain, and the blow made me see stars. I almost fell back but scrambled forward. My cheek felt hot. He took a step toward me and I took one back.

"That is a vile lie!"

"It is the truth, so help me God!"

"Whoreson!" He closed his fist this time and cocked back his arm.

I scuttled out of the way and edged away from him.

He seemed to be looking about for a weapon.

"No candlestick handy, eh?" But even as I said it, something adjusted in my brain. "Oi! I never mentioned a candlestick. It was you what said it."

"What are you talking about?"

"No. No, it was you. You said 'candlestick' very clearly when I had never mentioned it. That first time at the Tower. That's when you said it. I said he was hit on the head and you said 'hit with a candlestick' but I didn't remember it until now."

He lunged for me. I ducked and ran for the door. Uselessly, I pulled at the latch and ducked again when I saw the shadow of his arm swing toward me. He'd locked the damned door!

The window!

I got a leg under him and kicked upward. He tumbled to his backside with a loud exclamation. Leaping toward the window, I slipped the latch and jumped out, rolling a few times on the wet grass before I gained my footing. I didn't look back and ran and ran. Over the garden wall, and I was slapping the muddy streets of London, escaping toward Cornhill. Saint Dafydd's bollocks! I was in a fix now. What would de Mandeville do? By the saints. I still had no proof. I was little better off now than I was before!

It was the new Plan for certain now. It was all the justice I had left. I only hoped I would have the time to do it before all Hell broke loose.

I stopped running and grabbed onto a wobbly fence, gasping for breath. Well now. One thing at a time. If I could keep my head out of the noose for a whole day then I had a lot to do. Those money-lending knaves would be knocking at Alison's door at any moment. Time was running out. If there were only two of me!

CHAPTER TWENTY-FOUR

I TRIED TO appear casual making my way through London, but I'm known so well by some of the merchants that they follow me with their narrow-eyed gazes, clutching tight to their purse strings.

The gold and silversmiths blocked their doorways with their bodies, arms crossed against their chests. Some sent their apprentices to stand directly on the paths to their door. I felt a bit hurt. I mean, I done good business with most of them men. Fine time to desert me.

Still, I only had one path to follow that day, and that was to Master Arno. I noted that his shop was still shut up tight. I glanced over my shoulder. No one was following me. No sheriff's men, no disreputable knights, no murderous lords. Saint Dafydd! There seemed to be a long list these days.

Since all eyes were on me — and well I knew why — I could not just walk up to Master Arno' shop. No, that would not do. I changed directions and kept going. Just ahead of me was a cart laden with newly tanned hides, by the sharp smell of them. I slipped one off and threw it over my head, covering myself like a cloak. I trotted forth and got behind another cart, this one bearing fuel, sticks wrapped with cords. I tugged one until it fell softly from the cart. Then I tossed it over my shoulder and trudged back the way I had come, head down, different demeanor, different posture, and made a slow go of it right over the flagged stone path of Arno's shop. I was bent over, as if under a heavy burden, letting the hide shadow my face. I looked behind, and no one was looking at me at all. Well now!

I knocked. Waited. Knocked again.

Still nothing. "Master Arno!" I rasped. "It's me, Oswald."

I heard a shuffled step within. "Oswald? That you?"

"Aye. Let me in, you fool."

The bar scraped upward, the lock turned, and I was yanked inside. When he had barred the door once more, he turned and looked me up and down. "What are you supposed to be?"

"In disguise." I threw off the hide and the sticks and shook out my shoulders.

"Oh." He was just as nervous as he was the day before. "W-what do you want? Have you come to take these things away?"

"No. Well, a piece or two, if you will allow it. And some gold foil."

"Gold foil? What on earth for?"

I smiled. "To help you and me both."

And now I had one more stop to make.

——— • ———

THIS TIME, I sat in my own shop with the door barred. It wasn't a common thing, and so when Walter tried to enter, I heard him smacking against the door.

"What by God's toes is this?" he cried through the wood. "Oswald! Are you in there?"

I nodded to Geoff to open the door.

Walter bustled in, already in his cups. He stood unsteadily, looking around. I don't know what he expected to find, but Geoff with his polishing cloth and me at my workbench with Benet Chigwell beside me was not it.

"What are you doing? And why is he here?" he asked, gesturing to Benet.

"Just doing a bit of work, Walter."

"Good Master Wool Merchant," said Chigwell with a bow. He giggled and bent over the workbench again.

"Work? You? And him?" He stumbled toward me and my workbench and watched us. "What the devil are you doing?"

"I'm apprenticing this young alchemist, here," said Benet. "We are turning lead into gold."

And we were. I knew Chigwell would know the scheme. I could see it in his eyes. Many a canny alchemist fooled a client by claiming to have made the fabled philosopher's stone. He was right good with the foil. I watched as he carefully laid the gold foil over the lead ingot and smoothed it out with a brush. We already had three done and they looked wonderful.

"*Why* are you doing that?"

"There's a settlement that must be paid. And these will do it."

"What settlement? Oswald? What sort of trouble are you getting into now?"

"The same, Walter. These shiny objects are a trap for a large spider. Not just any fly will do."

"Fly? Spider? You mean…" and he whispered "…de Mandeville?"

"Aye, Walter. A spider can be deadly and needs squashing. And this…" I hefted it in my hand, feeling its solid weight. "This is just the thing to do it."

Walter stared at it for a long moment. "Oswald, whatever it is you are doing, don't! You will get yourself killed."

"Well, Walter, the thing of it is, if I don't do it, I'll likely get it somehow, somewhere when I least expect it. This way, it is done. One way or the other."

He bit his lip. Worry lines creased his brow.

————◆————

I WANTED TO meet alone with Alison. What we must do, I didn't want Walter or Geoff involved. We knew the risks and it was to be only our necks now.

I reached the Cockerel and Bullock, tied Walter's donkey to a ring, and pushed open the door. A scant crowd. I saw her near the back and I caught her eye.

I walked to a shadowed corner and, like a spirit, she swept toward me. I carefully schooled her. I never encountered a cleverer lass. Her eyes were filled with determination for we all knew that if this did not work, we would all surely hang.

I gave her one last look. "Now's the time to back out," I said.

Slowly, she shook her head. Her cheek was pale, but her lips were a blushing rose and I leaned in…but she stepped back, lifting her chin. Right then.

As the bells rang Terce from the nearby monastery, Alison left her alehouse and stepped out onto the muddy lane. It rained a light drizzle, a bit cold for April, but though she kept her hood up she let her hair free like I told her. Through the mud, she led Walter's donkey with its important sack slung over its haunches. I followed her, discreetly, of course, so I wouldn't be noticed. I had to make certain that all was well and no trouble befell her.

She picked her way down the lane, skirting a priest riding a fine horse and looking far ahead of him, never down in the mud. Some boys lugging baskets of salted fish rambled by her and nearly dropped them. A small girl with a white linen cap covering almost all her golden hair carried a box and walked sedately behind her mistress, but she seemed more distracted by a spotted dog following at her heels.

Alison led the donkey right before De Mandeville's great house and waited, not looking at me, for she was surely aware of me deep in the shadows. I knew she was frightened but I suppose desperation can make anyone a bit braver.

It was then when my attention was taken with soft eyes and long hair curled from the rain, that a rider emerged from under his gatehouse arch. It was the man, right enough, and Alison moved quickly, yanking the donkey's tether and spooking the beast so that he ran into de Mandeville's horse's path. The horse skittered to the side, nearly unhorsing him and the sack from the donkey fell to the ground, revealing one shining ingot.

De Mandeville reined in his horse and dismounted. He moved around the beast and it was then that Alison, lips red and wet from licking, gazed up at him. Ach, if only all that allure was directed to me. I, too, would have done what de Mandeville did, whether she was a peasant or a lady; he stooped to retrieve her bag, which she quickly pulled closed.

"I'm so sorry, my lord," she said with a deep curtsey. "I beg your mercy." She tied the sack to the donkey's back once more and shook her head in despair. Ah, she even managed to shed a tear. That was a good touch.

And de Mandeville noticed. "Lass, what ails you?" He had the temerity to tilt her chin up with his finger. I had fantasies of her biting it off.

"Oh good my lord, how can I trouble you with the worries of my like?"

"And what worries would a pretty thing like you have?" He eyed the sack with the same covetous gaze he directed at her. That was the man, right enough.

She sighed most piteously. "My lord, I must get coin for the goods in that sack for my mistress, but the place I must go to do it has forbidden me entrance. I tried to tell the shopkeeper it was for my mistress but he wouldn't hear of it."

"Why?"

"Because my husband, God rest his soul, cheated them and now I am helpless. I do not know what to do. She will turn me out if I cannot do as bid."

He edged closer to her and I could not hear his exchange, but a deep blush reddened her cheek. She continued to play him like a rebec, all smooth strings and sad notes. It was the twin sins of greed and lust that did him in. Alison was as comely as his own wife. They were a pair, them de Mandevilles! *And* he'd seen the gold foil-covered lead ingot with his own eyes, in the cover of rain and the distraction of a pretty face.

In his words, I owned him.

———◆———

THEY TRAVERSED DOWN the lane. He walked the horse by its lead and strolled alongside her, chatting amiably while Alison looked suitably grateful. It was as chivalrous a scene as might be woven into a tapestry or painted on a wall. But it was as false as could be.

I trotted behind, keeping to the shadows and skirting carts and horses. People looked at me curiously but I paid them no heed. I vowed to keep her safe and I meant to keep that vow.

We were almost there. She turned down the same lane as Arno's shop and I could tell that de Mandeville was growing alarmed. He even hesitated just outside of the man's pathway but she shook her head, pulling him along. *Not that one*, I imagined her saying. *But one farther down.*

"That's a lass," I whispered. "That's good. The net is thrown and even now he does not know he shall be struggling momentarily like a fish."

She found another shop and pointed. They stood at a distance but now I was close enough to eavesdrop all I desired.

"It's that one," she said, shy and sad at the same time. So irresistible.

He looked over the ramshackle cottage dubiously. "This is the place you would go?"

"Always, my lord." She leaned into him confidentially. "They pay almost twice the market."

"Oh?" He gave it another gaze, this time it was filled with admiration.

"But I am not allowed there. And I have these ingots. You are good to escort me, worrying over my safety, but now that I am here, what good does it do if I may not go in? Surely he's told the other goldsmiths as well. And the pawnbrokers. Who will help me?"

He shook his head.

Come on, man, I thought. *Say it. It must be your idea.*

"It seems a shame to go elsewhere when the price here is so good, as you say." He scanned the street, knowing every one of the gold and silversmiths, I'll wager. "But perhaps...perhaps *I* could do it for you."

"My lord?"

"I know it seems a silly thing, for we have only just met. But I hope to make more of our acquaintance, and what better way than to do you a service. And your mistress, of course."

She looked flabbergasted. "For *me*, my lord? You would do this for *me*?"

"That...and much more, fair Alison." He took her hand and kissed it. I cringed. Good lye soap will take care of washing demon spittle from decent flesh.

He began to untie the sack from the donkey. "That is most gracious of you, good my lord. But..."

He stopped, busy hands frozen over rope knots. "But?"

"My lord, I would feel better...it's nothing against you, you understand, it is just the business my husband taught me. If I were to hold your purse in surety, then I know my mistress would be satisfied. One mustn't be too careful."

He drew back and looked at her.

Bless me. Too far?

But he seemed to come back to himself, and even chuckled. He wagged a finger in her face. "You are a clever wench. I can see that you will not be cheated. Your mistress is quite fortunate to have you." He chuckled again and untied his money pouch from his belt. "Very well. I shall do my best transaction for you, to prove myself worthy."

"I've no doubt of that, my lord." She clutched the heavy purse to her chest and licked her lips. As he turned to walk up the path to the shop, her eye caught mine and I gave her a thumbs up. She heaved a big sigh and waited until he was inside the door to mount up and ride as fast as she could down one lane after another.

I straightened my tunic and walked forward. Now it was my turn.

———— ✦ ————

I HEARD THE voices as I neared the closed door.

"Who the hell are you?" came the first gruff voice.

"My name does not matter, masters. I am here to transact with you."

"Transact? We don't do no transacting with people we don't know."

De Mandeville seemed ruffled. I decided it was time for my entrance. I pulled open the door and the two knaves stood up. "You again!" cried one. Aye, they were the same two money lenders that dared put their hands on Alison. Are you keeping up?

De Mandeville turned and he wore the same expression. "What are you doing here, Welshman?"

"Surprised I'm not in prison, my lord?" Naw, I couldn't resist it. And the look on his face was priceless.

But then he sneered. "I was just on my way to the sheriffs myself. You have saved me the trouble."

I snorted and turned to the other knaves. The conclusion of my plan and my revenge was at hand. "Masters, you will recall that I told you just the other day, that there was a man claiming he had bought the owing of all your debtors and stole what was rightfully yours? Well, here is the man."

De Mandeville glared at me. "What are you talking about, knave?"

"It don't matter, my lord. All will become clear momentarily." I smiled at the money lenders, who had murder in their eyes. They slowly unsheathed their daggers.

"You've been stealing money from us."

De Mandeville thought at first that they were addressing me. He startled back when he discovered his error.

"What...what are you saying? Do you know who I am?" He laid a trembling hand on his sword hilt.

"We don't care who you are," said the man who I had coshed with my hammer. "Your business is done." He slid over his trestle table and approached de Mandeville with his dagger poised. The other lumbered around the table, Geoff's bite to his leg still causing a limp.

De Mandeville backed away. "Don't you see what this knave is doing? He is lying to you. He only wants his revenge on me. Don't be fools!"

"Who's the fool here?" said the man with the dagger. "This useless knave" –and he gestured toward me with his knife— "Or the fool who walked into the spider's web?"

"Oswald!" De Mandeville turned to me with a desperate face. "Tell them!"

"Tell them what, my lord? That you are a thief and a murderer?"

He lunged for me but I stepped back out of the way.

"Oswald!"

It was time for me to go. I was not fond of bloodshed. I slipped out the door and, just in time, Sir Henry and Sir Thomas arrived on their horses. They had gotten the missive I told Walter to write. They were to meet a contrite de Mandeville and divide the spoils, so the missive said.

"Right this way, my lords."

"What mischief is this, knave?" said Sir Thomas, dismounting.

De Mandeville shouted and we heard struggling and scraping. A sword was drawn but it sounded a bit too late.

The knights, those chivalrous men, ran inside, drawing their blades.

Once they were in, I closed the door and rolled a stone before it with my foot, propping it closed. I suppose it was a fairer fight now.

When I looked up, the rest of my plan was coming together. Walter had done his part again and had sent for the king's men-at-arms along with the sheriffs.

I bowed to Sheriff Nick and Sheriff Nigel.

"What is all this, Oswald?" said Sheriff Nick.

"My lord, here in this shop you will find the thieves that stole the king's treasure."

"Truly?" He looked confused, for he well knew it was me.

"Oh indeed, my Lord Sheriff. The truly guilty and sinful will find a bitter end. You will find proof within. There is a sack of false ingots but also in that sack you will find a crown belonging to the king."

Sheriff Nigel brushed his ginger locks from his cheeks impatiently. "But...but how can that be?"

They looked at one another, trying to reckon it out when they heard a horrible cry from within. Quickly, they motioned for the men-at-arms to enter. They cast the stone aside and threw open the door and a terrible scuffle ensued. I backed away. From what I could see between them money lenders, the two knights, and the king's men, there wouldn't be nobody left to hang. Not in one piece, anyway.

Sheriff Nick lifted a discarded sack and a gold crown tumbled out. No doubt, should they continue to search, they would find all the rest of the king's plunder in that humble shop. I made certain of that.

CHAPTER TWENTY-FIVE

A TAP ON the door and I quickly opened it. Alison. That gray fear that haunted her eyes was gone as was the dull pallor of her cheeks. All her worries were now for naught...as were our own. For the tidings had traveled quickly from one parish to another: Lord Percy de Mandeville and two of the king's knights were killed by the same ruffians who had stolen the king's crown jewels and they themselves were dispatched by the king's guards. It was so witnessed by both sheriffs of London. The king's treasure would be returned to his grace the king and all was well in London town again.

No mention of a wayward Welshman or his company. No mention of the silent rejoicing all over town from those released from the indenture of them money lenders. And no more sightings of two shadowy knights haunting the streets and lanes around Oswald of Harlech.

We were all safe. And even Walter could not argue how well my Plan worked this time.

Trev and Geoff sat side by side and, thank Christ, they were being discreet, unlike our fair king and his minions. I looked across the room at all their faces and felt proud. Even Walter and Benet were getting on. Aye, they were a good lot and it came out better than I'd hoped. A murderer had got his just deserts as well. And that sat well with the soul of Hugh Aubrey.

Alison took me aside. She pulled a leather pouch from her purse. It had been flattened and folded in half. "What shall we do with de Mandeville's purse?"

"Well, lass, you *could* return it to his wife, if you've a hankering to do so. But I say we should divide the spoils for our trouble."

"Can we do that?"

"Of course. These are our rules now. After all, lass, what did you think we would do with the king's treasure? Wear the crowns on our heads to market?"

Geoff guffawed. I smiled at him.

And so de Mandeville paid *all* his dues at last.

———•———

THEY COMMENCED MAKING a pottage. Geoff raised the turnips in the air and Trev brought over a big kettle filled with water. They were right drunk, them four, and occupied with putting vegetables into the soup pot—bits of turnips and leeks—the latter for me, of course—a skinned rabbit, and God knows what else. While they were busy with that, Alison tugged on my arm and dragged me outside to stand beside my neighbor's brazier. The flames had long ago gone down but the coals were still glowing red and kept us warmed, even as the sky lightened to a murky pink over the tower of St. Peter Cornhill church. She seemed shy of a sudden. Endearing. "Oswald, I wanted to thank you and bless you for what you did for me. It's a fresh start and I mean to make the most of it."

Her face was so bright that I almost forgot what her words meant. Fresh start? That meant no more Oswald. "Ah. Well. I wish good luck to you and God's blessings, Alison. And thank *you*, as well, for saving my miserable life."

She cocked her head, her eyes taking me apart and putting me back together. "That sounds a bit like…farewell."

I kicked the mud, dislodging a clod that rolled an inch or two. "Well…isn't it?"

Her eyes never stopped roving and her lips formed a thin, severe line. "I tell you true, Oswald. When you first proposed the burglary of the Tower, I thought you had lost your mind. And then we began and it all worked just as you said. Except for the moment it all fell apart."

"That wasn't my fault," I muttered, uselessly.

"I know it wasn't." I noticed with a burning in my belly that her hand rested on my arm. "It was a brilliant plan. A plan for the ages. Had the treasure been there it would have been truly divine."

My voice was rougher than usual. "Aye, it would have been."

"And you got us all out of it alive. That's an extra blessing for you."

I nodded. I did that, aye. I looked down on my scarred palms.

"And now you made us safe. Made *me* safe from those coin squeezers as well as the law. And I tell you true…I…I never had so much fun in my life."

"*Eh?*"

There was no jest in her face. Her eyes were clear and bright and her face as radiant as the sun glistening off the river.

"You…did?"

"Aye." She breathed deep, a clean, free sound. She leaned in.

I was so surprised I just stood there, even when her lips touched mine. But I moved quickly, my arms sliding around her and I pulled her close. Those sweet lips parted and I partook of such a feast that would have put King Solomon to shame. I tasted her and she tasted me, lips soft and wet and warm. She was all plump and sweet in my arms, round breasts crushed to my chest, supple hips under my hands. I wanted all of her and our kiss deepened, tongues caressing.

But alas. All good things must come to an end and slowly, she drew back from me. Her dark hair tangled on my cloak, stretched, and then fell away. My fingers longed to grasp those hips, to pull her back and sample that creamy neck, but she was dear to me and though I was loath to, I let her go.

I swallowed hard and blinked at her. "Well, lass," I said breathlessly. "Does this mean you wouldn't mind going along with my schemes again? Should the need arise."

Scandalized, she swatted my arm. "Oswald!" It gave her a good excuse to blush.

"It isn't always about the need. But about the challenge. It's true," I said to her skeptical expression. "For instance. There was that nice coin purse that you grabbed from Lord de Mandeville — rest his soul — with a sarding fortune inside. There was enough for the six of us, eh? At least enough to last a few months."

I reached into my own pouch and carefully pulled out a gleaming red gemstone, the size of a robin's egg. She clutched my arm. "Christ have mercy!" she gasped. "Oswald, where did you get that?"

"Oh, when I was slipping the king's treasure into those vile men's shop, one of the gems from a crown just…er…fell out."

"It *fell* out?"

"With the help of my eating knife." I grinned. "The point of the matter is, that I would never leave any of us with nothing. Not if I can help it. And this stone and that purse…well. We'll be good for a fair while. Until I get another Plan."

She shook her head at me and smiled right back. And I noticed she didn't say no.

AUTHOR'S AFTERWORD

THE TOWER OF London is a unique structure with many fascinating qualities. The fact that it is a castle in the middle of London (on a mound perhaps built on the very cradle of London when fur-clad Britons were running about), is made all the more interesting because, technically, it is still in use.

Besides the White Tower that William the Conqueror built, other structures were erected within the walls over the centuries, either being taken down or having burned down. Illustrious prisoners resided within. Some found their freedom while others found eternity. It was a mint, an armory, a royal residence, and the home of the crown jewels. And they're still there today.

The crown jewels are also shrouded in a bit of mystery. We know that in 1303, a former Keeper of the Wardrobe, Richard of Pudlicott, burgled them when they were ensconced in Westminster Abbey, apparently easily gotten to because of an appalling amount of corruption amongst the monks and the nobility in their complacence with their duties. Was it all recovered? Not likely. But a surprising amount of it was, what with pawnbrokers and jewelers returning them. Even fishermen fished them out of the Thames. But surely not all of it.

Then, there was that little episode in 1649 with the English Civil War. As Lord Protector, Oliver Cromwell couldn't abide the presence of royal accouterments and had the crowns and regalia melted down or broken up. The crowns and such we see today on display in the Tower are reproductions recreated when Charles II came to the throne restoring the monarchy, albeit gold and bejeweled reproductions. The only bit of regalia that survived, ironically, is the Ampullae or Golden Eagle and Golden Spoon, both used for the anointing oil for the monarch at their coronation. Take that, Cromwell!

There was once a separate building created to accommodate the treasury that abutted the White Tower but it no longer exists. One might assume that after yet another burglary, they would move it once more to safer ground well within the White Tower. During World War II, the jewels were removed from the Tower to safety…someplace. We know not where.

Pits? Traps? Real or fictional? According to the documentation of the heist at Westminster Abbey, they had such pits, so is it so unlikely to have the same at the Tower?

Also, a word about the names of the various towers and gates. The Lion Tower used to be and is no longer there at the southwest corner. St. Thomas' Tower (so named after Thomas Becket as he used to be chancellor of England under Henry II who built much of the tower's outer curtain walls and turrets) housed the gate at the Thames which we now know as Traitor's Gate, but in Oswald's London was known as Water Gate. It did not yet serve the parade of "traitors" that gave it its name.

The Bloody Tower, the main entrance to the Tower green, was called the Garden Tower which used to deposit entrants into the Constable's Garden. Wakefield Tower beside it was renamed in mid fourteenth century after William Wakefield, King's Clerk, who was appointed to hold custody of the Exchanges in the Tower in 1344. It was formerly known as the Records or Hall Tower. Many of the structures currently in the tower, including towers on towers, and the many buildings within the inner ward, were added much later.

I used the name de Mandeville for the Keeper's clerk in homage to the first Keeper of the Tower in 1140. It became a hereditary office. De Mandeville became the earl of Essex during the conflict between Empress Matilda and King Stephen. Later it seemed the custom to confer guardianship of the Tower to bishops who, in the twelfth century, might still be inclined to take up arms. They took to their office with particular zeal, especially Longchamp, Bishop of Ely under Richard Lionheart's absentee reign.

Thomas Bek, the Bishop of Lincoln was the Keeper of the Wardrobe for Edward II. There were probably many men losing sleep over the idea of stealing some of the king's treasure, but no one had succeeded like Richard of Pudlicott in 1303.

A word about homosexuality in the Middle Ages. Scholars still argue whether Edward II had intimate relations with his favorite, Piers Gaveston, though looking at those contemporary accounts it is hard to infer any other conclusion. He made Gaveston the Earl of Cornwall, a title customarily given to members of the royal family. He conferred this title shortly after his father, King Edward I died, bringing Gaveston back from the exile the old king decreed. In *Vita Edwardi Secundi*, the chronicler noted: "I do not remember to have heard that one man so loved another. Jonathan cherished David, Achilles loved Patroclus. But we do not read that they were immoderate. Our King, however, was incapable of moderate favour, and on account of Piers was said to forget himself, and so Piers was accounted a sorcerer." Indeed, it wasn't so much that both men might be homosexual, but that they flaunted it in the face of medieval morality and that the king conferred on Gaveston favors and privileges reserved for others of his status. That, along with Gaveston's arrogance and poor judgment, created a situation that could not be forgiven.

In the case of Geoff and Trev, homosexual acts of sodomy, though decried by the Church, were not necessarily criminal acts. It was a situation of don't ask, don't tell. Discretion was the key. Not until Henry VIII's Buggery Act of 1533 (yup, that's what it was

...led) designed specifically to address acts of sodomy of men, women, and animals was it decreed against the law.

But theft, however you couch it, *is* criminal. Fraud, cons, burglary. These are the things Oswald seems to excel at.

This book was always meant to be the beginning of a series, but since it could not seem to find a home with a publisher, I've had to rethink that. More recently, I dredged it from the vaults, polished it up, and decided to publish it under my own imprint Old London Press, the copy you now hold in your hands. I've always liked the first-person account and of his breaking the fourth wall, having the protagonist talk directly to the reader, dragging you into his plot. I do like to push the envelope when it comes to historical fiction, but perhaps a Medieval *Ocean's 11* was a little too much for traditional publishers. It seemed to give publishers conniptions, trying to figure out how to market it. So they just gave up.

Alas.

Thank *you* for reading. If you like a book, please review it. You can see all the rest of my books at **JeriWesterson.com**.

ABOUT THE AUTHOR

JERI WESTERSON is the author of the critically acclaimed Crispin Guest Medieval Noir mysteries. She also writes historical novels, several paranormal series, and a humorous rom/com LGBTQ mystery series under the pen name Haley Walsh. An award-winning author, her medieval mysteries were also nominated thirteen times for national mystery awards, from the Agatha to the Shamus. Jeri lives in Menifee, CA, mother to a gray senior kitty and a laconic tortoise.

JeriWesterson.com